# MY INCREDIBLE CAREER

## by
## Admiral
## A.J. Rimmer

JMC

*In the vast expanse of the cosmos,*
*where stars burn with celestial fervor*
*and nebulae weave tapestries of cosmic wonder,*
*there exists a tale, a tale so peculiar that it could only belong to one man*
*— Arnold Judas Rimmer.*

My Incredible Career
*By* Arnold J Rimmer

ISBN: 9798868494598

We gratefully acknowledge the following for the material and assistance they have
provided:
Grant Naylor Productions and The British Broadcasting Corporation

This edition has been prepared for publication in accordance with the Copyrights,
designs & Patents Act 1988 and the public information act 5 U.S code § 552 and
Open Parliament License V 3.0.

Cover art and typesetting by P .Wolfe

*So what is it?*

*It's a replica of the "My Incredible Career" masterpiece seen in Red Dwarfs 'Better than life' Season 2 Episode 2.*

*This book features a single chapter that replays endlessly. Why? Simply put, I lacked the motivation to pen the entire book.*

*This is a work of satire and not to be taken seriously.*

# CHAPTERS

# CHAPTER 1
# HUMBLE BEGINNINGS

It was just another sunny day on Io, spent jesting with my older brothers John, Howard, and Frank. God, we were close—the 'Four Musketeers,' as we used to call ourselves! Well, the three musketeers actually; they always let me be the queen of Spain. What fun we'd have! An occasional practical joke, of course—apple-pie beds, black-eye telescope. They even hid a small landmine in my sandpit! How were they supposed to know it would go off? However, on this particular day, we were all blissfully ignorant of the interstellar smeg about to hit my life!

As my mother casually revealed her plan to send me off to boarding school! My school grades had been gradually slipping, and my parents, having tried absolutely nothing and being fresh out of ideas, thought it would be best to let me be someone else's problem. I, in my infinite pubescent wisdom, hit her with the forceful question, 'Will I still get to see Bruno?' Bruno was the family dog, clearly. You could see where my main priorities lay.

In response, she crouched down, bless her heart—magnificent woman. Very prim, very proper; some say austere. Some people mistook her for being cold and thought she was aloof. Not a bit of it. She crouched down to my eye level, as if we were sharing the secrets of the universe. In a tone that probably sounded more dramatic than she intended, she explained that it was a boarding school on the other side of Io—pretty much as far away from them while still being on the same planet.

1

Turning to dear old Dad for an explanation or, at the very least, a distraction from the impending familial meltdown, the bearded git was engaged in a staring contest with the sky. It was as if he believed they held the secrets to a lifetime supply of cosmic beer. 'I don't want to go!' I declared, my voice dripping with the gravitas only a nine-year-old prophet could muster.

"Just a couple of years, Arnold, and you can come home for your birthday," she boldly declared, and Dad, ever the spectator in the family circus, continued his stoic gaze into the sky. He never was one for eye contact. Snapping his head, he interjected, "Don't get the weaselly smegger's hopes up." Classic Dad!

Undeterred by the lack of emotional support, she flung a promise of her triumphant return in time for my birthday, as if the universe itself would pause its dance to celebrate my existence. Hugging me, she hoisted me up. 'C'mon, let's get some quiche,' she declared, casting a glance at Dad, who remained emotionally disengaged; he never would give quiche a chance.

The next morning, I was hurled into a transport craft, sharing a seat with Fred 'Thicky' Holden, leaving me to ponder the cosmic absurdity of it all. Suddenly, the predictable rhythms of my boyhood were replaced by the unpredictable chaos of the universe. Leaving behind our modest house on Io — a perfect replica of an Earth house from the 19th and 20th centuries with its hectares of land. There were some parts I wouldn't miss: getting up early in the morning to feed the sheep and cows, and my pet Lemming. Dad's insistence on manual labor became the launching pad for my determination and my brothers to join the Space Corps.

Our house had witnessed the shenanigans of many generations of Rimmers, with stories galore about my great-great-grandfather, Jebediah Rimmer, who legend has it fought off native Ionians to build the house and gardens. Now maintained by my Dad and with help from the local gardener, Dungo. My dad couldn't stand Dungo, and could never understand why. Sure, he was slightly inept at times and egotistical, self-important, lacked confidence, and was socially awkward. But I always liked him; he had a strong moralistic attitude, and my mother always took a shine to him.

My father, a half-crazed military failure, spent his early years amidst the military pioneers. Growing up on Io, his childhood was an exercise in minimalism. Yet, he yearned to be an officer like his father. The dream almost turned into reality when he strutted onto Space Corps Academy grounds, fulfilling an ambition that had marinated in the spartan conditions of an Io upbringing. Grandpa, an eternal optimist, had dreams of his son treading the same starlit path. Destiny pulled a cosmic prank when he was one inch below Corps regulation height.

My mother was born into an austere family that considered space exploration a genetic trait. Her father was part of the Space Corps' third graduating class, and her mother was a part of the cybernautic division — a family with enough star power to make a pulsar blush.

Mum, with dreams of becoming an astrobiologist, found herself on a collision course with Dad in an Introduction to Space Corps History class. Oh, but the Space Corps Directive 2574 about students fraternizing with other students was stricter than a vegan at a butcher shop. They soon found themselves in front of the space corps instructor with a warning.

Fast forward to Dad's posting on the JMC Emerald Nebula. Despite the height restrictions, strings were pulled, and he was made a galley steward. The ship was still three months away from Earth. He'd stayed in touch with my mother throughout, and in a move that combined romantic flair with a dash of desperation, while on leave at Lunar City 7, Dad proposed to my mother. 'Everyone thought we were bloody mad,' Mum once said, 'Maybe it was the wine or the smell of the beef that had seeped into his clothes. But I just couldn't say no to those puppy dog eyes.' Ah, the cosmic irony of hindsight.

My mother was posted on Titan, and my dad was posted on the JMC Emerald Nebula. Over a year passed before she saw Dad again, and almost two more years before she donned the graduation cap and tossed it into the wind. Yet, fate, with its sense of humor, decided that she wouldn't be posted anywhere near my dad.

My mother was freshly stationed on the Axiom II; however, it wasn't long before she found she had a tiny stowaway on board. She was pregnant with my older brother, Frank! 'Your father was in the outer rim at the time; he nearly dropped his spatula,' she said, 'and by the time the message got to him, I was already as big as a cow

So Mum's Space Corps ambitions hit a speed bump; she took a leave of absence and went to shack up on Io with my paternal grandparents. Lacking her parental navigators, who had embarked on the ultimate road trip years earlier, she found herself surrounded by vast farmland of good old terrestrial adventure. Enter Frank, my elder sibling, making his grand entrance. The interstellar escapades of the next generation were officially underway.

With the cosmic clock ticking, Mum had a mere two Earth-bound years before Space Corp's relentless gravitational pull demanded her return. In those terrestrial years, she juggled the titles of astrobiologist and dedicated mum. 'I just felt shagged out all the time,' she reminisced. 'I missed little Frank; this wasn't what I wanted.' Parenthood, it turns out, is the ultimate improvisational act.

With parents who had charted the final frontier of life and having witnessed her mother resigning her commission to raise her and her brother solo during Dad's cosmic escapades as chief slop server, Mum found herself in a parenting predicament. 'I was bored out of my mind, but your dad's career was everything to him,' she admitted. She'd study where she could while my grandparents took care of Frank. 'Your grandparents were like Energizer bunnies,' she shared. Meanwhile, Dad, charting his course through the galactic highways aboard the JMC Emerald Nebula, missed Mum and Frank. As the countdown to Mum's return commenced, Dad, ever the master of cosmic shenanigans, pulled whatever strings he could to get her posted back to Io, where he had assumed the role of Restroom attendant.

Only for calamity to strike again after my Mum's grand return to the Space Corps. Surprise, surprise—John was on the way, stealing the spotlight as the next Rimmer headliner. Dad informing Captain Sulaco was less than thrilled. Shipboard nurseries were not on his playlist. But, that triggered Dad's decision. A message blinked in from the cosmic ether—Dad's old man had punched out his ticket to the great beyond when he was born. His career as a restroom attendant wasn't going anywhere fast. Cue the resignation letter to Space Corps—bye-bye dad's officer career. So from that point on, they began to settle into life on Io together. Mum later shot out my next brother Howard. Then, having a break, they focused on the house and garden, bringing local gardener Dungo to assist. It wasn't long after I arrived on the scene!

In the galactic years since, I've mulled over Dad's plot twist and how it flung my trajectory into the cosmic unknown. The cosmic yarn I spin for the masses: Dad ditching Space Corps lit the afterburners on John, Howard, Frank, and my career quest, filling the void he left.

My brothers, all being older, eventually signed up for the Space Corps, graduating with top marks in their classes. They all got commission postings on the fleet's best ships. John was an astro-navigator on the SSS Augustus, where he shared quarters with a certain Frank Hollister — a captain in the making.

Frank, the rising star in the Space Corps, snagged the first officer position aboard the Nova 4 when the previous first officer, Cheddar Flatheringson, decided he'd rather play captain. Six years of navigating the officer bureaucracy had Frank on a trajectory to break records and become the youngest captain in the Space Corps. But, as I've always said, 'Up, up, up the ziggurat lickety-split.

As for me, at the tender age of nine, my school grades were less than promising, and in a twist of cosmic fate, my parents decided it was better to wash their hands of me and ship me off to boarding school. As time ticked away, my envy for friends and their idyllic families turned me into a recluse. I found solace in the small things; I enjoyed listening to the Hammond organ, Morris Dancing, and building up my collection of 20th-century telegraph poles. You could always find me aimlessly wandering around the vast diesel decks at the local spaceport, attempting to rediscover the joy of getting lost. I even took up learning Esperanto in my sleep. But, as I looked up at the stars, where dreams of greatness shimmer like distant galaxies, my story was only just beginning. Arnold Judas Rimmer was destined for glory from the very fabric of stardust. My humble journey commenced not among the celestial bodies but within the labyrinth of obstacles — the very crucible of my stellar aspirations.

# CHAPTER 2
# STELLAR ASPIRATIONS

It was just another sunny day on Io, spent jesting with my older brothers John, Howard, and Frank. God, we were close — the 'Four Musketeers,' as we used to call ourselves! Well, the three musketeers actually; they always let me be the queen of Spain. What fun we'd have! An occasional practical joke, of course — apple-pie beds, black-eye telescope. They even hid a small landmine in my sandpit! How were they supposed to know it would go off? However, on this particular day, we were all blissfully ignorant of the interstellar smeg about to hit my life!

As my mother casually revealed her plan to send me off to boarding school! My school grades had been gradually slipping, and my parents, having tried absolutely nothing and being fresh out of ideas, thought it would be best to let me be someone else's problem. I, in my infinite pubescent wisdom, hit her with the forceful question, 'Will I still get to see Bruno?' Bruno was the family dog, clearly. You could see where my main priorities lay.

In response, she crouched down, bless her heart — magnificent woman. Very prim, very proper; some say austere. Some people mistook her for being cold and thought she was aloof. Not a bit of it. She crouched down to my eye level, as if we were sharing the secrets of the universe. In a tone that probably sounded more dramatic than she intended, she explained that it was a boarding school on the other side of Io — pretty much as far away from them while still being on the same planet.

Turning to dear old Dad for an explanation or, at the very least, a distraction from the impending familial meltdown, the bearded git was engaged in a staring contest with the sky. It was as if he believed they held the secrets to a lifetime supply of cosmic beer. 'I don't want to go!' I declared, my voice dripping with the gravitas only a nine-year-old prophet could muster.

"Just a couple of years, Arnold, and you can come home for your birthday," she boldly declared, and Dad, ever the spectator in the family circus, continued his stoic gaze into the sky. He never was one for eye contact. Snapping his head, he interjected, "Don't get the weaselly smegger's hopes up." Classic Dad!

Undeterred by the lack of emotional support, she flung a promise of her triumphant return in time for my birthday, as if the universe itself would pause its dance to celebrate my existence. Hugging me, she hoisted me up. 'C'mon, let's get some quiche,' she declared, casting a glance at Dad, who remained emotionally disengaged; he never would give quiche a chance.

The next morning, I was hurled into a transport craft, sharing a seat with Fred 'Thicky' Holden, leaving me to ponder the cosmic absurdity of it all. Suddenly, the predictable rhythms of my boyhood were replaced by the unpredictable chaos of the universe. Leaving behind our modest house on Io—a perfect replica of an Earth house from the 19th and 20th centuries with its hectares of land. There were some parts I wouldn't miss: getting up early in the morning to feed the sheep and cows, and my pet Lemming. Dad's insistence on manual labor became the launching pad for my determination and my brothers to join the Space Corps.

Our house had witnessed the shenanigans of many generations of Rimmers, with stories galore about my great-great-grandfather, Jebediah Rimmer, who legend has it fought off native Ionians to build the house and gardens. Now maintained by my Dad and with help from the local gardener, Dungo. My dad couldn't stand Dungo, and could never understand why. Sure, he was slightly inept at times and egotistical, self-important, lacked confidence, and was socially awkward. But I always liked him; he had a strong moralistic attitude, and my mother always took a shine to him.

My father, a half-crazed military failure, spent his early years amidst the military pioneers. Growing up on Io, his childhood was an exercise in minimalism. Yet, he yearned to be an officer like his father. The dream almost turned into reality when he strutted onto Space Corps Academy grounds, fulfilling an ambition that had marinated in the spartan conditions of an Io upbringing. Grandpa, an eternal optimist, had dreams of his son treading the same starlit path. Destiny pulled a cosmic prank when he was one inch below Corps regulation height.

My mother was born into an austere family that considered space exploration a genetic trait. Her father was part of the Space Corps' third graduating class, and her mother was a part of the cybernautic division — a family with enough star power to make a pulsar blush.

Mum, with dreams of becoming an astrobiologist, found herself on a collision course with Dad in an Introduction to Space Corps History class. Oh, but the Space Corps Directive 2574 about students fraternizing with other students was stricter than a vegan at a butcher shop. They soon found themselves in front of the space corps instructor with a warning.

Fast forward to Dad's posting on the JMC Emerald Nebula. Despite the height restrictions, strings were pulled, and he was made a galley steward. The ship was still three months away from Earth. He'd stayed in touch with my mother throughout, and in a move that combined romantic flair with a dash of desperation, while on leave at Lunar City 7, Dad proposed to my mother. 'Everyone thought we were bloody mad,' Mum once said, 'Maybe it was the wine or the smell of the beef that had seeped into his clothes. But I just couldn't say no to those puppy dog eyes.' Ah, the cosmic irony of hindsight.

My mother was posted on Titan, and my dad was posted on the JMC Emerald Nebula. Over a year passed before she saw Dad again, and almost two more years before she donned the graduation cap and tossed it into the wind. Yet, fate, with its sense of humor, decided that she wouldn't be posted anywhere near my dad.

My mother was freshly stationed on the Axiom II; however, it wasn't long before she found she had a tiny stowaway on board. She was pregnant with my older brother, Frank! 'Your father was in the outer rim at the time; he nearly dropped his spatula,' she said, 'and by the time the message got to him, I was already as big as a cow

So Mum's Space Corps ambitions hit a speed bump; she took a leave of absence and went to shack up on Io with my paternal grandparents. Lacking her parental navigators, who had embarked on the ultimate road trip years earlier, she found herself surrounded by vast farmland of good old terrestrial adventure. Enter Frank, my elder sibling, making his grand entrance. The interstellar escapades of the next generation were officially underway.

With the cosmic clock ticking, Mum had a mere two Earth-bound years before Space Corp's relentless gravitational pull demanded her return. In those terrestrial years, she juggled the titles of astrobiologist and dedicated mum. 'I just felt shagged out all the time,' she reminisced. 'I missed little Frank; this wasn't what I wanted.' Parenthood, it turns out, is the ultimate improvisational act.

With parents who had charted the final frontier of life and having witnessed her mother resigning her commission to raise her and her brother solo during Dad's cosmic escapades as chief slop server, Mum found herself in a parenting predicament. 'I was bored out of my mind, but your dad's career was everything to him,' she admitted. She'd study where she could while my grandparents took care of Frank. 'Your grandparents were like Energizer bunnies,' she shared. Meanwhile, Dad, charting his course through the galactic highways aboard the JMC Emerald Nebula, missed Mum and Frank. As the countdown to Mum's return commenced, Dad, ever the master of cosmic shenanigans, pulled whatever strings he could to get her posted back to Io, where he had assumed the role of Restroom attendant.

Only for calamity to strike again after my Mum's grand return to the Space Corps. Surprise, surprise—John was on the way, stealing the spotlight as the next Rimmer headliner. Dad informing Captain Sulaco was less than thrilled. Shipboard nurseries were not on his playlist. But, that triggered Dad's decision. A message blinked in from the cosmic ether—Dad's old man had punched out his ticket to the great beyond when he was born. His career as a restroom attendant wasn't going anywhere fast. Cue the resignation letter to Space Corps—bye-bye dad's officer career. So from that point on, they began to settle into life on Io together. Mum later shot out my next brother Howard. Then, having a break, they focused on the house and garden, bringing local gardener Dungo to assist. It wasn't long after I arrived on the scene!

In the galactic years since, I've mulled over Dad's plot twist and how it flung my trajectory into the cosmic unknown. The cosmic yarn I spin for the masses: Dad ditching Space Corps lit the afterburners on John, Howard, Frank, and my career quest, filling the void he left.

My brothers, all being older, eventually signed up for the Space Corps, graduating with top marks in their classes. They all got commission postings on the fleet's best ships. John was an astro-navigator on the SSS Augustus, where he shared quarters with a certain Frank Hollister—a captain in the making.

Frank, the rising star in the Space Corps, snagged the first officer position aboard the Nova 4 when the previous first officer, Cheddar Flatheringson, decided he'd rather play captain. Six years of navigating the officer bureaucracy had Frank on a trajectory to break records and become the youngest captain in the Space Corps. But, as I've always said, 'Up, up, up the ziggurat lickety-split.'

As for me, at the tender age of nine, my school grades were less than promising, and in a twist of cosmic fate, my parents decided it was better to wash their hands of me and ship me off to boarding school. As time ticked away, my envy for friends and their idyllic families turned me into a recluse. I found solace in the small things; I enjoyed listening to the Hammond organ, Morris Dancing, and building up my collection of 20th-century telegraph poles. You could always find me aimlessly wandering around the vast diesel decks at the local spaceport, attempting to rediscover the joy of getting lost. I even took up learning Esperanto in my sleep. But, as I looked up at the stars, where dreams of greatness shimmer like distant galaxies, my story was only just beginning. Arnold Judas Rimmer was destined for glory from the very fabric of stardust. My humble journey commenced not among the celestial bodies but within the labyrinth of obstacles—the very crucible of my stellar aspirations.

It was just another sunny day on Io, spent jesting with my older brothers John, Howard, and Frank. God, we were close—the 'Four Musketeers,' as we used to call ourselves! Well, the three musketeers actually; they always let me be the queen of Spain. What fun we'd have! An occasional practical joke, of course—apple-pie beds, black-eye telescope. They even hid a small landmine in my sandpit! How were they supposed to know it would go off? However, on this particular day, we were all blissfully ignorant of the interstellar smeg about to hit my life!

As my mother casually revealed her plan to send me off to boarding school! My school grades had been gradually slipping, and my parents, having tried absolutely nothing and being fresh out of ideas, thought it would be best to let me be someone else's problem. I, in my infinite pubescent wisdom, hit her with the forceful question, 'Will I still get to see Bruno?' Bruno was the family dog, clearly. You could see where my main priorities lay.

In response, she crouched down, bless her heart—magnificent woman. Very prim, very proper; some say austere. Some people mistook her for being cold and thought she was aloof. Not a bit of it. She crouched down to my eye level, as if we were sharing the secrets of the universe. In a tone that probably sounded more dramatic than she intended, she explained that it was a boarding school on the other side of Io—pretty much as far away from them while still being on the same planet.

Turning to dear old Dad for an explanation or, at the very least, a distraction from the impending familial meltdown, the bearded git was engaged in a staring contest with the sky. It was as if he believed they held the secrets to a lifetime supply of cosmic beer. 'I don't want to go!' I declared, my voice dripping with the gravitas only a nine-year-old prophet could muster.

"Just a couple of years, Arnold, and you can come home for your birthday," she boldly declared, and Dad, ever the spectator in the family circus, continued his stoic gaze into the sky. He never was one for eye contact. Snapping his head, he interjected, "Don't get the weaselly smegger's hopes up." Classic Dad!

Undeterred by the lack of emotional support, she flung a promise of her triumphant return in time for my birthday, as if the universe itself would pause its dance to celebrate my existence. Hugging me, she hoisted me up. 'C'mon, let's get some quiche,' she declared, casting a glance at Dad, who remained emotionally disengaged; he never would give quiche a chance.

The next morning, I was hurled into a transport craft, sharing a seat with Fred 'Thicky' Holden, leaving me to ponder the cosmic absurdity of it all. Suddenly, the predictable rhythms of my boyhood were replaced by the unpredictable chaos of the universe. Leaving behind our modest house on Io — a perfect replica of an Earth house from the 19th and 20th centuries with its hectares of land. There were some parts I wouldn't miss: getting up early in the morning to feed the sheep and cows, and my pet Lemming. Dad's insistence on manual labor became the launching pad for my determination and my brothers to join the Space Corps.

Our house had witnessed the shenanigans of many generations of Rimmers, with stories galore about my great-great-grandfather, Jebediah Rimmer, who legend has it fought off native Ionians to build the house and gardens. Now maintained by my Dad and with help from the local gardener, Dungo. My dad couldn't stand Dungo, and could never understand why. Sure, he was slightly inept at times and egotistical, self-important, lacked confidence, and was socially awkward. But I always liked him; he had a strong moralistic attitude, and my mother always took a shine to him.

My father, a half-crazed military failure, spent his early years amidst the military pioneers. Growing up on Io, his childhood was an exercise in minimalism. Yet, he yearned to be an officer like his father. The dream almost turned into reality when he strutted onto Space Corps Academy grounds, fulfilling an ambition that had marinated in the spartan conditions of an Io upbringing. Grandpa, an eternal optimist, had dreams of his son treading the same starlit path. Destiny pulled a cosmic prank when he was one inch below Corps regulation height.

My mother was born into an austere family that considered space exploration a genetic trait. Her father was part of the Space Corps' third graduating class, and her mother was a part of the cybernautic division — a family with enough star power to make a pulsar blush.

Mum, with dreams of becoming an astrobiologist, found herself on a collision course with Dad in an Introduction to Space Corps History class. Oh, but the Space Corps Directive 2574 about students fraternizing with other students was stricter than a vegan at a butcher shop. They soon found themselves in front of the space corps instructor with a warning.

Fast forward to Dad's posting on the JMC Emerald Nebula. Despite the height restrictions, strings were pulled, and he was made a galley steward. The ship was still three months away from Earth. He'd stayed in touch with my mother throughout, and in a move that combined romantic flair with a dash of desperation, while on leave at Lunar City 7, Dad proposed to my mother. 'Everyone thought we were bloody mad,' Mum once said, 'Maybe it was the wine or the smell of the beef that had seeped into his clothes. But I just couldn't say no to those puppy dog eyes.' Ah, the cosmic irony of hindsight.

My mother was posted on Titan, and my dad was posted on the JMC Emerald Nebula. Over a year passed before she saw Dad again, and almost two more years before she donned the graduation cap and tossed it into the wind. Yet, fate, with its sense of humor, decided that she wouldn't be posted anywhere near my dad.

My mother was freshly stationed on the Axiom II; however, it wasn't long before she found she had a tiny stowaway on board. She was pregnant with my older brother, Frank! 'Your father was in the outer rim at the time; he nearly dropped his spatula,' she said, 'and by the time the message got to him, I was already as big as a cow

So Mum's Space Corps ambitions hit a speed bump; she took a leave of absence and went to shack up on Io with my paternal grandparents. Lacking her parental navigators, who had embarked on the ultimate road trip years earlier, she found herself surrounded by vast farmland of good old terrestrial adventure. Enter Frank, my elder sibling, making his grand entrance. The interstellar escapades of the next generation were officially underway.

With the cosmic clock ticking, Mum had a mere two Earth-bound years before Space Corp's relentless gravitational pull demanded her return. In those terrestrial years, she juggled the titles of astrobiologist and dedicated mum. 'I just felt shagged out all the time,' she reminisced. 'I missed little Frank; this wasn't what I wanted.' Parenthood, it turns out, is the ultimate improvisational act.

With parents who had charted the final frontier of life and having witnessed her mother resigning her commission to raise her and her brother solo during Dad's cosmic escapades as chief slop server, Mum found herself in a parenting predicament. 'I was bored out of my mind,

but your dad's career was everything to him,' she admitted. She'd study where she could while my grandparents took care of Frank. 'Your grandparents were like Energizer bunnies,' she shared. Meanwhile, Dad, charting his course through the galactic highways aboard the JMC Emerald Nebula, missed Mum and Frank. As the countdown to Mum's return commenced, Dad, ever the master of cosmic shenanigans, pulled whatever strings he could to get her posted back to Io, where he had assumed the role of Restroom attendant.

Only for calamity to strike again after my Mum's grand return to the Space Corps. Surprise, surprise—John was on the way, stealing the spotlight as the next Rimmer headliner. Dad informing Captain Sulaco was less than thrilled. Shipboard nurseries were not on his playlist. But, that triggered Dad's decision. A message blinked in from the cosmic ether—Dad's old man had punched out his ticket to the great beyond when he was born. His career as a restroom attendant wasn't going anywhere fast. Cue the resignation letter to Space Corps—bye-bye dad's officer career. So from that point on, they began to settle into life on Io together. Mum later shot out my next brother Howard. Then, having a break, they focused on the house and garden, bringing local gardener Dungo to assist. It wasn't long after I arrived on the scene!

In the galactic years since, I've mulled over Dad's plot twist and how it flung my trajectory into the cosmic unknown. The cosmic yarn I spin for the masses: Dad ditching Space Corps lit the afterburners on John, Howard, Frank, and my career quest, filling the void he left.

My brothers, all being older, eventually signed up for the Space Corps, graduating with top marks in their classes. They all got commission postings on the fleet's best ships. John was an astro-navigator on the SSS Augustus, where he shared quarters with a certain Frank Hollister—a captain in the making.

17

Frank, the rising star in the Space Corps, snagged the first officer position aboard the Nova 4 when the previous first officer, Cheddar Flatheringson, decided he'd rather play captain. Six years of navigating the officer bureaucracy had Frank on a trajectory to break records and become the youngest captain in the Space Corps. But, as I've always said, 'Up, up, up the ziggurat lickety-split.

As for me, at the tender age of nine, my school grades were less than promising, and in a twist of cosmic fate, my parents decided it was better to wash their hands of me and ship me off to boarding school. As time ticked away, my envy for friends and their idyllic families turned me into a recluse. I found solace in the small things; I enjoyed listening to the Hammond organ, Morris Dancing, and building up my collection of 20th-century telegraph poles. You could always find me aimlessly wandering around the vast diesel decks at the local spaceport, attempting to rediscover the joy of getting lost. I even took up learning Esperanto in my sleep. But, as I looked up at the stars, where dreams of greatness shimmer like distant galaxies, my story was only just beginning. Arnold Judas Rimmer was destined for glory from the very fabric of stardust. My humble journey commenced not among the celestial bodies but within the labyrinth of obstacles—the very crucible of my stellar aspirations.

It was just another sunny day on Io, spent jesting with my older brothers John, Howard, and Frank. God, we were close—the 'Four Musketeers,' as we used to call ourselves! Well, the three musketeers actually; they always let me be the queen of Spain. What fun we'd have! An occasional practical joke, of course—apple-pie beds, black-eye telescope. They even hid a small landmine in my sandpit! How were they supposed to know it would go off? However, on this particular day, we were all blissfully ignorant of the interstellar smeg about to hit my life!

As my mother casually revealed her plan to send me off to boarding school! My school grades had been gradually slipping, and my parents, having tried absolutely nothing and being fresh out of ideas, thought it would be best to let me be someone else's problem. I, in my infinite pubescent wisdom, hit her with the forceful question, 'Will I still get to see Bruno?' Bruno was the family dog, clearly. You could see where my main priorities lay.

In response, she crouched down, bless her heart—magnificent woman. Very prim, very proper; some say austere. Some people mistook her for being cold and thought she was aloof. Not a bit of it. She crouched down to my eye level, as if we were sharing the secrets of the universe. In a tone that probably sounded more dramatic than she intended, she explained that it was a boarding school on the other side of Io—pretty much as far away from them while still being on the same planet.

Turning to dear old Dad for an explanation or, at the very least, a distraction from the impending familial meltdown, the bearded git was engaged in a staring contest with the sky. It was as if he believed they held the secrets to a lifetime supply of cosmic beer. 'I don't want to go!' I declared, my voice dripping with the gravitas only a nine-year-old prophet could muster.

"Just a couple of years, Arnold, and you can come home for your birthday," she boldly declared, and Dad, ever the spectator in the family circus, continued his stoic gaze into the sky. He never was one for eye contact. Snapping his head, he interjected, "Don't get the weaselly smegger's hopes up." Classic Dad!

Undeterred by the lack of emotional support, she flung a promise of her triumphant return in time for my birthday, as if the universe itself would pause its dance to celebrate my existence. Hugging me, she hoisted me up. 'C'mon, let's get some quiche,' she declared, casting a glance at Dad, who remained emotionally disengaged; he never would give quiche a chance.

The next morning, I was hurled into a transport craft, sharing a seat with Fred 'Thicky' Holden, leaving me to ponder the cosmic absurdity of it all. Suddenly, the predictable rhythms of my boyhood were replaced by the unpredictable chaos of the universe. Leaving behind our modest house on Io — a perfect replica of an Earth house from the 19th and 20th centuries with its hectares of land. There were some parts I wouldn't miss: getting up early in the morning to feed the sheep and cows, and my pet Lemming. Dad's insistence on manual labor became the launching pad for my determination and my brothers to join the Space Corps.

Our house had witnessed the shenanigans of many generations of Rimmers, with stories galore about my great-great-grandfather, Jebediah Rimmer, who legend has it fought off native Ionians to build the house and gardens. Now maintained by my Dad and with help from the local gardener, Dungo. My dad couldn't stand Dungo, and could never understand why. Sure, he was slightly inept at times and egotistical, self-important, lacked confidence, and was socially awkward. But I always liked him; he had a strong moralistic attitude, and my mother always took a shine to him.

My father, a half-crazed military failure, spent his early years amidst the military pioneers. Growing up on Io, his childhood was an exercise in minimalism. Yet, he yearned to be an officer like his father. The dream almost turned into reality when he strutted onto Space Corps Academy grounds, fulfilling an ambition that had marinated in the spartan

conditions of an Io upbringing. Grandpa, an eternal optimist, had dreams of his son treading the same starlit path. Destiny pulled a cosmic prank when he was one inch below Corps regulation height.

My mother was born into an austere family that considered space exploration a genetic trait. Her father was part of the Space Corps' third graduating class, and her mother was a part of the cybernautic division — a family with enough star power to make a pulsar blush.

Mum, with dreams of becoming an astrobiologist, found herself on a collision course with Dad in an Introduction to Space Corps History class. Oh, but the Space Corps Directive 2574 about students fraternizing with other students was stricter than a vegan at a butcher shop. They soon found themselves in front of the space corps instructor with a warning.

Fast forward to Dad's posting on the JMC Emerald Nebula. Despite the height restrictions, strings were pulled, and he was made a galley steward. The ship was still three months away from Earth. He'd stayed in touch with my mother throughout, and in a move that combined romantic flair with a dash of desperation, while on leave at Lunar City 7, Dad proposed to my mother. 'Everyone thought we were bloody mad,' Mum once said, 'Maybe it was the wine or the smell of the beef that had seeped into his clothes. But I just couldn't say no to those puppy dog eyes.' Ah, the cosmic irony of hindsight.

My mother was posted on Titan, and my dad was posted on the JMC Emerald Nebula. Over a year passed before she saw Dad again, and almost two more years before she donned the graduation cap and tossed it into the wind. Yet, fate, with its sense of humor, decided that she wouldn't be posted anywhere near my dad.

My mother was freshly stationed on the Axiom II; however, it wasn't long before she found she had a tiny stowaway on board. She was pregnant with my older brother, Frank! 'Your father was in the outer rim at the time; he nearly dropped his spatula,' she said, 'and by the time the message got to him, I was already as big as a cow

So Mum's Space Corps ambitions hit a speed bump; she took a leave of absence and went to shack up on Io with my paternal grandparents. Lacking her parental navigators, who had embarked on the ultimate road trip years earlier, she found herself surrounded by vast farmland of good old terrestrial adventure. Enter Frank, my elder sibling, making his grand entrance. The interstellar escapades of the next generation were officially underway.

With the cosmic clock ticking, Mum had a mere two Earth-bound years before Space Corp's relentless gravitational pull demanded her return. In those terrestrial years, she juggled the titles of astrobiologist and dedicated mum. 'I just felt shagged out all the time,' she reminisced. 'I missed little Frank; this wasn't what I wanted.' Parenthood, it turns out, is the ultimate improvisational act.

With parents who had charted the final frontier of life and having witnessed her mother resigning her commission to raise her and her brother solo during Dad's cosmic escapades as chief slop server, Mum found herself in a parenting predicament. 'I was bored out of my mind, but your dad's career was everything to him,' she admitted. She'd study where she could while my grandparents took care of Frank. 'Your grandparents were like Energizer bunnies,' she shared. Meanwhile, Dad, charting his course through the galactic highways aboard the JMC Emerald Nebula, missed Mum and Frank. As the countdown to Mum's return commenced, Dad, ever the master of cosmic shenanigans, pulled whatever strings he could to get her posted back to Io, where he had assumed the role of Restroom attendant.

Only for calamity to strike again after my Mum's grand return to the Space Corps. Surprise, surprise—John was on the way, stealing the spotlight as the next Rimmer headliner. Dad informing Captain Sulaco was less than thrilled. Shipboard nurseries were not on his playlist. But, that triggered Dad's decision. A message blinked in from the cosmic ether—Dad's old man had punched out his ticket to the great beyond when he was born. His career as a restroom attendant wasn't going anywhere fast. Cue the resignation letter to Space Corps—bye-bye dad's officer career. So from that point on, they began to settle into life on Io together. Mum later shot out my next brother Howard. Then, having a break, they focused on the house and garden, bringing local gardener Dungo to assist. It wasn't long after I arrived on the scene!

In the galactic years since, I've mulled over Dad's plot twist and how it flung my trajectory into the cosmic unknown. The cosmic yarn I spin for the masses: Dad ditching Space Corps lit the afterburners on John, Howard, Frank, and my career quest, filling the void he left.

My brothers, all being older, eventually signed up for the Space Corps, graduating with top marks in their classes. They all got commission postings on the fleet's best ships. John was an astro-navigator on the SSS Augustus, where he shared quarters with a certain Frank Hollister—a captain in the making.

Frank, the rising star in the Space Corps, snagged the first officer position aboard the Nova 4 when the previous first officer, Cheddar Flatheringson, decided he'd rather play captain. Six years of navigating the officer bureaucracy had Frank on a trajectory to break records and become the youngest captain in the Space Corps. But, as I've always said, 'Up, up, up the ziggurat lickety-split.

As for me, at the tender age of nine, my school grades were less than promising, and in a twist of cosmic fate, my parents decided it was better to wash their hands of me and ship me off to boarding school. As time ticked away, my envy for friends and their idyllic families turned me into a recluse. I found solace in the small things; I enjoyed listening to the Hammond organ, Morris Dancing, and building up my collection of 20th-century telegraph poles. You could always find me aimlessly wandering around the vast diesel decks at the local spaceport, attempting to rediscover the joy of getting lost. I even took up learning Esperanto in my sleep. But, as I looked up at the stars, where dreams of greatness shimmer like distant galaxies, my story was only just beginning. Arnold Judas Rimmer was destined for glory from the very fabric of stardust. My humble journey commenced not among the celestial bodies but within the labyrinth of obstacles — the very crucible of my stellar aspirations.

It was just another sunny day on Io, spent jesting with my older brothers John, Howard, and Frank. God, we were close — the 'Four Musketeers,' as we used to call ourselves! Well, the three musketeers actually; they always let me be the queen of Spain. What fun we'd have! An occasional practical joke, of course — apple-pie beds, black-eye telescope. They even hid a small landmine in my sandpit! How were they supposed to know it would go off? However, on this particular day, we were all blissfully ignorant of the interstellar smeg about to hit my life!

As my mother casually revealed her plan to send me off to boarding school! My school grades had been gradually slipping, and my parents, having tried absolutely nothing and being fresh out of ideas, thought it would be best to let me be someone else's problem. I, in my infinite pubescent wisdom, hit her with the forceful question, 'Will I still get to see Bruno?' Bruno was the family dog, clearly. You could see where my main priorities lay.

In response, she crouched down, bless her heart—magnificent woman. Very prim, very proper; some say austere. Some people mistook her for being cold and thought she was aloof. Not a bit of it. She crouched down to my eye level, as if we were sharing the secrets of the universe. In a tone that probably sounded more dramatic than she intended, she explained that it was a boarding school on the other side of Io—pretty much as far away from them while still being on the same planet.

Turning to dear old Dad for an explanation or, at the very least, a distraction from the impending familial meltdown, the bearded git was engaged in a staring contest with the sky. It was as if he believed they held the secrets to a lifetime supply of cosmic beer. 'I don't want to go!' I declared, my voice dripping with the gravitas only a nine-year-old prophet could muster.

"Just a couple of years, Arnold, and you can come home for your birthday," she boldly declared, and Dad, ever the spectator in the family circus, continued his stoic gaze into the sky. He never was one for eye contact. Snapping his head, he interjected, "Don't get the weaselly smegger's hopes up." Classic Dad!

Undeterred by the lack of emotional support, she flung a promise of her triumphant return in time for my birthday, as if the universe itself would pause its dance to celebrate my existence. Hugging me, she hoisted me up. 'C'mon, let's get some quiche,' she declared, casting a glance at Dad, who remained emotionally disengaged; he never would give quiche a chance.

The next morning, I was hurled into a transport craft, sharing a seat with Fred 'Thicky' Holden, leaving me to ponder the cosmic absurdity of it all. Suddenly, the predictable rhythms of my boyhood were replaced by the unpredictable chaos of the universe. Leaving behind our modest house

on Io — a perfect replica of an Earth house from the 19th and 20th centuries with its hectares of land. There were some parts I wouldn't miss: getting up early in the morning to feed the sheep and cows, and my pet Lemming. Dad's insistence on manual labor became the launching pad for my determination and my brothers to join the Space Corps.

Our house had witnessed the shenanigans of many generations of Rimmers, with stories galore about my great-great-grandfather, Jebediah Rimmer, who legend has it fought off native Ionians to build the house and gardens. Now maintained by my Dad and with help from the local gardener, Dungo. My dad couldn't stand Dungo, and could never understand why. Sure, he was slightly inept at times and egotistical, self-important, lacked confidence, and was socially awkward. But I always liked him; he had a strong moralistic attitude, and my mother always took a shine to him.

My father, a half-crazed military failure, spent his early years amidst the military pioneers. Growing up on Io, his childhood was an exercise in minimalism. Yet, he yearned to be an officer like his father. The dream almost turned into reality when he strutted onto Space Corps Academy grounds, fulfilling an ambition that had marinated in the spartan conditions of an Io upbringing. Grandpa, an eternal optimist, had dreams of his son treading the same starlit path. Destiny pulled a cosmic prank when he was one inch below Corps regulation height.

My mother was born into an austere family that considered space exploration a genetic trait. Her father was part of the Space Corps' third graduating class, and her mother was a part of the cybernautic division — a family with enough star power to make a pulsar blush.

Mum, with dreams of becoming an astrobiologist, found herself on a collision course with Dad in an Introduction to Space Corps History class. Oh, but the Space Corps Directive 2574 about students fraternizing with other students was stricter than a vegan at a butcher shop. They soon found themselves in front of the space corps instructor with a warning.

Fast forward to Dad's posting on the JMC Emerald Nebula. Despite the height restrictions, strings were pulled, and he was made a galley steward. The ship was still three months away from Earth. He'd stayed in touch with my mother throughout, and in a move that combined romantic flair with a dash of desperation, while on leave at Lunar City 7, Dad proposed to my mother. 'Everyone thought we were bloody mad,' Mum once said, 'Maybe it was the wine or the smell of the beef that had seeped into his clothes. But I just couldn't say no to those puppy dog eyes.' Ah, the cosmic irony of hindsight.

My mother was posted on Titan, and my dad was posted on the JMC Emerald Nebula. Over a year passed before she saw Dad again, and almost two more years before she donned the graduation cap and tossed it into the wind. Yet, fate, with its sense of humor, decided that she wouldn't be posted anywhere near my dad.

My mother was freshly stationed on the Axiom II; however, it wasn't long before she found she had a tiny stowaway on board. She was pregnant with my older brother, Frank! 'Your father was in the outer rim at the time; he nearly dropped his spatula,' she said, 'and by the time the message got to him, I was already as big as a cow

So Mum's Space Corps ambitions hit a speed bump; she took a leave of absence and went to shack up on Io with my paternal grandparents. Lacking her parental navigators, who had embarked on the ultimate road

trip years earlier, she found herself surrounded by vast farmland of good old terrestrial adventure. Enter Frank, my elder sibling, making his grand entrance. The interstellar escapades of the next generation were officially underway.

With the cosmic clock ticking, Mum had a mere two Earth-bound years before Space Corp's relentless gravitational pull demanded her return. In those terrestrial years, she juggled the titles of astrobiologist and dedicated mum. 'I just felt shagged out all the time,' she reminisced. 'I missed little Frank; this wasn't what I wanted.' Parenthood, it turns out, is the ultimate improvisational act.

With parents who had charted the final frontier of life and having witnessed her mother resigning her commission to raise her and her brother solo during Dad's cosmic escapades as chief slop server, Mum found herself in a parenting predicament. 'I was bored out of my mind, but your dad's career was everything to him,' she admitted. She'd study where she could while my grandparents took care of Frank. 'Your grandparents were like Energizer bunnies,' she shared. Meanwhile, Dad, charting his course through the galactic highways aboard the JMC Emerald Nebula, missed Mum and Frank. As the countdown to Mum's return commenced, Dad, ever the master of cosmic shenanigans, pulled whatever strings he could to get her posted back to Io, where he had assumed the role of Restroom attendant.

Only for calamity to strike again after my Mum's grand return to the Space Corps. Surprise, surprise—John was on the way, stealing the spotlight as the next Rimmer headliner. Dad informing Captain Sulaco was less than thrilled. Shipboard nurseries were not on his playlist. But, that triggered Dad's decision. A message blinked in from the cosmic ether—Dad's old man had punched out his ticket to the great beyond when he was born. His career as a restroom attendant wasn't going anywhere fast. Cue the resignation letter to Space Corps — bye-bye dad's officer career. So from that point on, they began to settle into life on Io together. Mum later shot out my next brother Howard. Then, having a break, they focused on the house and garden, bringing local gardener Dungo to assist. It wasn't long after I arrived on the scene!

In the galactic years since, I've mulled over Dad's plot twist and how it flung my trajectory into the cosmic unknown. The cosmic yarn I spin for the masses: Dad ditching Space Corps lit the afterburners on John, Howard, Frank, and my career quest, filling the void he left.

My brothers, all being older, eventually signed up for the Space Corps, graduating with top marks in their classes. They all got commission postings on the fleet's best ships. John was an astro-navigator on the SSS Augustus, where he shared quarters with a certain Frank Hollister — a captain in the making.

Frank, the rising star in the Space Corps, snagged the first officer position aboard the Nova 4 when the previous first officer, Cheddar Flatheringson, decided he'd rather play captain. Six years of navigating the officer bureaucracy had Frank on a trajectory to break records and become the youngest captain in the Space Corps. But, as I've always said, 'Up, up, up the ziggurat lickety-split.

As for me, at the tender age of nine, my school grades were less than promising, and in a twist of cosmic fate, my parents decided it was better to wash their hands of me and ship me off to boarding school. As time ticked away, my envy for friends and their idyllic families turned me into a recluse. I found solace in the small things; I enjoyed listening to the Hammond organ, Morris Dancing, and building up my collection of 20th-century telegraph poles. You could always find me aimlessly wandering around the vast diesel decks at the local spaceport, attempting to rediscover the joy of getting lost. I even took up learning Esperanto in my sleep. But, as I looked up at the stars, where dreams of greatness shimmer like distant galaxies, my story was only just beginning. Arnold Judas Rimmer was destined for glory from the very fabric of stardust. My humble journey commenced not among the celestial bodies but within the labyrinth of obstacles — the very crucible of my stellar aspirations.

# CHAPTER 3
# CRISIS OF CONFIDENCE

It was just another sunny day on Io, spent jesting with my older brothers John, Howard, and Frank. God, we were close—the 'Four Musketeers,' as we used to call ourselves! Well, the three musketeers actually; they always let me be the queen of Spain. What fun we'd have! An occasional practical joke, of course—apple-pie beds, black-eye telescope. They even hid a small landmine in my sandpit! How were they supposed to know it would go off? However, on this particular day, we were all blissfully ignorant of the interstellar smeg about to hit my life!

As my mother casually revealed her plan to send me off to boarding school! My school grades had been gradually slipping, and my parents, having tried absolutely nothing and being fresh out of ideas, thought it would be best to let me be someone else's problem. I, in my infinite pubescent wisdom, hit her with the forceful question, 'Will I still get to see Bruno?' Bruno was the family dog, clearly. You could see where my main priorities lay.

In response, she crouched down, bless her heart—magnificent woman. Very prim, very proper; some say austere. Some people mistook her for being cold and thought she was aloof. Not a bit of it. She crouched down to my eye level, as if we were sharing the secrets of the universe. In a tone that probably sounded more dramatic than she intended, she explained that it was a boarding school on the other side of Io—pretty much as far away from them while still being on the same planet.

Turning to dear old Dad for an explanation or, at the very least, a distraction from the impending familial meltdown, the bearded git was engaged in a staring contest with the sky. It was as if he believed they held the secrets to a lifetime supply of cosmic beer. 'I don't want to go!' I declared, my voice dripping with the gravitas only a nine-year-old prophet could muster.

"Just a couple of years, Arnold, and you can come home for your birthday," she boldly declared, and Dad, ever the spectator in the family circus, continued his stoic gaze into the sky. He never was one for eye contact. Snapping his head, he interjected, "Don't get the weaselly smegger's hopes up." Classic Dad!

Undeterred by the lack of emotional support, she flung a promise of her triumphant return in time for my birthday, as if the universe itself would pause its dance to celebrate my existence. Hugging me, she hoisted me up. 'C'mon, let's get some quiche,' she declared, casting a glance at Dad, who remained emotionally disengaged; he never would give quiche a chance.

The next morning, I was hurled into a transport craft, sharing a seat with Fred 'Thicky' Holden, leaving me to ponder the cosmic absurdity of it all. Suddenly, the predictable rhythms of my boyhood were replaced by the unpredictable chaos of the universe. Leaving behind our modest house on Io — a perfect replica of an Earth house from the 19th and 20th centuries with its hectares of land. There were some parts I wouldn't miss: getting up early in the morning to feed the sheep and cows, and my pet Lemming. Dad's insistence on manual labor became the launching pad for my determination and my brothers to join the Space Corps.

Our house had witnessed the shenanigans of many generations of Rimmers, with stories galore about my great-great-grandfather, Jebediah Rimmer, who legend has it fought off native Ionians to build the house and gardens. Now maintained by my Dad and with help from the local gardener, Dungo. My dad couldn't stand Dungo, and could never understand why. Sure, he was slightly inept at times and egotistical, self-important, lacked confidence, and was socially awkward. But I always liked him; he had a strong moralistic attitude, and my mother always took a shine to him.

My father, a half-crazed military failure, spent his early years amidst the military pioneers. Growing up on Io, his childhood was an exercise in minimalism. Yet, he yearned to be an officer like his father. The dream almost turned into reality when he strutted onto Space Corps Academy grounds, fulfilling an ambition that had marinated in the spartan conditions of an Io upbringing. Grandpa, an eternal optimist, had dreams of his son treading the same starlit path. Destiny pulled a cosmic prank when he was one inch below Corps regulation height.

My mother was born into an austere family that considered space exploration a genetic trait. Her father was part of the Space Corps' third graduating class, and her mother was a part of the cybernautic division — a family with enough star power to make a pulsar blush.

Mum, with dreams of becoming an astrobiologist, found herself on a collision course with Dad in an Introduction to Space Corps History class. Oh, but the Space Corps Directive 2574 about students fraternizing with other students was stricter than a vegan at a butcher shop. They soon found themselves in front of the space corps instructor with a warning.

Fast forward to Dad's posting on the JMC Emerald Nebula. Despite the height restrictions, strings were pulled, and he was made a galley steward. The ship was still three months away from Earth. He'd stayed in touch with my mother throughout, and in a move that combined romantic flair with a dash of desperation, while on leave at Lunar City 7, Dad proposed to my mother. 'Everyone thought we were bloody mad,' Mum once said, 'Maybe it was the wine or the smell of the beef that had seeped into his clothes. But I just couldn't say no to those puppy dog eyes.' Ah, the cosmic irony of hindsight.

My mother was posted on Titan, and my dad was posted on the JMC Emerald Nebula. Over a year passed before she saw Dad again, and almost two more years before she donned the graduation cap and tossed it into the wind. Yet, fate, with its sense of humor, decided that she wouldn't be posted anywhere near my dad.

My mother was freshly stationed on the Axiom II; however, it wasn't long before she found she had a tiny stowaway on board. She was pregnant with my older brother, Frank! 'Your father was in the outer rim at the time; he nearly dropped his spatula,' she said, 'and by the time the message got to him, I was already as big as a cow

So Mum's Space Corps ambitions hit a speed bump; she took a leave of absence and went to shack up on Io with my paternal grandparents. Lacking her parental navigators, who had embarked on the ultimate road trip years earlier, she found herself surrounded by vast farmland of good old terrestrial adventure. Enter Frank, my elder sibling, making his grand entrance. The interstellar escapades of the next generation were officially underway.

With the cosmic clock ticking, Mum had a mere two Earth-bound years before Space Corp's relentless gravitational pull demanded her return. In those terrestrial years, she juggled the titles of astrobiologist and dedicated mum. 'I just felt shagged out all the time,' she reminisced. 'I missed little Frank; this wasn't what I wanted.' Parenthood, it turns out, is the ultimate improvisational act.

With parents who had charted the final frontier of life and having witnessed her mother resigning her commission to raise her and her brother solo during Dad's cosmic escapades as chief slop server, Mum found herself in a parenting predicament. 'I was bored out of my mind, but your dad's career was everything to him,' she admitted. She'd study where she could while my grandparents took care of Frank. 'Your grandparents were like Energizer bunnies,' she shared. Meanwhile, Dad, charting his course through the galactic highways aboard the JMC Emerald Nebula, missed Mum and Frank. As the countdown to Mum's return commenced, Dad, ever the master of cosmic shenanigans, pulled whatever strings he could to get her posted back to Io, where he had assumed the role of Restroom attendant.

Only for calamity to strike again after my Mum's grand return to the Space Corps. Surprise, surprise—John was on the way, stealing the spotlight as the next Rimmer headliner. Dad informing Captain Sulaco was less than thrilled. Shipboard nurseries were not on his playlist. But, that triggered Dad's decision. A message blinked in from the cosmic ether—Dad's old man had punched out his ticket to the great beyond when he was born. His career as a restroom attendant wasn't going anywhere fast. Cue the resignation letter to Space Corps—bye-bye dad's officer career. So from that point on, they began to settle into life on Io together. Mum later shot out my next brother Howard. Then, having a break, they focused on the house and garden, bringing local gardener Dungo to assist. It wasn't long after I arrived on the scene!

In the galactic years since, I've mulled over Dad's plot twist and how it flung my trajectory into the cosmic unknown. The cosmic yarn I spin for the masses: Dad ditching Space Corps lit the afterburners on John, Howard, Frank, and my career quest, filling the void he left.

My brothers, all being older, eventually signed up for the Space Corps, graduating with top marks in their classes. They all got commission postings on the fleet's best ships. John was an astro-navigator on the SSS Augustus, where he shared quarters with a certain Frank Hollister—a captain in the making.

Frank, the rising star in the Space Corps, snagged the first officer position aboard the Nova 4 when the previous first officer, Cheddar Flatheringson, decided he'd rather play captain. Six years of navigating the officer bureaucracy had Frank on a trajectory to break records and become the youngest captain in the Space Corps. But, as I've always said, 'Up, up, up the ziggurat lickety-split.

As for me, at the tender age of nine, my school grades were less than promising, and in a twist of cosmic fate, my parents decided it was better to wash their hands of me and ship me off to boarding school. As time ticked away, my envy for friends and their idyllic families turned me into a recluse. I found solace in the small things; I enjoyed listening to the Hammond organ, Morris Dancing, and building up my collection of 20th-century telegraph poles. You could always find me aimlessly wandering around the vast diesel decks at the local spaceport, attempting to rediscover the joy of getting lost. I even took up learning Esperanto in my sleep. But, as I looked up at the stars, where dreams of greatness shimmer like distant galaxies, my story was only just beginning. Arnold Judas Rimmer was destined for glory from the very fabric of stardust. My humble journey commenced not among the celestial bodies but within the labyrinth of obstacles—the very crucible of my stellar aspirations.

It was just another sunny day on Io, spent jesting with my older brothers John, Howard, and Frank. God, we were close—the 'Four Musketeers,' as we used to call ourselves! Well, the three musketeers actually; they always let me be the queen of Spain. What fun we'd have! An occasional practical joke, of course—apple-pie beds, black-eye telescope. They even hid a small landmine in my sandpit! How were they supposed to know it would go off? However, on this particular day, we were all blissfully ignorant of the interstellar smeg about to hit my life!

As my mother casually revealed her plan to send me off to boarding school! My school grades had been gradually slipping, and my parents, having tried absolutely nothing and being fresh out of ideas, thought it would be best to let me be someone else's problem. I, in my infinite pubescent wisdom, hit her with the forceful question, 'Will I still get to see Bruno?' Bruno was the family dog, clearly. You could see where my main priorities lay.

In response, she crouched down, bless her heart—magnificent woman. Very prim, very proper; some say austere. Some people mistook her for being cold and thought she was aloof. Not a bit of it. She crouched down to my eye level, as if we were sharing the secrets of the universe. In a tone that probably sounded more dramatic than she intended, she explained that it was a boarding school on the other side of Io—pretty much as far away from them while still being on the same planet.

Turning to dear old Dad for an explanation or, at the very least, a distraction from the impending familial meltdown, the bearded git was engaged in a staring contest with the sky. It was as if he believed they held the secrets to a lifetime supply of cosmic beer. 'I don't want to go!' I declared, my voice dripping with the gravitas only a nine-year-old prophet could muster.

"Just a couple of years, Arnold, and you can come home for your birthday," she boldly declared, and Dad, ever the spectator in the family circus, continued his stoic gaze into the sky. He never was one for eye contact. Snapping his head, he interjected, "Don't get the weaselly smegger's hopes up." Classic Dad!

Undeterred by the lack of emotional support, she flung a promise of her triumphant return in time for my birthday, as if the universe itself would pause its dance to celebrate my existence. Hugging me, she hoisted me up. 'C'mon, let's get some quiche,' she declared, casting a glance at Dad, who remained emotionally disengaged; he never would give quiche a chance.

The next morning, I was hurled into a transport craft, sharing a seat with Fred 'Thicky' Holden, leaving me to ponder the cosmic absurdity of it all. Suddenly, the predictable rhythms of my boyhood were replaced by the unpredictable chaos of the universe. Leaving behind our modest house on Io — a perfect replica of an Earth house from the 19th and 20th centuries with its hectares of land. There were some parts I wouldn't miss: getting up early in the morning to feed the sheep and cows, and my pet Lemming. Dad's insistence on manual labor became the launching pad for my determination and my brothers to join the Space Corps.

Our house had witnessed the shenanigans of many generations of Rimmers, with stories galore about my great-great-grandfather, Jebediah Rimmer, who legend has it fought off native Ionians to build the house and gardens. Now maintained by my Dad and with help from the local gardener, Dungo. My dad couldn't stand Dungo, and could never understand why. Sure, he was slightly inept at times and egotistical, self-important, lacked confidence, and was socially awkward. But I always liked him; he had a strong moralistic attitude, and my mother always took a shine to him.

My father, a half-crazed military failure, spent his early years amidst the military pioneers. Growing up on Io, his childhood was an exercise in minimalism. Yet, he yearned to be an officer like his father. The dream almost turned into reality when he strutted onto Space Corps Academy grounds, fulfilling an ambition that had marinated in the spartan conditions of an Io upbringing. Grandpa, an eternal optimist, had dreams of his son treading the same starlit path. Destiny pulled a cosmic prank when he was one inch below Corps regulation height.

My mother was born into an austere family that considered space exploration a genetic trait. Her father was part of the Space Corps' third graduating class, and her mother was a part of the cybernautic division — a family with enough star power to make a pulsar blush.

Mum, with dreams of becoming an astrobiologist, found herself on a collision course with Dad in an Introduction to Space Corps History class. Oh, but the Space Corps Directive 2574 about students fraternizing with other students was stricter than a vegan at a butcher shop. They soon found themselves in front of the space corps instructor with a warning.

Fast forward to Dad's posting on the JMC Emerald Nebula. Despite the height restrictions, strings were pulled, and he was made a galley steward. The ship was still three months away from Earth. He'd stayed in touch with my mother throughout, and in a move that combined romantic flair with a dash of desperation, while on leave at Lunar City 7, Dad proposed to my mother. 'Everyone thought we were bloody mad,' Mum once said, 'Maybe it was the wine or the smell of the beef that had seeped into his clothes. But I just couldn't say no to those puppy dog eyes.' Ah, the cosmic irony of hindsight.

My mother was posted on Titan, and my dad was posted on the JMC Emerald Nebula. Over a year passed before she saw Dad again, and almost two more years before she donned the graduation cap and tossed it into the wind. Yet, fate, with its sense of humor, decided that she wouldn't be posted anywhere near my dad.

My mother was freshly stationed on the Axiom II; however, it wasn't long before she found she had a tiny stowaway on board. She was pregnant with my older brother, Frank! 'Your father was in the outer rim at the time; he nearly dropped his spatula,' she said, 'and by the time the message got to him, I was already as big as a cow

So Mum's Space Corps ambitions hit a speed bump; she took a leave of absence and went to shack up on Io with my paternal grandparents. Lacking her parental navigators, who had embarked on the ultimate road trip years earlier, she found herself surrounded by vast farmland of good old terrestrial adventure. Enter Frank, my elder sibling, making his grand entrance. The interstellar escapades of the next generation were officially underway.

With the cosmic clock ticking, Mum had a mere two Earth-bound years before Space Corp's relentless gravitational pull demanded her return. In those terrestrial years, she juggled the titles of astrobiologist and dedicated mum. 'I just felt shagged out all the time,' she reminisced. 'I missed little Frank; this wasn't what I wanted.' Parenthood, it turns out, is the ultimate improvisational act.

With parents who had charted the final frontier of life and having witnessed her mother resigning her commission to raise her and her brother solo during Dad's cosmic escapades as chief slop server, Mum found herself in a parenting predicament. 'I was bored out of my mind, but your dad's career was everything to him,' she admitted. She'd study

where she could while my grandparents took care of Frank. 'Your grandparents were like Energizer bunnies,' she shared. Meanwhile, Dad, charting his course through the galactic highways aboard the JMC Emerald Nebula, missed Mum and Frank. As the countdown to Mum's return commenced, Dad, ever the master of cosmic shenanigans, pulled whatever strings he could to get her posted back to Io, where he had assumed the role of Restroom attendant.

Only for calamity to strike again after my Mum's grand return to the Space Corps. Surprise, surprise—John was on the way, stealing the spotlight as the next Rimmer headliner. Dad informing Captain Sulaco was less than thrilled. Shipboard nurseries were not on his playlist. But, that triggered Dad's decision. A message blinked in from the cosmic ether—Dad's old man had punched out his ticket to the great beyond when he was born. His career as a restroom attendant wasn't going anywhere fast. Cue the resignation letter to Space Corps—bye-bye dad's officer career. So from that point on, they began to settle into life on Io together. Mum later shot out my next brother Howard. Then, having a break, they focused on the house and garden, bringing local gardener Dungo to assist. It wasn't long after I arrived on the scene!

In the galactic years since, I've mulled over Dad's plot twist and how it flung my trajectory into the cosmic unknown. The cosmic yarn I spin for the masses: Dad ditching Space Corps lit the afterburners on John, Howard, Frank, and my career quest, filling the void he left.

My brothers, all being older, eventually signed up for the Space Corps, graduating with top marks in their classes. They all got commission postings on the fleet's best ships. John was an astro-navigator on the SSS Augustus, where he shared quarters with a certain Frank Hollister—a captain in the making.

Frank, the rising star in the Space Corps, snagged the first officer position aboard the Nova 4 when the previous first officer, Cheddar Flatheringson, decided he'd rather play captain. Six years of navigating the officer bureaucracy had Frank on a trajectory to break records and become the youngest captain in the Space Corps. But, as I've always said, 'Up, up, up the ziggurat lickety-split.

As for me, at the tender age of nine, my school grades were less than promising, and in a twist of cosmic fate, my parents decided it was better to wash their hands of me and ship me off to boarding school. As time ticked away, my envy for friends and their idyllic families turned me into a recluse. I found solace in the small things; I enjoyed listening to the Hammond organ, Morris Dancing, and building up my collection of 20th-century telegraph poles. You could always find me aimlessly wandering around the vast diesel decks at the local spaceport, attempting to rediscover the joy of getting lost. I even took up learning Esperanto in my sleep. But, as I looked up at the stars, where dreams of greatness shimmer like distant galaxies, my story was only just beginning. Arnold Judas Rimmer was destined for glory from the very fabric of stardust. My humble journey commenced not among the celestial bodies but within the labyrinth of obstacles — the very crucible of my stellar aspirations.

It was just another sunny day on Io, spent jesting with my older brothers John, Howard, and Frank. God, we were close — the 'Four Musketeers,' as we used to call ourselves! Well, the three musketeers actually; they always let me be the queen of Spain. What fun we'd have! An occasional practical joke, of course — apple-pie beds, black-eye telescope. They even hid a small landmine in my sandpit! How were they supposed to know it would go off? However, on this particular day, we were all blissfully ignorant of the interstellar smeg about to hit my life!

As my mother casually revealed her plan to send me off to boarding school! My school grades had been gradually slipping, and my parents, having tried absolutely nothing and being fresh out of ideas, thought it would be best to let me be someone else's problem. I, in my infinite pubescent wisdom, hit her with the forceful question, 'Will I still get to see Bruno?' Bruno was the family dog, clearly. You could see where my main priorities lay.

In response, she crouched down, bless her heart — magnificent woman. Very prim, very proper; some say austere. Some people mistook her for being cold and thought she was aloof. Not a bit of it. She crouched down to my eye level, as if we were sharing the secrets of the universe. In a tone that probably sounded more dramatic than she intended, she explained that it was a boarding school on the other side of Io — pretty much as far away from them while still being on the same planet.

Turning to dear old Dad for an explanation or, at the very least, a distraction from the impending familial meltdown, the bearded git was engaged in a staring contest with the sky. It was as if he believed they held the secrets to a lifetime supply of cosmic beer. 'I don't want to go!' I declared, my voice dripping with the gravitas only a nine-year-old prophet could muster.

"Just a couple of years, Arnold, and you can come home for your birthday," she boldly declared, and Dad, ever the spectator in the family circus, continued his stoic gaze into the sky. He never was one for eye contact. Snapping his head, he interjected, "Don't get the weaselly smegger's hopes up." Classic Dad!

Undeterred by the lack of emotional support, she flung a promise of her triumphant return in time for my birthday, as if the universe itself would pause its dance to celebrate my existence. Hugging me, she hoisted me up. 'C'mon, let's get some quiche,' she declared, casting a glance at Dad, who remained emotionally disengaged; he never would give quiche a chance.

The next morning, I was hurled into a transport craft, sharing a seat with Fred 'Thicky' Holden, leaving me to ponder the cosmic absurdity of it all. Suddenly, the predictable rhythms of my boyhood were replaced by the unpredictable chaos of the universe. Leaving behind our modest house on Io — a perfect replica of an Earth house from the 19th and 20th centuries with its hectares of land. There were some parts I wouldn't miss: getting up early in the morning to feed the sheep and cows, and my pet Lemming. Dad's insistence on manual labor became the launching pad for my determination and my brothers to join the Space Corps.

Our house had witnessed the shenanigans of many generations of Rimmers, with stories galore about my great-great-grandfather, Jebediah Rimmer, who legend has it fought off native Ionians to build the house and gardens. Now maintained by my Dad and with help from the local gardener, Dungo. My dad couldn't stand Dungo, and could never understand why. Sure, he was slightly inept at times and egotistical, self-important, lacked confidence, and was socially awkward. But I always liked him; he had a strong moralistic attitude, and my mother always took a shine to him.

My father, a half-crazed military failure, spent his early years amidst the military pioneers. Growing up on Io, his childhood was an exercise in minimalism. Yet, he yearned to be an officer like his father. The dream almost turned into reality when he strutted onto Space Corps Academy grounds, fulfilling an ambition that had marinated in the spartan

conditions of an Io upbringing. Grandpa, an eternal optimist, had dreams of his son treading the same starlit path. Destiny pulled a cosmic prank when he was one inch below Corps regulation height.

My mother was born into an austere family that considered space exploration a genetic trait. Her father was part of the Space Corps' third graduating class, and her mother was a part of the cybernautic division — a family with enough star power to make a pulsar blush.

Mum, with dreams of becoming an astrobiologist, found herself on a collision course with Dad in an Introduction to Space Corps History class. Oh, but the Space Corps Directive 2574 about students fraternizing with other students was stricter than a vegan at a butcher shop. They soon found themselves in front of the space corps instructor with a warning.

Fast forward to Dad's posting on the JMC Emerald Nebula. Despite the height restrictions, strings were pulled, and he was made a galley steward. The ship was still three months away from Earth. He'd stayed in touch with my mother throughout, and in a move that combined romantic flair with a dash of desperation, while on leave at Lunar City 7, Dad proposed to my mother. 'Everyone thought we were bloody mad,' Mum once said, 'Maybe it was the wine or the smell of the beef that had seeped into his clothes. But I just couldn't say no to those puppy dog eyes.' Ah, the cosmic irony of hindsight.

My mother was posted on Titan, and my dad was posted on the JMC Emerald Nebula. Over a year passed before she saw Dad again, and almost two more years before she donned the graduation cap and tossed it into the wind. Yet, fate, with its sense of humor, decided that she wouldn't be posted anywhere near my dad.

My mother was freshly stationed on the Axiom II; however, it wasn't long before she found she had a tiny stowaway on board. She was pregnant with my older brother, Frank! 'Your father was in the outer rim at the time; he nearly dropped his spatula,' she said, 'and by the time the message got to him, I was already as big as a cow

So Mum's Space Corps ambitions hit a speed bump; she took a leave of absence and went to shack up on Io with my paternal grandparents. Lacking her parental navigators, who had embarked on the ultimate road trip years earlier, she found herself surrounded by vast farmland of good old terrestrial adventure. Enter Frank, my elder sibling, making his grand entrance. The interstellar escapades of the next generation were officially underway.

With the cosmic clock ticking, Mum had a mere two Earth-bound years before Space Corp's relentless gravitational pull demanded her return. In those terrestrial years, she juggled the titles of astrobiologist and dedicated mum. 'I just felt shagged out all the time,' she reminisced. 'I missed little Frank; this wasn't what I wanted.' Parenthood, it turns out, is the ultimate improvisational act.

With parents who had charted the final frontier of life and having witnessed her mother resigning her commission to raise her and her brother solo during Dad's cosmic escapades as chief slop server, Mum found herself in a parenting predicament. 'I was bored out of my mind, but your dad's career was everything to him,' she admitted. She'd study where she could while my grandparents took care of Frank. 'Your grandparents were like Energizer bunnies,' she shared. Meanwhile, Dad, charting his course through the galactic highways aboard the JMC Emerald Nebula, missed Mum and Frank. As the countdown to Mum's return commenced, Dad, ever the master of cosmic shenanigans, pulled whatever strings he could to get her posted back to Io, where he had assumed the role of Restroom attendant.

Only for calamity to strike again after my Mum's grand return to the Space Corps. Surprise, surprise — John was on the way, stealing the spotlight as the next Rimmer headliner. Dad informing Captain Sulaco was less than thrilled. Shipboard nurseries were not on his playlist. But, that triggered Dad's decision. A message blinked in from the cosmic ether — Dad's old man had punched out his ticket to the great beyond when he was born. His career as a restroom attendant wasn't going anywhere fast. Cue the resignation letter to Space Corps — bye-bye dad's officer career. So from that point on, they began to settle into life on Io together. Mum later shot out my next brother Howard. Then, having a break, they focused on the house and garden, bringing local gardener Dungo to assist. It wasn't long after I arrived on the scene!

In the galactic years since, I've mulled over Dad's plot twist and how it flung my trajectory into the cosmic unknown. The cosmic yarn I spin for the masses: Dad ditching Space Corps lit the afterburners on John, Howard, Frank, and my career quest, filling the void he left.

My brothers, all being older, eventually signed up for the Space Corps, graduating with top marks in their classes. They all got commission postings on the fleet's best ships. John was an astro-navigator on the SSS Augustus, where he shared quarters with a certain Frank Hollister — a captain in the making.

Frank, the rising star in the Space Corps, snagged the first officer position aboard the Nova 4 when the previous first officer, Cheddar Flatheringson, decided he'd rather play captain. Six years of navigating the officer bureaucracy had Frank on a trajectory to break records and become the youngest captain in the Space Corps. But, as I've always said, 'Up, up, up the ziggurat lickety-split.

As for me, at the tender age of nine, my school grades were less than promising, and in a twist of cosmic fate, my parents decided it was better to wash their hands of me and ship me off to boarding school. As time ticked away, my envy for friends and their idyllic families turned me into a recluse. I found solace in the small things; I enjoyed listening to the Hammond organ, Morris Dancing, and building up my collection of 20th-century telegraph poles. You could always find me aimlessly wandering around the vast diesel decks at the local spaceport, attempting to rediscover the joy of getting lost. I even took up learning Esperanto in my sleep. But, as I looked up at the stars, where dreams of greatness shimmer like distant galaxies, my story was only just beginning. Arnold Judas Rimmer was destined for glory from the very fabric of stardust. My humble journey commenced not among the celestial bodies but within the labyrinth of obstacles — the very crucible of my stellar aspirations.

It was just another sunny day on Io, spent jesting with my older brothers John, Howard, and Frank. God, we were close — the 'Four Musketeers,' as we used to call ourselves! Well, the three musketeers actually; they always let me be the queen of Spain. What fun we'd have! An occasional practical joke, of course — apple-pie beds, black-eye telescope. They even hid a small landmine in my sandpit! How were they supposed to know it would go off? However, on this particular day, we were all blissfully ignorant of the interstellar smeg about to hit my life!

As my mother casually revealed her plan to send me off to boarding school! My school grades had been gradually slipping, and my parents, having tried absolutely nothing and being fresh out of ideas, thought it would be best to let me be someone else's problem. I, in my infinite pubescent wisdom, hit her with the forceful question, 'Will I still get to see Bruno?' Bruno was the family dog, clearly. You could see where my main priorities lay.

In response, she crouched down, bless her heart—magnificent woman. Very prim, very proper; some say austere. Some people mistook her for being cold and thought she was aloof. Not a bit of it. She crouched down to my eye level, as if we were sharing the secrets of the universe. In a tone that probably sounded more dramatic than she intended, she explained that it was a boarding school on the other side of Io—pretty much as far away from them while still being on the same planet.

Turning to dear old Dad for an explanation or, at the very least, a distraction from the impending familial meltdown, the bearded git was engaged in a staring contest with the sky. It was as if he believed they held the secrets to a lifetime supply of cosmic beer. 'I don't want to go!' I declared, my voice dripping with the gravitas only a nine-year-old prophet could muster.

"Just a couple of years, Arnold, and you can come home for your birthday," she boldly declared, and Dad, ever the spectator in the family circus, continued his stoic gaze into the sky. He never was one for eye contact. Snapping his head, he interjected, "Don't get the weaselly smegger's hopes up." Classic Dad!

Undeterred by the lack of emotional support, she flung a promise of her triumphant return in time for my birthday, as if the universe itself would pause its dance to celebrate my existence. Hugging me, she hoisted me up. 'C'mon, let's get some quiche,' she declared, casting a glance at Dad, who remained emotionally disengaged; he never would give quiche a chance.

The next morning, I was hurled into a transport craft, sharing a seat with Fred 'Thicky' Holden, leaving me to ponder the cosmic absurdity of it all. Suddenly, the predictable rhythms of my boyhood were replaced by the unpredictable chaos of the universe. Leaving behind our modest house

on Io — a perfect replica of an Earth house from the 19th and 20th centuries with its hectares of land. There were some parts I wouldn't miss: getting up early in the morning to feed the sheep and cows, and my pet Lemming. Dad's insistence on manual labor became the launching pad for my determination and my brothers to join the Space Corps.

Our house had witnessed the shenanigans of many generations of Rimmers, with stories galore about my great-great-grandfather, Jebediah Rimmer, who legend has it fought off native Ionians to build the house and gardens. Now maintained by my Dad and with help from the local gardener, Dungo. My dad couldn't stand Dungo, and could never understand why. Sure, he was slightly inept at times and egotistical, self-important, lacked confidence, and was socially awkward. But I always liked him; he had a strong moralistic attitude, and my mother always took a shine to him.

My father, a half-crazed military failure, spent his early years amidst the military pioneers. Growing up on Io, his childhood was an exercise in minimalism. Yet, he yearned to be an officer like his father. The dream almost turned into reality when he strutted onto Space Corps Academy grounds, fulfilling an ambition that had marinated in the spartan conditions of an Io upbringing. Grandpa, an eternal optimist, had dreams of his son treading the same starlit path. Destiny pulled a cosmic prank when he was one inch below Corps regulation height.

My mother was born into an austere family that considered space exploration a genetic trait. Her father was part of the Space Corps' third graduating class, and her mother was a part of the cybernautic division — a family with enough star power to make a pulsar blush.

Mum, with dreams of becoming an astrobiologist, found herself on a collision course with Dad in an Introduction to Space Corps History class. Oh, but the Space Corps Directive 2574 about students fraternizing with other students was stricter than a vegan at a butcher shop. They soon found themselves in front of the space corps instructor with a warning.

Fast forward to Dad's posting on the JMC Emerald Nebula. Despite the height restrictions, strings were pulled, and he was made a galley steward. The ship was still three months away from Earth. He'd stayed in touch with my mother throughout, and in a move that combined romantic flair with a dash of desperation, while on leave at Lunar City 7, Dad proposed to my mother. 'Everyone thought we were bloody mad,' Mum once said, 'Maybe it was the wine or the smell of the beef that had seeped into his clothes. But I just couldn't say no to those puppy dog eyes.' Ah, the cosmic irony of hindsight.

My mother was posted on Titan, and my dad was posted on the JMC Emerald Nebula. Over a year passed before she saw Dad again, and almost two more years before she donned the graduation cap and tossed it into the wind. Yet, fate, with its sense of humor, decided that she wouldn't be posted anywhere near my dad.

My mother was freshly stationed on the Axiom II; however, it wasn't long before she found she had a tiny stowaway on board. She was pregnant with my older brother, Frank! 'Your father was in the outer rim at the time; he nearly dropped his spatula,' she said, 'and by the time the message got to him, I was already as big as a cow

So Mum's Space Corps ambitions hit a speed bump; she took a leave of absence and went to shack up on Io with my paternal grandparents. Lacking her parental navigators, who had embarked on the ultimate road

trip years earlier, she found herself surrounded by vast farmland of good old terrestrial adventure. Enter Frank, my elder sibling, making his grand entrance. The interstellar escapades of the next generation were officially underway.

With the cosmic clock ticking, Mum had a mere two Earth-bound years before Space Corp's relentless gravitational pull demanded her return. In those terrestrial years, she juggled the titles of astrobiologist and dedicated mum. 'I just felt shagged out all the time,' she reminisced. 'I missed little Frank; this wasn't what I wanted.' Parenthood, it turns out, is the ultimate improvisational act.

With parents who had charted the final frontier of life and having witnessed her mother resigning her commission to raise her and her brother solo during Dad's cosmic escapades as chief slop server, Mum found herself in a parenting predicament. 'I was bored out of my mind, but your dad's career was everything to him,' she admitted. She'd study where she could while my grandparents took care of Frank. 'Your grandparents were like Energizer bunnies,' she shared. Meanwhile, Dad, charting his course through the galactic highways aboard the JMC Emerald Nebula, missed Mum and Frank. As the countdown to Mum's return commenced, Dad, ever the master of cosmic shenanigans, pulled whatever strings he could to get her posted back to Io, where he had assumed the role of Restroom attendant.

Only for calamity to strike again after my Mum's grand return to the Space Corps. Surprise, surprise—John was on the way, stealing the spotlight as the next Rimmer headliner. Dad informing Captain Sulaco was less than thrilled. Shipboard nurseries were not on his playlist. But, that triggered Dad's decision. A message blinked in from the cosmic ether—Dad's old man had punched out his ticket to the great beyond when he was born. His career as a restroom attendant wasn't going anywhere fast. Cue the resignation letter to Space Corps—bye-bye dad's

officer career. So from that point on, they began to settle into life on Io together. Mum later shot out my next brother Howard. Then, having a break, they focused on the house and garden, bringing local gardener Dungo to assist. It wasn't long after I arrived on the scene!

In the galactic years since, I've mulled over Dad's plot twist and how it flung my trajectory into the cosmic unknown. The cosmic yarn I spin for the masses: Dad ditching Space Corps lit the afterburners on John, Howard, Frank, and my career quest, filling the void he left.

My brothers, all being older, eventually signed up for the Space Corps, graduating with top marks in their classes. They all got commission postings on the fleet's best ships. John was an astro-navigator on the SSS Augustus, where he shared quarters with a certain Frank Hollister — a captain in the making.

Frank, the rising star in the Space Corps, snagged the first officer position aboard the Nova 4 when the previous first officer, Cheddar Flatheringson, decided he'd rather play captain. Six years of navigating the officer bureaucracy had Frank on a trajectory to break records and become the youngest captain in the Space Corps. But, as I've always said, 'Up, up, up the ziggurat lickety-split.

As for me, at the tender age of nine, my school grades were less than promising, and in a twist of cosmic fate, my parents decided it was better to wash their hands of me and ship me off to boarding school. As time ticked away, my envy for friends and their idyllic families turned me into a recluse. I found solace in the small things; I enjoyed listening to the Hammond organ, Morris Dancing, and building up my collection of 20th-century telegraph poles. You could always find me aimlessly wandering around the vast diesel decks at the local spaceport, attempting to rediscover the joy of getting lost. I even took up learning Esperanto in my

sleep. But, as I looked up at the stars, where dreams of greatness shimmer like distant galaxies, my story was only just beginning. Arnold Judas Rimmer was destined for glory from the very fabric of stardust. My humble journey commenced not among the celestial bodies but within the labyrinth of obstacles—the very crucible of my stellar aspirations.

It was just another sunny day on Io, spent jesting with my older brothers John, Howard, and Frank. God, we were close—the 'Four Musketeers,' as we used to call ourselves! Well, the three musketeers actually; they always let me be the queen of Spain. What fun we'd have! An occasional practical joke, of course—apple-pie beds, black-eye telescope. They even hid a small landmine in my sandpit! How were they supposed to know it would go off? However, on this particular day, we were all blissfully ignorant of the interstellar smeg about to hit my life!

As my mother casually revealed her plan to send me off to boarding school! My school grades had been gradually slipping, and my parents, having tried absolutely nothing and being fresh out of ideas, thought it would be best to let me be someone else's problem. I, in my infinite pubescent wisdom, hit her with the forceful question, 'Will I still get to see Bruno?' Bruno was the family dog, clearly. You could see where my main priorities lay.

In response, she crouched down, bless her heart—magnificent woman. Very prim, very proper; some say austere. Some people mistook her for being cold and thought she was aloof. Not a bit of it. She crouched down to my eye level, as if we were sharing the secrets of the universe. In a tone that probably sounded more dramatic than she intended, she explained that it was a boarding school on the other side of Io—pretty much as far away from them while still being on the same planet.

Turning to dear old Dad for an explanation or, at the very least, a distraction from the impending familial meltdown, the bearded git was engaged in a staring contest with the sky. It was as if he believed they held the secrets to a lifetime supply of cosmic beer. 'I don't want to go!' I declared, my voice dripping with the gravitas only a nine-year-old prophet could muster.

"Just a couple of years, Arnold, and you can come home for your birthday," she boldly declared, and Dad, ever the spectator in the family circus, continued his stoic gaze into the sky. He never was one for eye contact. Snapping his head, he interjected, "Don't get the weaselly smegger's hopes up." Classic Dad!

Undeterred by the lack of emotional support, she flung a promise of her triumphant return in time for my birthday, as if the universe itself would pause its dance to celebrate my existence. Hugging me, she hoisted me up. 'C'mon, let's get some quiche,' she declared, casting a glance at Dad, who remained emotionally disengaged; he never would give quiche a chance.

The next morning, I was hurled into a transport craft, sharing a seat with Fred 'Thicky' Holden, leaving me to ponder the cosmic absurdity of it all. Suddenly, the predictable rhythms of my boyhood were replaced by the unpredictable chaos of the universe. Leaving behind our modest house on Io — a perfect replica of an Earth house from the 19th and 20th centuries with its hectares of land. There were some parts I wouldn't miss: getting up early in the morning to feed the sheep and cows, and my pet Lemming. Dad's insistence on manual labor became the launching pad for my determination and my brothers to join the Space Corps.

Our house had witnessed the shenanigans of many generations of Rimmers, with stories galore about my great-great-grandfather, Jebediah Rimmer, who legend has it fought off native Ionians to build the house and gardens. Now maintained by my Dad and with help from the local gardener, Dungo. My dad couldn't stand Dungo, and could never understand why. Sure, he was slightly inept at times and egotistical, self-important, lacked confidence, and was socially awkward. But I always liked him; he had a strong moralistic attitude, and my mother always took a shine to him.

My father, a half-crazed military failure, spent his early years amidst the military pioneers. Growing up on Io, his childhood was an exercise in minimalism. Yet, he yearned to be an officer like his father. The dream almost turned into reality when he strutted onto Space Corps Academy grounds, fulfilling an ambition that had marinated in the spartan conditions of an Io upbringing. Grandpa, an eternal optimist, had dreams of his son treading the same starlit path. Destiny pulled a cosmic prank when he was one inch below Corps regulation height.

My mother was born into an austere family that considered space exploration a genetic trait. Her father was part of the Space Corps' third graduating class, and her mother was a part of the cybernautic division — a family with enough star power to make a pulsar blush.

Mum, with dreams of becoming an astrobiologist, found herself on a collision course with Dad in an Introduction to Space Corps History class. Oh, but the Space Corps Directive 2574 about students fraternizing with other students was stricter than a vegan at a butcher shop. They soon found themselves in front of the space corps instructor with a warning.

Fast forward to Dad's posting on the JMC Emerald Nebula. Despite the height restrictions, strings were pulled, and he was made a galley steward. The ship was still three months away from Earth. He'd stayed in touch with my mother throughout, and in a move that combined romantic flair with a dash of desperation, while on leave at Lunar City 7, Dad proposed to my mother. 'Everyone thought we were bloody mad,' Mum once said, 'Maybe it was the wine or the smell of the beef that had seeped into his clothes. But I just couldn't say no to those puppy dog eyes.' Ah, the cosmic irony of hindsight.

My mother was posted on Titan, and my dad was posted on the JMC Emerald Nebula. Over a year passed before she saw Dad again, and almost two more years before she donned the graduation cap and tossed it into the wind. Yet, fate, with its sense of humor, decided that she wouldn't be posted anywhere near my dad.

My mother was freshly stationed on the Axiom II; however, it wasn't long before she found she had a tiny stowaway on board. She was pregnant with my older brother, Frank! 'Your father was in the outer rim at the time; he nearly dropped his spatula,' she said, 'and by the time the message got to him, I was already as big as a cow

So Mum's Space Corps ambitions hit a speed bump; she took a leave of absence and went to shack up on Io with my paternal grandparents. Lacking her parental navigators, who had embarked on the ultimate road trip years earlier, she found herself surrounded by vast farmland of good old terrestrial adventure. Enter Frank, my elder sibling, making his grand entrance. The interstellar escapades of the next generation were officially underway.

With the cosmic clock ticking, Mum had a mere two Earth-bound years before Space Corp's relentless gravitational pull demanded her return. In those terrestrial years, she juggled the titles of astrobiologist and dedicated mum. 'I just felt shagged out all the time,' she reminisced. 'I missed little Frank; this wasn't what I wanted.' Parenthood, it turns out, is the ultimate improvisational act.

With parents who had charted the final frontier of life and having witnessed her mother resigning her commission to raise her and her brother solo during Dad's cosmic escapades as chief slop server, Mum found herself in a parenting predicament. 'I was bored out of my mind, but your dad's career was everything to him,' she admitted. She'd study where she could while my grandparents took care of Frank. 'Your grandparents were like Energizer bunnies,' she shared. Meanwhile, Dad, charting his course through the galactic highways aboard the JMC Emerald Nebula, missed Mum and Frank. As the countdown to Mum's return commenced, Dad, ever the master of cosmic shenanigans, pulled whatever strings he could to get her posted back to Io, where he had assumed the role of Restroom attendant.

Only for calamity to strike again after my Mum's grand return to the Space Corps. Surprise, surprise—John was on the way, stealing the spotlight as the next Rimmer headliner. Dad informing Captain Sulaco was less than thrilled. Shipboard nurseries were not on his playlist. But, that triggered Dad's decision. A message blinked in from the cosmic ether—Dad's old man had punched out his ticket to the great beyond when he was born. His career as a restroom attendant wasn't going anywhere fast. Cue the resignation letter to Space Corps—bye-bye dad's officer career. So from that point on, they began to settle into life on Io together. Mum later shot out my next brother Howard. Then, having a break, they focused on the house and garden, bringing local gardener Dungo to assist. It wasn't long after I arrived on the scene!

In the galactic years since, I've mulled over Dad's plot twist and how it flung my trajectory into the cosmic unknown. The cosmic yarn I spin for the masses: Dad ditching Space Corps lit the afterburners on John, Howard, Frank, and my career quest, filling the void he left.

My brothers, all being older, eventually signed up for the Space Corps, graduating with top marks in their classes. They all got commission postings on the fleet's best ships. John was an astro-navigator on the SSS Augustus, where he shared quarters with a certain Frank Hollister — a captain in the making.

Frank, the rising star in the Space Corps, snagged the first officer position aboard the Nova 4 when the previous first officer, Cheddar Flatheringson, decided he'd rather play captain. Six years of navigating the officer bureaucracy had Frank on a trajectory to break records and become the youngest captain in the Space Corps. But, as I've always said, 'Up, up, up the ziggurat lickety-split.

As for me, at the tender age of nine, my school grades were less than promising, and in a twist of cosmic fate, my parents decided it was better to wash their hands of me and ship me off to boarding school. As time ticked away, my envy for friends and their idyllic families turned me into a recluse. I found solace in the small things; I enjoyed listening to the Hammond organ, Morris Dancing, and building up my collection of 20th-century telegraph poles. You could always find me aimlessly wandering around the vast diesel decks at the local spaceport, attempting to rediscover the joy of getting lost. I even took up learning Esperanto in my sleep. But, as I looked up at the stars, where dreams of greatness shimmer like distant galaxies, my story was only just beginning. Arnold Judas Rimmer was destined for glory from the very fabric of stardust. My humble journey commenced not among the celestial bodies but within the labyrinth of obstacles — the very crucible of my stellar aspirations.

# CHAPTER 4
# THE RIMMER DIRECTIVE:
# A GUIDE TO LEADERSHIP

It was just another sunny day on Io, spent jesting with my older brothers John, Howard, and Frank. God, we were close — the 'Four Musketeers,' as we used to call ourselves! Well, the three musketeers actually; they always let me be the queen of Spain. What fun we'd have! An occasional practical joke, of course — apple-pie beds, black-eye telescope. They even hid a small landmine in my sandpit! How were they supposed to know it would go off? However, on this particular day, we were all blissfully ignorant of the interstellar smeg about to hit my life!

As my mother casually revealed her plan to send me off to boarding school! My school grades had been gradually slipping, and my parents, having tried absolutely nothing and being fresh out of ideas, thought it would be best to let me be someone else's problem. I, in my infinite pubescent wisdom, hit her with the forceful question, 'Will I still get to see Bruno?' Bruno was the family dog, clearly. You could see where my main priorities lay.

In response, she crouched down, bless her heart — magnificent woman. Very prim, very proper; some say austere. Some people mistook her for being cold and thought she was aloof. Not a bit of it. She crouched down to my eye level, as if we were sharing the secrets of the universe. In a tone that probably sounded more dramatic than she intended, she explained that it was a boarding school on the other side of Io — pretty much as far away from them while still being on the same planet.

Turning to dear old Dad for an explanation or, at the very least, a distraction from the impending familial meltdown, the bearded git was engaged in a staring contest with the sky. It was as if he believed they held the secrets to a lifetime supply of cosmic beer. 'I don't want to go!' I declared, my voice dripping with the gravitas only a nine-year-old prophet could muster.

"Just a couple of years, Arnold, and you can come home for your birthday," she boldly declared, and Dad, ever the spectator in the family circus, continued his stoic gaze into the sky. He never was one for eye contact. Snapping his head, he interjected, "Don't get the weaselly smegger's hopes up." Classic Dad!

Undeterred by the lack of emotional support, she flung a promise of her triumphant return in time for my birthday, as if the universe itself would pause its dance to celebrate my existence. Hugging me, she hoisted me up. 'C'mon, let's get some quiche,' she declared, casting a glance at Dad, who remained emotionally disengaged; he never would give quiche a chance.

The next morning, I was hurled into a transport craft, sharing a seat with Fred 'Thicky' Holden, leaving me to ponder the cosmic absurdity of it all. Suddenly, the predictable rhythms of my boyhood were replaced by the unpredictable chaos of the universe. Leaving behind our modest house on Io — a perfect replica of an Earth house from the 19th and 20th centuries with its hectares of land. There were some parts I wouldn't miss: getting up early in the morning to feed the sheep and cows, and my pet Lemming. Dad's insistence on manual labor became the launching pad for my determination and my brothers to join the Space Corps.

Our house had witnessed the shenanigans of many generations of Rimmers, with stories galore about my great-great-grandfather, Jebediah Rimmer, who legend has it fought off native Ionians to build the house and gardens. Now maintained by my Dad and with help from the local gardener, Dungo. My dad couldn't stand Dungo, and could never understand why. Sure, he was slightly inept at times and egotistical, self-important, lacked confidence, and was socially awkward. But I always liked him; he had a strong moralistic attitude, and my mother always took a shine to him.

My father, a half-crazed military failure, spent his early years amidst the military pioneers. Growing up on Io, his childhood was an exercise in minimalism. Yet, he yearned to be an officer like his father. The dream almost turned into reality when he strutted onto Space Corps Academy grounds, fulfilling an ambition that had marinated in the spartan conditions of an Io upbringing. Grandpa, an eternal optimist, had dreams of his son treading the same starlit path. Destiny pulled a cosmic prank when he was one inch below Corps regulation height.

My mother was born into an austere family that considered space exploration a genetic trait. Her father was part of the Space Corps' third graduating class, and her mother was a part of the cybernautic division — a family with enough star power to make a pulsar blush.

Mum, with dreams of becoming an astrobiologist, found herself on a collision course with Dad in an Introduction to Space Corps History class. Oh, but the Space Corps Directive 2574 about students fraternizing with other students was stricter than a vegan at a butcher shop. They soon found themselves in front of the space corps instructor with a warning.

Fast forward to Dad's posting on the JMC Emerald Nebula. Despite the height restrictions, strings were pulled, and he was made a galley steward. The ship was still three months away from Earth. He'd stayed in touch with my mother throughout, and in a move that combined romantic flair with a dash of desperation, while on leave at Lunar City 7, Dad proposed to my mother. 'Everyone thought we were bloody mad,' Mum once said, 'Maybe it was the wine or the smell of the beef that had seeped into his clothes. But I just couldn't say no to those puppy dog eyes.' Ah, the cosmic irony of hindsight.

My mother was posted on Titan, and my dad was posted on the JMC Emerald Nebula. Over a year passed before she saw Dad again, and almost two more years before she donned the graduation cap and tossed it into the wind. Yet, fate, with its sense of humor, decided that she wouldn't be posted anywhere near my dad.

My mother was freshly stationed on the Axiom II; however, it wasn't long before she found she had a tiny stowaway on board. She was pregnant with my older brother, Frank! 'Your father was in the outer rim at the time; he nearly dropped his spatula,' she said, 'and by the time the message got to him, I was already as big as a cow

So Mum's Space Corps ambitions hit a speed bump; she took a leave of absence and went to shack up on Io with my paternal grandparents. Lacking her parental navigators, who had embarked on the ultimate road trip years earlier, she found herself surrounded by vast farmland of good old terrestrial adventure. Enter Frank, my elder sibling, making his grand entrance. The interstellar escapades of the next generation were officially underway.

With the cosmic clock ticking, Mum had a mere two Earth-bound years before Space Corp's relentless gravitational pull demanded her return. In those terrestrial years, she juggled the titles of astrobiologist and dedicated mum. 'I just felt shagged out all the time,' she reminisced. 'I missed little Frank; this wasn't what I wanted.' Parenthood, it turns out, is the ultimate improvisational act.

With parents who had charted the final frontier of life and having witnessed her mother resigning her commission to raise her and her brother solo during Dad's cosmic escapades as chief slop server, Mum found herself in a parenting predicament. 'I was bored out of my mind, but your dad's career was everything to him,' she admitted. She'd study where she could while my grandparents took care of Frank. 'Your grandparents were like Energizer bunnies,' she shared. Meanwhile, Dad, charting his course through the galactic highways aboard the JMC Emerald Nebula, missed Mum and Frank. As the countdown to Mum's return commenced, Dad, ever the master of cosmic shenanigans, pulled whatever strings he could to get her posted back to Io, where he had assumed the role of Restroom attendant.

Only for calamity to strike again after my Mum's grand return to the Space Corps. Surprise, surprise—John was on the way, stealing the spotlight as the next Rimmer headliner. Dad informing Captain Sulaco was less than thrilled. Shipboard nurseries were not on his playlist. But, that triggered Dad's decision. A message blinked in from the cosmic ether—Dad's old man had punched out his ticket to the great beyond when he was born. His career as a restroom attendant wasn't going anywhere fast. Cue the resignation letter to Space Corps—bye-bye dad's officer career. So from that point on, they began to settle into life on Io together. Mum later shot out my next brother Howard. Then, having a break, they focused on the house and garden, bringing local gardener Dungo to assist. It wasn't long after I arrived on the scene!

In the galactic years since, I've mulled over Dad's plot twist and how it flung my trajectory into the cosmic unknown. The cosmic yarn I spin for the masses: Dad ditching Space Corps lit the afterburners on John, Howard, Frank, and my career quest, filling the void he left.

My brothers, all being older, eventually signed up for the Space Corps, graduating with top marks in their classes. They all got commission postings on the fleet's best ships. John was an astro-navigator on the SSS Augustus, where he shared quarters with a certain Frank Hollister — a captain in the making.

Frank, the rising star in the Space Corps, snagged the first officer position aboard the Nova 4 when the previous first officer, Cheddar Flatheringson, decided he'd rather play captain. Six years of navigating the officer bureaucracy had Frank on a trajectory to break records and become the youngest captain in the Space Corps. But, as I've always said, 'Up, up, up the ziggurat lickety-split.

As for me, at the tender age of nine, my school grades were less than promising, and in a twist of cosmic fate, my parents decided it was better to wash their hands of me and ship me off to boarding school. As time ticked away, my envy for friends and their idyllic families turned me into a recluse. I found solace in the small things; I enjoyed listening to the Hammond organ, Morris Dancing, and building up my collection of 20th-century telegraph poles. You could always find me aimlessly wandering around the vast diesel decks at the local spaceport, attempting to rediscover the joy of getting lost. I even took up learning Esperanto in my sleep. But, as I looked up at the stars, where dreams of greatness shimmer like distant galaxies, my story was only just beginning. Arnold Judas Rimmer was destined for glory from the very fabric of stardust. My humble journey commenced not among the celestial bodies but within the labyrinth of obstacles — the very crucible of my stellar aspirations.

It was just another sunny day on Io, spent jesting with my older brothers John, Howard, and Frank. God, we were close—the 'Four Musketeers,' as we used to call ourselves! Well, the three musketeers actually; they always let me be the queen of Spain. What fun we'd have! An occasional practical joke, of course—apple-pie beds, black-eye telescope. They even hid a small landmine in my sandpit! How were they supposed to know it would go off? However, on this particular day, we were all blissfully ignorant of the interstellar smeg about to hit my life!

As my mother casually revealed her plan to send me off to boarding school! My school grades had been gradually slipping, and my parents, having tried absolutely nothing and being fresh out of ideas, thought it would be best to let me be someone else's problem. I, in my infinite pubescent wisdom, hit her with the forceful question, 'Will I still get to see Bruno?' Bruno was the family dog, clearly. You could see where my main priorities lay.

In response, she crouched down, bless her heart—magnificent woman. Very prim, very proper; some say austere. Some people mistook her for being cold and thought she was aloof. Not a bit of it. She crouched down to my eye level, as if we were sharing the secrets of the universe. In a tone that probably sounded more dramatic than she intended, she explained that it was a boarding school on the other side of Io—pretty much as far away from them while still being on the same planet.

Turning to dear old Dad for an explanation or, at the very least, a distraction from the impending familial meltdown, the bearded git was engaged in a staring contest with the sky. It was as if he believed they held the secrets to a lifetime supply of cosmic beer. 'I don't want to go!' I declared, my voice dripping with the gravitas only a nine-year-old prophet could muster.

"Just a couple of years, Arnold, and you can come home for your birthday," she boldly declared, and Dad, ever the spectator in the family circus, continued his stoic gaze into the sky. He never was one for eye contact. Snapping his head, he interjected, "Don't get the weaselly smegger's hopes up." Classic Dad!

Undeterred by the lack of emotional support, she flung a promise of her triumphant return in time for my birthday, as if the universe itself would pause its dance to celebrate my existence. Hugging me, she hoisted me up. 'C'mon, let's get some quiche,' she declared, casting a glance at Dad, who remained emotionally disengaged; he never would give quiche a chance.

The next morning, I was hurled into a transport craft, sharing a seat with Fred 'Thicky' Holden, leaving me to ponder the cosmic absurdity of it all. Suddenly, the predictable rhythms of my boyhood were replaced by the unpredictable chaos of the universe. Leaving behind our modest house on Io — a perfect replica of an Earth house from the 19th and 20th centuries with its hectares of land. There were some parts I wouldn't miss: getting up early in the morning to feed the sheep and cows, and my pet Lemming. Dad's insistence on manual labor became the launching pad for my determination and my brothers to join the Space Corps.

Our house had witnessed the shenanigans of many generations of Rimmers, with stories galore about my great-great-grandfather, Jebediah Rimmer, who legend has it fought off native Ionians to build the house and gardens. Now maintained by my Dad and with help from the local gardener, Dungo. My dad couldn't stand Dungo, and could never understand why. Sure, he was slightly inept at times and egotistical, self-important, lacked confidence, and was socially awkward. But I always liked him; he had a strong moralistic attitude, and my mother always took a shine to him.

My father, a half-crazed military failure, spent his early years amidst the military pioneers. Growing up on Io, his childhood was an exercise in minimalism. Yet, he yearned to be an officer like his father. The dream almost turned into reality when he strutted onto Space Corps Academy grounds, fulfilling an ambition that had marinated in the spartan conditions of an Io upbringing. Grandpa, an eternal optimist, had dreams of his son treading the same starlit path. Destiny pulled a cosmic prank when he was one inch below Corps regulation height.

My mother was born into an austere family that considered space exploration a genetic trait. Her father was part of the Space Corps' third graduating class, and her mother was a part of the cybernautic division — a family with enough star power to make a pulsar blush.

Mum, with dreams of becoming an astrobiologist, found herself on a collision course with Dad in an Introduction to Space Corps History class. Oh, but the Space Corps Directive 2574 about students fraternizing with other students was stricter than a vegan at a butcher shop. They soon found themselves in front of the space corps instructor with a warning.

Fast forward to Dad's posting on the JMC Emerald Nebula. Despite the height restrictions, strings were pulled, and he was made a galley steward. The ship was still three months away from Earth. He'd stayed in touch with my mother throughout, and in a move that combined romantic flair with a dash of desperation, while on leave at Lunar City 7, Dad proposed to my mother. 'Everyone thought we were bloody mad,' Mum once said, 'Maybe it was the wine or the smell of the beef that had seeped into his clothes. But I just couldn't say no to those puppy dog eyes.' Ah, the cosmic irony of hindsight.

My mother was posted on Titan, and my dad was posted on the JMC Emerald Nebula. Over a year passed before she saw Dad again, and almost two more years before she donned the graduation cap and tossed it into the wind. Yet, fate, with its sense of humor, decided that she wouldn't be posted anywhere near my dad.

My mother was freshly stationed on the Axiom II; however, it wasn't long before she found she had a tiny stowaway on board. She was pregnant with my older brother, Frank! 'Your father was in the outer rim at the time; he nearly dropped his spatula,' she said, 'and by the time the message got to him, I was already as big as a cow

So Mum's Space Corps ambitions hit a speed bump; she took a leave of absence and went to shack up on Io with my paternal grandparents. Lacking her parental navigators, who had embarked on the ultimate road trip years earlier, she found herself surrounded by vast farmland of good old terrestrial adventure. Enter Frank, my elder sibling, making his grand entrance. The interstellar escapades of the next generation were officially underway.

With the cosmic clock ticking, Mum had a mere two Earth-bound years before Space Corp's relentless gravitational pull demanded her return. In those terrestrial years, she juggled the titles of astrobiologist and dedicated mum. 'I just felt shagged out all the time,' she reminisced. 'I missed little Frank; this wasn't what I wanted.' Parenthood, it turns out, is the ultimate improvisational act.

With parents who had charted the final frontier of life and having witnessed her mother resigning her commission to raise her and her brother solo during Dad's cosmic escapades as chief slop server, Mum found herself in a parenting predicament. 'I was bored out of my mind,

69

but your dad's career was everything to him,' she admitted. She'd study where she could while my grandparents took care of Frank. 'Your grandparents were like Energizer bunnies,' she shared. Meanwhile, Dad, charting his course through the galactic highways aboard the JMC Emerald Nebula, missed Mum and Frank. As the countdown to Mum's return commenced, Dad, ever the master of cosmic shenanigans, pulled whatever strings he could to get her posted back to Io, where he had assumed the role of Restroom attendant.

Only for calamity to strike again after my Mum's grand return to the Space Corps. Surprise, surprise — John was on the way, stealing the spotlight as the next Rimmer headliner. Dad informing Captain Sulaco was less than thrilled. Shipboard nurseries were not on his playlist. But, that triggered Dad's decision. A message blinked in from the cosmic ether — Dad's old man had punched out his ticket to the great beyond when he was born. His career as a restroom attendant wasn't going anywhere fast. Cue the resignation letter to Space Corps — bye-bye dad's officer career. So from that point on, they began to settle into life on Io together. Mum later shot out my next brother Howard. Then, having a break, they focused on the house and garden, bringing local gardener Dungo to assist. It wasn't long after I arrived on the scene!

In the galactic years since, I've mulled over Dad's plot twist and how it flung my trajectory into the cosmic unknown. The cosmic yarn I spin for the masses: Dad ditching Space Corps lit the afterburners on John, Howard, Frank, and my career quest, filling the void he left.

My brothers, all being older, eventually signed up for the Space Corps, graduating with top marks in their classes. They all got commission postings on the fleet's best ships. John was an astro-navigator on the SSS Augustus, where he shared quarters with a certain Frank Hollister — a captain in the making.

70

Frank, the rising star in the Space Corps, snagged the first officer position aboard the Nova 4 when the previous first officer, Cheddar Flatheringson, decided he'd rather play captain. Six years of navigating the officer bureaucracy had Frank on a trajectory to break records and become the youngest captain in the Space Corps. But, as I've always said, 'Up, up, up the ziggurat lickety-split.'

As for me, at the tender age of nine, my school grades were less than promising, and in a twist of cosmic fate, my parents decided it was better to wash their hands of me and ship me off to boarding school. As time ticked away, my envy for friends and their idyllic families turned me into a recluse. I found solace in the small things; I enjoyed listening to the Hammond organ, Morris Dancing, and building up my collection of 20th-century telegraph poles. You could always find me aimlessly wandering around the vast diesel decks at the local spaceport, attempting to rediscover the joy of getting lost. I even took up learning Esperanto in my sleep. But, as I looked up at the stars, where dreams of greatness shimmer like distant galaxies, my story was only just beginning. Arnold Judas Rimmer was destined for glory from the very fabric of stardust. My humble journey commenced not among the celestial bodies but within the labyrinth of obstacles—the very crucible of my stellar aspirations.

It was just another sunny day on Io, spent jesting with my older brothers John, Howard, and Frank. God, we were close—the 'Four Musketeers,' as we used to call ourselves! Well, the three musketeers actually; they always let me be the queen of Spain. What fun we'd have! An occasional practical joke, of course—apple-pie beds, black-eye telescope. They even hid a small landmine in my sandpit! How were they supposed to know it would go off? However, on this particular day, we were all blissfully ignorant of the interstellar smeg about to hit my life!

As my mother casually revealed her plan to send me off to boarding school! My school grades had been gradually slipping, and my parents, having tried absolutely nothing and being fresh out of ideas, thought it would be best to let me be someone else's problem. I, in my infinite pubescent wisdom, hit her with the forceful question, 'Will I still get to see Bruno?' Bruno was the family dog, clearly. You could see where my main priorities lay.

In response, she crouched down, bless her heart — magnificent woman. Very prim, very proper; some say austere. Some people mistook her for being cold and thought she was aloof. Not a bit of it. She crouched down to my eye level, as if we were sharing the secrets of the universe. In a tone that probably sounded more dramatic than she intended, she explained that it was a boarding school on the other side of Io — pretty much as far away from them while still being on the same planet.

Turning to dear old Dad for an explanation or, at the very least, a distraction from the impending familial meltdown, the bearded git was engaged in a staring contest with the sky. It was as if he believed they held the secrets to a lifetime supply of cosmic beer. 'I don't want to go!' I declared, my voice dripping with the gravitas only a nine-year-old prophet could muster.

"Just a couple of years, Arnold, and you can come home for your birthday," she boldly declared, and Dad, ever the spectator in the family circus, continued his stoic gaze into the sky. He never was one for eye contact. Snapping his head, he interjected, "Don't get the weaselly smegger's hopes up." Classic Dad!

Undeterred by the lack of emotional support, she flung a promise of her triumphant return in time for my birthday, as if the universe itself would pause its dance to celebrate my existence. Hugging me, she hoisted me up. 'C'mon, let's get some quiche,' she declared, casting a glance at Dad, who remained emotionally disengaged; he never would give quiche a chance.

The next morning, I was hurled into a transport craft, sharing a seat with Fred 'Thicky' Holden, leaving me to ponder the cosmic absurdity of it all. Suddenly, the predictable rhythms of my boyhood were replaced by the unpredictable chaos of the universe. Leaving behind our modest house on Io — a perfect replica of an Earth house from the 19th and 20th centuries with its hectares of land. There were some parts I wouldn't miss: getting up early in the morning to feed the sheep and cows, and my pet Lemming. Dad's insistence on manual labor became the launching pad for my determination and my brothers to join the Space Corps.

Our house had witnessed the shenanigans of many generations of Rimmers, with stories galore about my great-great-grandfather, Jebediah Rimmer, who legend has it fought off native Ionians to build the house and gardens. Now maintained by my Dad and with help from the local gardener, Dungo. My dad couldn't stand Dungo, and could never understand why. Sure, he was slightly inept at times and egotistical, self-important, lacked confidence, and was socially awkward. But I always liked him; he had a strong moralistic attitude, and my mother always took a shine to him.

My father, a half-crazed military failure, spent his early years amidst the military pioneers. Growing up on Io, his childhood was an exercise in minimalism. Yet, he yearned to be an officer like his father. The dream almost turned into reality when he strutted onto Space Corps Academy grounds, fulfilling an ambition that had marinated in the spartan

conditions of an Io upbringing. Grandpa, an eternal optimist, had dreams of his son treading the same starlit path. Destiny pulled a cosmic prank when he was one inch below Corps regulation height.

My mother was born into an austere family that considered space exploration a genetic trait. Her father was part of the Space Corps' third graduating class, and her mother was a part of the cybernautic division — a family with enough star power to make a pulsar blush.

Mum, with dreams of becoming an astrobiologist, found herself on a collision course with Dad in an Introduction to Space Corps History class. Oh, but the Space Corps Directive 2574 about students fraternizing with other students was stricter than a vegan at a butcher shop. They soon found themselves in front of the space corps instructor with a warning.

Fast forward to Dad's posting on the JMC Emerald Nebula. Despite the height restrictions, strings were pulled, and he was made a galley steward. The ship was still three months away from Earth. He'd stayed in touch with my mother throughout, and in a move that combined romantic flair with a dash of desperation, while on leave at Lunar City 7, Dad proposed to my mother. 'Everyone thought we were bloody mad,' Mum once said, 'Maybe it was the wine or the smell of the beef that had seeped into his clothes. But I just couldn't say no to those puppy dog eyes.' Ah, the cosmic irony of hindsight.

My mother was posted on Titan, and my dad was posted on the JMC Emerald Nebula. Over a year passed before she saw Dad again, and almost two more years before she donned the graduation cap and tossed it into the wind. Yet, fate, with its sense of humor, decided that she wouldn't be posted anywhere near my dad.

My mother was freshly stationed on the Axiom II; however, it wasn't long before she found she had a tiny stowaway on board. She was pregnant with my older brother, Frank! 'Your father was in the outer rim at the time; he nearly dropped his spatula,' she said, 'and by the time the message got to him, I was already as big as a cow

So Mum's Space Corps ambitions hit a speed bump; she took a leave of absence and went to shack up on Io with my paternal grandparents. Lacking her parental navigators, who had embarked on the ultimate road trip years earlier, she found herself surrounded by vast farmland of good old terrestrial adventure. Enter Frank, my elder sibling, making his grand entrance. The interstellar escapades of the next generation were officially underway.

With the cosmic clock ticking, Mum had a mere two Earth-bound years before Space Corp's relentless gravitational pull demanded her return. In those terrestrial years, she juggled the titles of astrobiologist and dedicated mum. 'I just felt shagged out all the time,' she reminisced. 'I missed little Frank; this wasn't what I wanted.' Parenthood, it turns out, is the ultimate improvisational act.

With parents who had charted the final frontier of life and having witnessed her mother resigning her commission to raise her and her brother solo during Dad's cosmic escapades as chief slop server, Mum found herself in a parenting predicament. 'I was bored out of my mind, but your dad's career was everything to him,' she admitted. She'd study where she could while my grandparents took care of Frank. 'Your grandparents were like Energizer bunnies,' she shared. Meanwhile, Dad, charting his course through the galactic highways aboard the JMC Emerald Nebula, missed Mum and Frank. As the countdown to Mum's return commenced, Dad, ever the master of cosmic shenanigans, pulled whatever strings he could to get her posted back to Io, where he had assumed the role of Restroom attendant.

Only for calamity to strike again after my Mum's grand return to the Space Corps. Surprise, surprise—John was on the way, stealing the spotlight as the next Rimmer headliner. Dad informing Captain Sulaco was less than thrilled. Shipboard nurseries were not on his playlist. But, that triggered Dad's decision. A message blinked in from the cosmic ether—Dad's old man had punched out his ticket to the great beyond when he was born. His career as a restroom attendant wasn't going anywhere fast. Cue the resignation letter to Space Corps—bye-bye dad's officer career. So from that point on, they began to settle into life on Io together. Mum later shot out my next brother Howard. Then, having a break, they focused on the house and garden, bringing local gardener Dungo to assist. It wasn't long after I arrived on the scene!

In the galactic years since, I've mulled over Dad's plot twist and how it flung my trajectory into the cosmic unknown. The cosmic yarn I spin for the masses: Dad ditching Space Corps lit the afterburners on John, Howard, Frank, and my career quest, filling the void he left.

My brothers, all being older, eventually signed up for the Space Corps, graduating with top marks in their classes. They all got commission postings on the fleet's best ships. John was an astro-navigator on the SSS Augustus, where he shared quarters with a certain Frank Hollister—a captain in the making.

Frank, the rising star in the Space Corps, snagged the first officer position aboard the Nova 4 when the previous first officer, Cheddar Flatheringson, decided he'd rather play captain. Six years of navigating the officer bureaucracy had Frank on a trajectory to break records and become the youngest captain in the Space Corps. But, as I've always said, 'Up, up, up the ziggurat lickety-split.

As for me, at the tender age of nine, my school grades were less than promising, and in a twist of cosmic fate, my parents decided it was better to wash their hands of me and ship me off to boarding school. As time ticked away, my envy for friends and their idyllic families turned me into a recluse. I found solace in the small things; I enjoyed listening to the Hammond organ, Morris Dancing, and building up my collection of 20th-century telegraph poles. You could always find me aimlessly wandering around the vast diesel decks at the local spaceport, attempting to rediscover the joy of getting lost. I even took up learning Esperanto in my sleep. But, as I looked up at the stars, where dreams of greatness shimmer like distant galaxies, my story was only just beginning. Arnold Judas Rimmer was destined for glory from the very fabric of stardust. My humble journey commenced not among the celestial bodies but within the labyrinth of obstacles—the very crucible of my stellar aspirations.

It was just another sunny day on Io, spent jesting with my older brothers John, Howard, and Frank. God, we were close—the 'Four Musketeers,' as we used to call ourselves! Well, the three musketeers actually; they always let me be the queen of Spain. What fun we'd have! An occasional practical joke, of course—apple-pie beds, black-eye telescope. They even hid a small landmine in my sandpit! How were they supposed to know it would go off? However, on this particular day, we were all blissfully ignorant of the interstellar smeg about to hit my life!

As my mother casually revealed her plan to send me off to boarding school! My school grades had been gradually slipping, and my parents, having tried absolutely nothing and being fresh out of ideas, thought it would be best to let me be someone else's problem. I, in my infinite pubescent wisdom, hit her with the forceful question, 'Will I still get to see Bruno?' Bruno was the family dog, clearly. You could see where my main priorities lay.

In response, she crouched down, bless her heart—magnificent woman. Very prim, very proper; some say austere. Some people mistook her for being cold and thought she was aloof. Not a bit of it. She crouched down to my eye level, as if we were sharing the secrets of the universe. In a tone that probably sounded more dramatic than she intended, she explained that it was a boarding school on the other side of Io—pretty much as far away from them while still being on the same planet.

Turning to dear old Dad for an explanation or, at the very least, a distraction from the impending familial meltdown, the bearded git was engaged in a staring contest with the sky. It was as if he believed they held the secrets to a lifetime supply of cosmic beer. 'I don't want to go!' I declared, my voice dripping with the gravitas only a nine-year-old prophet could muster.

"Just a couple of years, Arnold, and you can come home for your birthday," she boldly declared, and Dad, ever the spectator in the family circus, continued his stoic gaze into the sky. He never was one for eye contact. Snapping his head, he interjected, "Don't get the weaselly smegger's hopes up." Classic Dad!

Undeterred by the lack of emotional support, she flung a promise of her triumphant return in time for my birthday, as if the universe itself would pause its dance to celebrate my existence. Hugging me, she hoisted me up. 'C'mon, let's get some quiche,' she declared, casting a glance at Dad, who remained emotionally disengaged; he never would give quiche a chance.

The next morning, I was hurled into a transport craft, sharing a seat with Fred 'Thicky' Holden, leaving me to ponder the cosmic absurdity of it all. Suddenly, the predictable rhythms of my boyhood were replaced by the unpredictable chaos of the universe. Leaving behind our modest house

on Io—a perfect replica of an Earth house from the 19th and 20th centuries with its hectares of land. There were some parts I wouldn't miss: getting up early in the morning to feed the sheep and cows, and my pet Lemming. Dad's insistence on manual labor became the launching pad for my determination and my brothers to join the Space Corps.

Our house had witnessed the shenanigans of many generations of Rimmers, with stories galore about my great-great-grandfather, Jebediah Rimmer, who legend has it fought off native Ionians to build the house and gardens. Now maintained by my Dad and with help from the local gardener, Dungo. My dad couldn't stand Dungo, and could never understand why. Sure, he was slightly inept at times and egotistical, self-important, lacked confidence, and was socially awkward. But I always liked him; he had a strong moralistic attitude, and my mother always took a shine to him.

My father, a half-crazed military failure, spent his early years amidst the military pioneers. Growing up on Io, his childhood was an exercise in minimalism. Yet, he yearned to be an officer like his father. The dream almost turned into reality when he strutted onto Space Corps Academy grounds, fulfilling an ambition that had marinated in the spartan conditions of an Io upbringing. Grandpa, an eternal optimist, had dreams of his son treading the same starlit path. Destiny pulled a cosmic prank when he was one inch below Corps regulation height.

My mother was born into an austere family that considered space exploration a genetic trait. Her father was part of the Space Corps' third graduating class, and her mother was a part of the cybernautic division— a family with enough star power to make a pulsar blush.

Mum, with dreams of becoming an astrobiologist, found herself on a collision course with Dad in an Introduction to Space Corps History class. Oh, but the Space Corps Directive 2574 about students fraternizing with other students was stricter than a vegan at a butcher shop. They soon found themselves in front of the space corps instructor with a warning.

Fast forward to Dad's posting on the JMC Emerald Nebula. Despite the height restrictions, strings were pulled, and he was made a galley steward. The ship was still three months away from Earth. He'd stayed in touch with my mother throughout, and in a move that combined romantic flair with a dash of desperation, while on leave at Lunar City 7, Dad proposed to my mother. 'Everyone thought we were bloody mad,' Mum once said, 'Maybe it was the wine or the smell of the beef that had seeped into his clothes. But I just couldn't say no to those puppy dog eyes.' Ah, the cosmic irony of hindsight.

My mother was posted on Titan, and my dad was posted on the JMC Emerald Nebula. Over a year passed before she saw Dad again, and almost two more years before she donned the graduation cap and tossed it into the wind. Yet, fate, with its sense of humor, decided that she wouldn't be posted anywhere near my dad.

My mother was freshly stationed on the Axiom II; however, it wasn't long before she found she had a tiny stowaway on board. She was pregnant with my older brother, Frank! 'Your father was in the outer rim at the time; he nearly dropped his spatula,' she said, 'and by the time the message got to him, I was already as big as a cow

So Mum's Space Corps ambitions hit a speed bump; she took a leave of absence and went to shack up on Io with my paternal grandparents. Lacking her parental navigators, who had embarked on the ultimate road

trip years earlier, she found herself surrounded by vast farmland of good old terrestrial adventure. Enter Frank, my elder sibling, making his grand entrance. The interstellar escapades of the next generation were officially underway.

With the cosmic clock ticking, Mum had a mere two Earth-bound years before Space Corp's relentless gravitational pull demanded her return. In those terrestrial years, she juggled the titles of astrobiologist and dedicated mum. 'I just felt shagged out all the time,' she reminisced. 'I missed little Frank; this wasn't what I wanted.' Parenthood, it turns out, is the ultimate improvisational act.

With parents who had charted the final frontier of life and having witnessed her mother resigning her commission to raise her and her brother solo during Dad's cosmic escapades as chief slop server, Mum found herself in a parenting predicament. 'I was bored out of my mind, but your dad's career was everything to him,' she admitted. She'd study where she could while my grandparents took care of Frank. 'Your grandparents were like Energizer bunnies,' she shared. Meanwhile, Dad, charting his course through the galactic highways aboard the JMC Emerald Nebula, missed Mum and Frank. As the countdown to Mum's return commenced, Dad, ever the master of cosmic shenanigans, pulled whatever strings he could to get her posted back to Io, where he had assumed the role of Restroom attendant.

Only for calamity to strike again after my Mum's grand return to the Space Corps. Surprise, surprise—John was on the way, stealing the spotlight as the next Rimmer headliner. Dad informing Captain Sulaco was less than thrilled. Shipboard nurseries were not on his playlist. But, that triggered Dad's decision. A message blinked in from the cosmic ether—Dad's old man had punched out his ticket to the great beyond when he was born. His career as a restroom attendant wasn't going anywhere fast. Cue the resignation letter to Space Corps—bye-bye dad's

officer career. So from that point on, they began to settle into life on Io together. Mum later shot out my next brother Howard. Then, having a break, they focused on the house and garden, bringing local gardener Dungo to assist. It wasn't long after I arrived on the scene!

In the galactic years since, I've mulled over Dad's plot twist and how it flung my trajectory into the cosmic unknown. The cosmic yarn I spin for the masses: Dad ditching Space Corps lit the afterburners on John, Howard, Frank, and my career quest, filling the void he left.

My brothers, all being older, eventually signed up for the Space Corps, graduating with top marks in their classes. They all got commission postings on the fleet's best ships. John was an astro-navigator on the SSS Augustus, where he shared quarters with a certain Frank Hollister — a captain in the making.

Frank, the rising star in the Space Corps, snagged the first officer position aboard the Nova 4 when the previous first officer, Cheddar Flatheringson, decided he'd rather play captain. Six years of navigating the officer bureaucracy had Frank on a trajectory to break records and become the youngest captain in the Space Corps. But, as I've always said, 'Up, up, up the ziggurat lickety-split.

As for me, at the tender age of nine, my school grades were less than promising, and in a twist of cosmic fate, my parents decided it was better to wash their hands of me and ship me off to boarding school. As time ticked away, my envy for friends and their idyllic families turned me into a recluse. I found solace in the small things; I enjoyed listening to the Hammond organ, Morris Dancing, and building up my collection of 20th-century telegraph poles. You could always find me aimlessly wandering around the vast diesel decks at the local spaceport, attempting to rediscover the joy of getting lost. I even took up learning Esperanto in my

sleep. But, as I looked up at the stars, where dreams of greatness shimmer like distant galaxies, my story was only just beginning. Arnold Judas Rimmer was destined for glory from the very fabric of stardust. My humble journey commenced not among the celestial bodies but within the labyrinth of obstacles—the very crucible of my stellar aspirations.

It was just another sunny day on Io, spent jesting with my older brothers John, Howard, and Frank. God, we were close—the 'Four Musketeers,' as we used to call ourselves! Well, the three musketeers actually; they always let me be the queen of Spain. What fun we'd have! An occasional practical joke, of course—apple-pie beds, black-eye telescope. They even hid a small landmine in my sandpit! How were they supposed to know it would go off? However, on this particular day, we were all blissfully ignorant of the interstellar smeg about to hit my life!

As my mother casually revealed her plan to send me off to boarding school! My school grades had been gradually slipping, and my parents, having tried absolutely nothing and being fresh out of ideas, thought it would be best to let me be someone else's problem. I, in my infinite pubescent wisdom, hit her with the forceful question, 'Will I still get to see Bruno?' Bruno was the family dog, clearly. You could see where my main priorities lay.

In response, she crouched down, bless her heart—magnificent woman. Very prim, very proper; some say austere. Some people mistook her for being cold and thought she was aloof. Not a bit of it. She crouched down to my eye level, as if we were sharing the secrets of the universe. In a tone that probably sounded more dramatic than she intended, she explained that it was a boarding school on the other side of Io—pretty much as far away from them while still being on the same planet.

Turning to dear old Dad for an explanation or, at the very least, a distraction from the impending familial meltdown, the bearded git was engaged in a staring contest with the sky. It was as if he believed they held the secrets to a lifetime supply of cosmic beer. 'I don't want to go!' I declared, my voice dripping with the gravitas only a nine-year-old prophet could muster.

"Just a couple of years, Arnold, and you can come home for your birthday," she boldly declared, and Dad, ever the spectator in the family circus, continued his stoic gaze into the sky. He never was one for eye contact. Snapping his head, he interjected, "Don't get the weaselly smegger's hopes up." Classic Dad!

Undeterred by the lack of emotional support, she flung a promise of her triumphant return in time for my birthday, as if the universe itself would pause its dance to celebrate my existence. Hugging me, she hoisted me up. 'C'mon, let's get some quiche,' she declared, casting a glance at Dad, who remained emotionally disengaged; he never would give quiche a chance.

The next morning, I was hurled into a transport craft, sharing a seat with Fred 'Thicky' Holden, leaving me to ponder the cosmic absurdity of it all. Suddenly, the predictable rhythms of my boyhood were replaced by the unpredictable chaos of the universe. Leaving behind our modest house on Io—a perfect replica of an Earth house from the 19th and 20th centuries with its hectares of land. There were some parts I wouldn't miss: getting up early in the morning to feed the sheep and cows, and my pet Lemming. Dad's insistence on manual labor became the launching pad for my determination and my brothers to join the Space Corps.

Our house had witnessed the shenanigans of many generations of Rimmers, with stories galore about my great-great-grandfather, Jebediah Rimmer, who legend has it fought off native Ionians to build the house and gardens. Now maintained by my Dad and with help from the local gardener, Dungo. My dad couldn't stand Dungo, and could never understand why. Sure, he was slightly inept at times and egotistical, self-important, lacked confidence, and was socially awkward. But I always liked him; he had a strong moralistic attitude, and my mother always took a shine to him.

My father, a half-crazed military failure, spent his early years amidst the military pioneers. Growing up on Io, his childhood was an exercise in minimalism. Yet, he yearned to be an officer like his father. The dream almost turned into reality when he strutted onto Space Corps Academy grounds, fulfilling an ambition that had marinated in the spartan conditions of an Io upbringing. Grandpa, an eternal optimist, had dreams of his son treading the same starlit path. Destiny pulled a cosmic prank when he was one inch below Corps regulation height.

My mother was born into an austere family that considered space exploration a genetic trait. Her father was part of the Space Corps' third graduating class, and her mother was a part of the cybernautic division — a family with enough star power to make a pulsar blush.

Mum, with dreams of becoming an astrobiologist, found herself on a collision course with Dad in an Introduction to Space Corps History class. Oh, but the Space Corps Directive 2574 about students fraternizing with other students was stricter than a vegan at a butcher shop. They soon found themselves in front of the space corps instructor with a warning.

Fast forward to Dad's posting on the JMC Emerald Nebula. Despite the height restrictions, strings were pulled, and he was made a galley steward. The ship was still three months away from Earth. He'd stayed in touch with my mother throughout, and in a move that combined romantic flair with a dash of desperation, while on leave at Lunar City 7, Dad proposed to my mother. 'Everyone thought we were bloody mad,' Mum once said, 'Maybe it was the wine or the smell of the beef that had seeped into his clothes. But I just couldn't say no to those puppy dog eyes.' Ah, the cosmic irony of hindsight.

My mother was posted on Titan, and my dad was posted on the JMC Emerald Nebula. Over a year passed before she saw Dad again, and almost two more years before she donned the graduation cap and tossed it into the wind. Yet, fate, with its sense of humor, decided that she wouldn't be posted anywhere near my dad.

My mother was freshly stationed on the Axiom II; however, it wasn't long before she found she had a tiny stowaway on board. She was pregnant with my older brother, Frank! 'Your father was in the outer rim at the time; he nearly dropped his spatula,' she said, 'and by the time the message got to him, I was already as big as a cow

So Mum's Space Corps ambitions hit a speed bump; she took a leave of absence and went to shack up on Io with my paternal grandparents. Lacking her parental navigators, who had embarked on the ultimate road trip years earlier, she found herself surrounded by vast farmland of good old terrestrial adventure. Enter Frank, my elder sibling, making his grand entrance. The interstellar escapades of the next generation were officially underway.

With the cosmic clock ticking, Mum had a mere two Earth-bound years before Space Corp's relentless gravitational pull demanded her return. In those terrestrial years, she juggled the titles of astrobiologist and dedicated mum. 'I just felt shagged out all the time,' she reminisced. 'I missed little Frank; this wasn't what I wanted.' Parenthood, it turns out, is the ultimate improvisational act.

With parents who had charted the final frontier of life and having witnessed her mother resigning her commission to raise her and her brother solo during Dad's cosmic escapades as chief slop server, Mum found herself in a parenting predicament. 'I was bored out of my mind, but your dad's career was everything to him,' she admitted. She'd study where she could while my grandparents took care of Frank. 'Your grandparents were like Energizer bunnies,' she shared. Meanwhile, Dad, charting his course through the galactic highways aboard the JMC Emerald Nebula, missed Mum and Frank. As the countdown to Mum's return commenced, Dad, ever the master of cosmic shenanigans, pulled whatever strings he could to get her posted back to Io, where he had assumed the role of Restroom attendant.

Only for calamity to strike again after my Mum's grand return to the Space Corps. Surprise, surprise—John was on the way, stealing the spotlight as the next Rimmer headliner. Dad informing Captain Sulaco was less than thrilled. Shipboard nurseries were not on his playlist. But, that triggered Dad's decision. A message blinked in from the cosmic ether—Dad's old man had punched out his ticket to the great beyond when he was born. His career as a restroom attendant wasn't going anywhere fast. Cue the resignation letter to Space Corps—bye-bye dad's officer career. So from that point on, they began to settle into life on Io together. Mum later shot out my next brother Howard. Then, having a break, they focused on the house and garden, bringing local gardener Dungo to assist. It wasn't long after I arrived on the scene!

In the galactic years since, I've mulled over Dad's plot twist and how it flung my trajectory into the cosmic unknown. The cosmic yarn I spin for the masses: Dad ditching Space Corps lit the afterburners on John, Howard, Frank, and my career quest, filling the void he left.

My brothers, all being older, eventually signed up for the Space Corps, graduating with top marks in their classes. They all got commission postings on the fleet's best ships. John was an astro-navigator on the SSS Augustus, where he shared quarters with a certain Frank Hollister—a captain in the making.

Frank, the rising star in the Space Corps, snagged the first officer position aboard the Nova 4 when the previous first officer, Cheddar Flatheringson, decided he'd rather play captain. Six years of navigating the officer bureaucracy had Frank on a trajectory to break records and become the youngest captain in the Space Corps. But, as I've always said, 'Up, up, up the ziggurat lickety-split.

As for me, at the tender age of nine, my school grades were less than promising, and in a twist of cosmic fate, my parents decided it was better to wash their hands of me and ship me off to boarding school. As time ticked away, my envy for friends and their idyllic families turned me into a recluse. I found solace in the small things; I enjoyed listening to the Hammond organ, Morris Dancing, and building up my collection of 20th-century telegraph poles. You could always find me aimlessly wandering around the vast diesel decks at the local spaceport, attempting to rediscover the joy of getting lost. I even took up learning Esperanto in my sleep. But, as I looked up at the stars, where dreams of greatness shimmer like distant galaxies, my story was only just beginning. Arnold Judas Rimmer was destined for glory from the very fabric of stardust. My humble journey commenced not among the celestial bodies but within the labyrinth of obstacles—the very crucible of my stellar aspirations.

# CHAPTER 5
# THE COSMIC SYMPHONY UNVEILED

It was just another sunny day on Io, spent jesting with my older brothers John, Howard, and Frank. God, we were close—the 'Four Musketeers,' as we used to call ourselves! Well, the three musketeers actually; they always let me be the queen of Spain. What fun we'd have! An occasional practical joke, of course—apple-pie beds, black-eye telescope. They even hid a small landmine in my sandpit! How were they supposed to know it would go off? However, on this particular day, we were all blissfully ignorant of the interstellar smeg about to hit my life!

As my mother casually revealed her plan to send me off to boarding school! My school grades had been gradually slipping, and my parents, having tried absolutely nothing and being fresh out of ideas, thought it would be best to let me be someone else's problem. I, in my infinite pubescent wisdom, hit her with the forceful question, 'Will I still get to see Bruno?' Bruno was the family dog, clearly. You could see where my main priorities lay.

In response, she crouched down, bless her heart—magnificent woman. Very prim, very proper; some say austere. Some people mistook her for being cold and thought she was aloof. Not a bit of it. She crouched down to my eye level, as if we were sharing the secrets of the universe. In a tone that probably sounded more dramatic than she intended, she explained that it was a boarding school on the other side of Io—pretty much as far away from them while still being on the same planet.

Turning to dear old Dad for an explanation or, at the very least, a distraction from the impending familial meltdown, the bearded git was engaged in a staring contest with the sky. It was as if he believed they held the secrets to a lifetime supply of cosmic beer. 'I don't want to go!' I declared, my voice dripping with the gravitas only a nine-year-old prophet could muster.

"Just a couple of years, Arnold, and you can come home for your birthday," she boldly declared, and Dad, ever the spectator in the family circus, continued his stoic gaze into the sky. He never was one for eye contact. Snapping his head, he interjected, "Don't get the weaselly smegger's hopes up." Classic Dad!

Undeterred by the lack of emotional support, she flung a promise of her triumphant return in time for my birthday, as if the universe itself would pause its dance to celebrate my existence. Hugging me, she hoisted me up. 'C'mon, let's get some quiche,' she declared, casting a glance at Dad, who remained emotionally disengaged; he never would give quiche a chance.

The next morning, I was hurled into a transport craft, sharing a seat with Fred 'Thicky' Holden, leaving me to ponder the cosmic absurdity of it all. Suddenly, the predictable rhythms of my boyhood were replaced by the unpredictable chaos of the universe. Leaving behind our modest house on Io — a perfect replica of an Earth house from the 19th and 20th centuries with its hectares of land. There were some parts I wouldn't miss: getting up early in the morning to feed the sheep and cows, and my pet Lemming. Dad's insistence on manual labor became the launching pad for my determination and my brothers to join the Space Corps.

Our house had witnessed the shenanigans of many generations of Rimmers, with stories galore about my great-great-grandfather, Jebediah Rimmer, who legend has it fought off native Ionians to build the house and gardens. Now maintained by my Dad and with help from the local gardener, Dungo. My dad couldn't stand Dungo, and could never understand why. Sure, he was slightly inept at times and egotistical, self-important, lacked confidence, and was socially awkward. But I always liked him; he had a strong moralistic attitude, and my mother always took a shine to him.

My father, a half-crazed military failure, spent his early years amidst the military pioneers. Growing up on Io, his childhood was an exercise in minimalism. Yet, he yearned to be an officer like his father. The dream almost turned into reality when he strutted onto Space Corps Academy grounds, fulfilling an ambition that had marinated in the spartan conditions of an Io upbringing. Grandpa, an eternal optimist, had dreams of his son treading the same starlit path. Destiny pulled a cosmic prank when he was one inch below Corps regulation height.

My mother was born into an austere family that considered space exploration a genetic trait. Her father was part of the Space Corps' third graduating class, and her mother was a part of the cybernautic division — a family with enough star power to make a pulsar blush.

Mum, with dreams of becoming an astrobiologist, found herself on a collision course with Dad in an Introduction to Space Corps History class. Oh, but the Space Corps Directive 2574 about students fraternizing with other students was stricter than a vegan at a butcher shop. They soon found themselves in front of the space corps instructor with a warning.

Fast forward to Dad's posting on the JMC Emerald Nebula. Despite the height restrictions, strings were pulled, and he was made a galley steward. The ship was still three months away from Earth. He'd stayed in touch with my mother throughout, and in a move that combined romantic flair with a dash of desperation, while on leave at Lunar City 7, Dad proposed to my mother. 'Everyone thought we were bloody mad,' Mum once said, 'Maybe it was the wine or the smell of the beef that had seeped into his clothes. But I just couldn't say no to those puppy dog eyes.' Ah, the cosmic irony of hindsight.

My mother was posted on Titan, and my dad was posted on the JMC Emerald Nebula. Over a year passed before she saw Dad again, and almost two more years before she donned the graduation cap and tossed it into the wind. Yet, fate, with its sense of humor, decided that she wouldn't be posted anywhere near my dad.

My mother was freshly stationed on the Axiom II; however, it wasn't long before she found she had a tiny stowaway on board. She was pregnant with my older brother, Frank! 'Your father was in the outer rim at the time; he nearly dropped his spatula,' she said, 'and by the time the message got to him, I was already as big as a cow

So Mum's Space Corps ambitions hit a speed bump; she took a leave of absence and went to shack up on Io with my paternal grandparents. Lacking her parental navigators, who had embarked on the ultimate road trip years earlier, she found herself surrounded by vast farmland of good old terrestrial adventure. Enter Frank, my elder sibling, making his grand entrance. The interstellar escapades of the next generation were officially underway.

With the cosmic clock ticking, Mum had a mere two Earth-bound years before Space Corp's relentless gravitational pull demanded her return. In those terrestrial years, she juggled the titles of astrobiologist and dedicated mum. 'I just felt shagged out all the time,' she reminisced. 'I missed little Frank; this wasn't what I wanted.' Parenthood, it turns out, is the ultimate improvisational act.

With parents who had charted the final frontier of life and having witnessed her mother resigning her commission to raise her and her brother solo during Dad's cosmic escapades as chief slop server, Mum found herself in a parenting predicament. 'I was bored out of my mind, but your dad's career was everything to him,' she admitted. She'd study where she could while my grandparents took care of Frank. 'Your grandparents were like Energizer bunnies,' she shared. Meanwhile, Dad, charting his course through the galactic highways aboard the JMC Emerald Nebula, missed Mum and Frank. As the countdown to Mum's return commenced, Dad, ever the master of cosmic shenanigans, pulled whatever strings he could to get her posted back to Io, where he had assumed the role of Restroom attendant.

Only for calamity to strike again after my Mum's grand return to the Space Corps. Surprise, surprise—John was on the way, stealing the spotlight as the next Rimmer headliner. Dad informing Captain Sulaco was less than thrilled. Shipboard nurseries were not on his playlist. But, that triggered Dad's decision. A message blinked in from the cosmic ether—Dad's old man had punched out his ticket to the great beyond when he was born. His career as a restroom attendant wasn't going anywhere fast. Cue the resignation letter to Space Corps—bye-bye dad's officer career. So from that point on, they began to settle into life on Io together. Mum later shot out my next brother Howard. Then, having a break, they focused on the house and garden, bringing local gardener Dungo to assist. It wasn't long after I arrived on the scene!

In the galactic years since, I've mulled over Dad's plot twist and how it flung my trajectory into the cosmic unknown. The cosmic yarn I spin for the masses: Dad ditching Space Corps lit the afterburners on John, Howard, Frank, and my career quest, filling the void he left.

My brothers, all being older, eventually signed up for the Space Corps, graduating with top marks in their classes. They all got commission postings on the fleet's best ships. John was an astro-navigator on the SSS Augustus, where he shared quarters with a certain Frank Hollister—a captain in the making.

Frank, the rising star in the Space Corps, snagged the first officer position aboard the Nova 4 when the previous first officer, Cheddar Flatheringson, decided he'd rather play captain. Six years of navigating the officer bureaucracy had Frank on a trajectory to break records and become the youngest captain in the Space Corps. But, as I've always said, 'Up, up, up the ziggurat lickety-split.

As for me, at the tender age of nine, my school grades were less than promising, and in a twist of cosmic fate, my parents decided it was better to wash their hands of me and ship me off to boarding school. As time ticked away, my envy for friends and their idyllic families turned me into a recluse. I found solace in the small things; I enjoyed listening to the Hammond organ, Morris Dancing, and building up my collection of 20th-century telegraph poles. You could always find me aimlessly wandering around the vast diesel decks at the local spaceport, attempting to rediscover the joy of getting lost. I even took up learning Esperanto in my sleep. But, as I looked up at the stars, where dreams of greatness shimmer like distant galaxies, my story was only just beginning. Arnold Judas Rimmer was destined for glory from the very fabric of stardust. My humble journey commenced not among the celestial bodies but within the labyrinth of obstacles—the very crucible of my stellar aspirations.

It was just another sunny day on Io, spent jesting with my older brothers John, Howard, and Frank. God, we were close—the 'Four Musketeers,' as we used to call ourselves! Well, the three musketeers actually; they always let me be the queen of Spain. What fun we'd have! An occasional practical joke, of course—apple-pie beds, black-eye telescope. They even hid a small landmine in my sandpit! How were they supposed to know it would go off? However, on this particular day, we were all blissfully ignorant of the interstellar smeg about to hit my life!

As my mother casually revealed her plan to send me off to boarding school! My school grades had been gradually slipping, and my parents, having tried absolutely nothing and being fresh out of ideas, thought it would be best to let me be someone else's problem. I, in my infinite pubescent wisdom, hit her with the forceful question, 'Will I still get to see Bruno?' Bruno was the family dog, clearly. You could see where my main priorities lay.

In response, she crouched down, bless her heart—magnificent woman. Very prim, very proper; some say austere. Some people mistook her for being cold and thought she was aloof. Not a bit of it. She crouched down to my eye level, as if we were sharing the secrets of the universe. In a tone that probably sounded more dramatic than she intended, she explained that it was a boarding school on the other side of Io—pretty much as far away from them while still being on the same planet.

Turning to dear old Dad for an explanation or, at the very least, a distraction from the impending familial meltdown, the bearded git was engaged in a staring contest with the sky. It was as if he believed they held the secrets to a lifetime supply of cosmic beer. 'I don't want to go!' I declared, my voice dripping with the gravitas only a nine-year-old prophet could muster.

"Just a couple of years, Arnold, and you can come home for your birthday," she boldly declared, and Dad, ever the spectator in the family circus, continued his stoic gaze into the sky. He never was one for eye contact. Snapping his head, he interjected, "Don't get the weaselly smegger's hopes up." Classic Dad!

Undeterred by the lack of emotional support, she flung a promise of her triumphant return in time for my birthday, as if the universe itself would pause its dance to celebrate my existence. Hugging me, she hoisted me up. 'C'mon, let's get some quiche,' she declared, casting a glance at Dad, who remained emotionally disengaged; he never would give quiche a chance.

The next morning, I was hurled into a transport craft, sharing a seat with Fred 'Thicky' Holden, leaving me to ponder the cosmic absurdity of it all. Suddenly, the predictable rhythms of my boyhood were replaced by the unpredictable chaos of the universe. Leaving behind our modest house on Io—a perfect replica of an Earth house from the 19th and 20th centuries with its hectares of land. There were some parts I wouldn't miss: getting up early in the morning to feed the sheep and cows, and my pet Lemming. Dad's insistence on manual labor became the launching pad for my determination and my brothers to join the Space Corps.

Our house had witnessed the shenanigans of many generations of Rimmers, with stories galore about my great-great-grandfather, Jebediah Rimmer, who legend has it fought off native Ionians to build the house and gardens. Now maintained by my Dad and with help from the local gardener, Dungo. My dad couldn't stand Dungo, and could never understand why. Sure, he was slightly inept at times and egotistical, self-important, lacked confidence, and was socially awkward. But I always liked him; he had a strong moralistic attitude, and my mother always took a shine to him.

My father, a half-crazed military failure, spent his early years amidst the military pioneers. Growing up on Io, his childhood was an exercise in minimalism. Yet, he yearned to be an officer like his father. The dream almost turned into reality when he strutted onto Space Corps Academy grounds, fulfilling an ambition that had marinated in the spartan conditions of an Io upbringing. Grandpa, an eternal optimist, had dreams of his son treading the same starlit path. Destiny pulled a cosmic prank when he was one inch below Corps regulation height.

My mother was born into an austere family that considered space exploration a genetic trait. Her father was part of the Space Corps' third graduating class, and her mother was a part of the cybernautic division — a family with enough star power to make a pulsar blush.

Mum, with dreams of becoming an astrobiologist, found herself on a collision course with Dad in an Introduction to Space Corps History class. Oh, but the Space Corps Directive 2574 about students fraternizing with other students was stricter than a vegan at a butcher shop. They soon found themselves in front of the space corps instructor with a warning.

Fast forward to Dad's posting on the JMC Emerald Nebula. Despite the height restrictions, strings were pulled, and he was made a galley steward. The ship was still three months away from Earth. He'd stayed in touch with my mother throughout, and in a move that combined romantic flair with a dash of desperation, while on leave at Lunar City 7, Dad proposed to my mother. 'Everyone thought we were bloody mad,' Mum once said, 'Maybe it was the wine or the smell of the beef that had seeped into his clothes. But I just couldn't say no to those puppy dog eyes.' Ah, the cosmic irony of hindsight.

My mother was posted on Titan, and my dad was posted on the JMC Emerald Nebula. Over a year passed before she saw Dad again, and almost two more years before she donned the graduation cap and tossed it into the wind. Yet, fate, with its sense of humor, decided that she wouldn't be posted anywhere near my dad.

My mother was freshly stationed on the Axiom II; however, it wasn't long before she found she had a tiny stowaway on board. She was pregnant with my older brother, Frank! 'Your father was in the outer rim at the time; he nearly dropped his spatula,' she said, 'and by the time the message got to him, I was already as big as a cow

So Mum's Space Corps ambitions hit a speed bump; she took a leave of absence and went to shack up on Io with my paternal grandparents. Lacking her parental navigators, who had embarked on the ultimate road trip years earlier, she found herself surrounded by vast farmland of good old terrestrial adventure. Enter Frank, my elder sibling, making his grand entrance. The interstellar escapades of the next generation were officially underway.

With the cosmic clock ticking, Mum had a mere two Earth-bound years before Space Corp's relentless gravitational pull demanded her return. In those terrestrial years, she juggled the titles of astrobiologist and dedicated mum. 'I just felt shagged out all the time,' she reminisced. 'I missed little Frank; this wasn't what I wanted.' Parenthood, it turns out, is the ultimate improvisational act.

With parents who had charted the final frontier of life and having witnessed her mother resigning her commission to raise her and her brother solo during Dad's cosmic escapades as chief slop server, Mum found herself in a parenting predicament. 'I was bored out of my mind, but your dad's career was everything to him,' she admitted. She'd study

where she could while my grandparents took care of Frank. 'Your grandparents were like Energizer bunnies,' she shared. Meanwhile, Dad, charting his course through the galactic highways aboard the JMC Emerald Nebula, missed Mum and Frank. As the countdown to Mum's return commenced, Dad, ever the master of cosmic shenanigans, pulled whatever strings he could to get her posted back to Io, where he had assumed the role of Restroom attendant.

Only for calamity to strike again after my Mum's grand return to the Space Corps. Surprise, surprise—John was on the way, stealing the spotlight as the next Rimmer headliner. Dad informing Captain Sulaco was less than thrilled. Shipboard nurseries were not on his playlist. But, that triggered Dad's decision. A message blinked in from the cosmic ether—Dad's old man had punched out his ticket to the great beyond when he was born. His career as a restroom attendant wasn't going anywhere fast. Cue the resignation letter to Space Corps—bye-bye dad's officer career. So from that point on, they began to settle into life on Io together. Mum later shot out my next brother Howard. Then, having a break, they focused on the house and garden, bringing local gardener Dungo to assist. It wasn't long after I arrived on the scene!

In the galactic years since, I've mulled over Dad's plot twist and how it flung my trajectory into the cosmic unknown. The cosmic yarn I spin for the masses: Dad ditching Space Corps lit the afterburners on John, Howard, Frank, and my career quest, filling the void he left.

My brothers, all being older, eventually signed up for the Space Corps, graduating with top marks in their classes. They all got commission postings on the fleet's best ships. John was an astro-navigator on the SSS Augustus, where he shared quarters with a certain Frank Hollister—a captain in the making.

Frank, the rising star in the Space Corps, snagged the first officer position aboard the Nova 4 when the previous first officer, Cheddar Flatheringson, decided he'd rather play captain. Six years of navigating the officer bureaucracy had Frank on a trajectory to break records and become the youngest captain in the Space Corps. But, as I've always said, 'Up, up, up the ziggurat lickety-split.

As for me, at the tender age of nine, my school grades were less than promising, and in a twist of cosmic fate, my parents decided it was better to wash their hands of me and ship me off to boarding school. As time ticked away, my envy for friends and their idyllic families turned me into a recluse. I found solace in the small things; I enjoyed listening to the Hammond organ, Morris Dancing, and building up my collection of 20th-century telegraph poles. You could always find me aimlessly wandering around the vast diesel decks at the local spaceport, attempting to rediscover the joy of getting lost. I even took up learning Esperanto in my sleep. But, as I looked up at the stars, where dreams of greatness shimmer like distant galaxies, my story was only just beginning. Arnold Judas Rimmer was destined for glory from the very fabric of stardust. My humble journey commenced not among the celestial bodies but within the labyrinth of obstacles—the very crucible of my stellar aspirations.

It was just another sunny day on Io, spent jesting with my older brothers John, Howard, and Frank. God, we were close—the 'Four Musketeers,' as we used to call ourselves! Well, the three musketeers actually; they always let me be the queen of Spain. What fun we'd have! An occasional practical joke, of course—apple-pie beds, black-eye telescope. They even hid a small landmine in my sandpit! How were they supposed to know it would go off? However, on this particular day, we were all blissfully ignorant of the interstellar smeg about to hit my life!

As my mother casually revealed her plan to send me off to boarding school! My school grades had been gradually slipping, and my parents, having tried absolutely nothing and being fresh out of ideas, thought it would be best to let me be someone else's problem. I, in my infinite pubescent wisdom, hit her with the forceful question, 'Will I still get to see Bruno?' Bruno was the family dog, clearly. You could see where my main priorities lay.

In response, she crouched down, bless her heart—magnificent woman. Very prim, very proper; some say austere. Some people mistook her for being cold and thought she was aloof. Not a bit of it. She crouched down to my eye level, as if we were sharing the secrets of the universe. In a tone that probably sounded more dramatic than she intended, she explained that it was a boarding school on the other side of Io—pretty much as far away from them while still being on the same planet.

Turning to dear old Dad for an explanation or, at the very least, a distraction from the impending familial meltdown, the bearded git was engaged in a staring contest with the sky. It was as if he believed they held the secrets to a lifetime supply of cosmic beer. 'I don't want to go!' I declared, my voice dripping with the gravitas only a nine-year-old prophet could muster.

"Just a couple of years, Arnold, and you can come home for your birthday," she boldly declared, and Dad, ever the spectator in the family circus, continued his stoic gaze into the sky. He never was one for eye contact. Snapping his head, he interjected, "Don't get the weaselly smegger's hopes up." Classic Dad!

Undeterred by the lack of emotional support, she flung a promise of her triumphant return in time for my birthday, as if the universe itself would pause its dance to celebrate my existence. Hugging me, she hoisted me up. 'C'mon, let's get some quiche,' she declared, casting a glance at Dad, who remained emotionally disengaged; he never would give quiche a chance.

The next morning, I was hurled into a transport craft, sharing a seat with Fred 'Thicky' Holden, leaving me to ponder the cosmic absurdity of it all. Suddenly, the predictable rhythms of my boyhood were replaced by the unpredictable chaos of the universe. Leaving behind our modest house on Io — a perfect replica of an Earth house from the 19th and 20th centuries with its hectares of land. There were some parts I wouldn't miss: getting up early in the morning to feed the sheep and cows, and my pet Lemming. Dad's insistence on manual labor became the launching pad for my determination and my brothers to join the Space Corps.

Our house had witnessed the shenanigans of many generations of Rimmers, with stories galore about my great-great-grandfather, Jebediah Rimmer, who legend has it fought off native Ionians to build the house and gardens. Now maintained by my Dad and with help from the local gardener, Dungo. My dad couldn't stand Dungo, and could never understand why. Sure, he was slightly inept at times and egotistical, self-important, lacked confidence, and was socially awkward. But I always liked him; he had a strong moralistic attitude, and my mother always took a shine to him.

My father, a half-crazed military failure, spent his early years amidst the military pioneers. Growing up on Io, his childhood was an exercise in minimalism. Yet, he yearned to be an officer like his father. The dream almost turned into reality when he strutted onto Space Corps Academy grounds, fulfilling an ambition that had marinated in the spartan

conditions of an Io upbringing. Grandpa, an eternal optimist, had dreams of his son treading the same starlit path. Destiny pulled a cosmic prank when he was one inch below Corps regulation height.

My mother was born into an austere family that considered space exploration a genetic trait. Her father was part of the Space Corps' third graduating class, and her mother was a part of the cybernautic division — a family with enough star power to make a pulsar blush.

Mum, with dreams of becoming an astrobiologist, found herself on a collision course with Dad in an Introduction to Space Corps History class. Oh, but the Space Corps Directive 2574 about students fraternizing with other students was stricter than a vegan at a butcher shop. They soon found themselves in front of the space corps instructor with a warning.

Fast forward to Dad's posting on the JMC Emerald Nebula. Despite the height restrictions, strings were pulled, and he was made a galley steward. The ship was still three months away from Earth. He'd stayed in touch with my mother throughout, and in a move that combined romantic flair with a dash of desperation, while on leave at Lunar City 7, Dad proposed to my mother. 'Everyone thought we were bloody mad,' Mum once said, 'Maybe it was the wine or the smell of the beef that had seeped into his clothes. But I just couldn't say no to those puppy dog eyes.' Ah, the cosmic irony of hindsight.

My mother was posted on Titan, and my dad was posted on the JMC Emerald Nebula. Over a year passed before she saw Dad again, and almost two more years before she donned the graduation cap and tossed it into the wind. Yet, fate, with its sense of humor, decided that she wouldn't be posted anywhere near my dad.

My mother was freshly stationed on the Axiom II; however, it wasn't long before she found she had a tiny stowaway on board. She was pregnant with my older brother, Frank! 'Your father was in the outer rim at the time; he nearly dropped his spatula,' she said, 'and by the time the message got to him, I was already as big as a cow

So Mum's Space Corps ambitions hit a speed bump; she took a leave of absence and went to shack up on Io with my paternal grandparents. Lacking her parental navigators, who had embarked on the ultimate road trip years earlier, she found herself surrounded by vast farmland of good old terrestrial adventure. Enter Frank, my elder sibling, making his grand entrance. The interstellar escapades of the next generation were officially underway.

With the cosmic clock ticking, Mum had a mere two Earth-bound years before Space Corp's relentless gravitational pull demanded her return. In those terrestrial years, she juggled the titles of astrobiologist and dedicated mum. 'I just felt shagged out all the time,' she reminisced. 'I missed little Frank; this wasn't what I wanted.' Parenthood, it turns out, is the ultimate improvisational act.

With parents who had charted the final frontier of life and having witnessed her mother resigning her commission to raise her and her brother solo during Dad's cosmic escapades as chief slop server, Mum found herself in a parenting predicament. 'I was bored out of my mind, but your dad's career was everything to him,' she admitted. She'd study where she could while my grandparents took care of Frank. 'Your grandparents were like Energizer bunnies,' she shared. Meanwhile, Dad, charting his course through the galactic highways aboard the JMC Emerald Nebula, missed Mum and Frank. As the countdown to Mum's return commenced, Dad, ever the master of cosmic shenanigans, pulled whatever strings he could to get her posted back to Io, where he had assumed the role of Restroom attendant.

Only for calamity to strike again after my Mum's grand return to the Space Corps. Surprise, surprise—John was on the way, stealing the spotlight as the next Rimmer headliner. Dad informing Captain Sulaco was less than thrilled. Shipboard nurseries were not on his playlist. But, that triggered Dad's decision. A message blinked in from the cosmic ether—Dad's old man had punched out his ticket to the great beyond when he was born. His career as a restroom attendant wasn't going anywhere fast. Cue the resignation letter to Space Corps—bye-bye dad's officer career. So from that point on, they began to settle into life on Io together. Mum later shot out my next brother Howard. Then, having a break, they focused on the house and garden, bringing local gardener Dungo to assist. It wasn't long after I arrived on the scene!

In the galactic years since, I've mulled over Dad's plot twist and how it flung my trajectory into the cosmic unknown. The cosmic yarn I spin for the masses: Dad ditching Space Corps lit the afterburners on John, Howard, Frank, and my career quest, filling the void he left.

My brothers, all being older, eventually signed up for the Space Corps, graduating with top marks in their classes. They all got commission postings on the fleet's best ships. John was an astro-navigator on the SSS Augustus, where he shared quarters with a certain Frank Hollister—a captain in the making.

Frank, the rising star in the Space Corps, snagged the first officer position aboard the Nova 4 when the previous first officer, Cheddar Flatheringson, decided he'd rather play captain. Six years of navigating the officer bureaucracy had Frank on a trajectory to break records and become the youngest captain in the Space Corps. But, as I've always said, 'Up, up, up the ziggurat lickety-split.

As for me, at the tender age of nine, my school grades were less than promising, and in a twist of cosmic fate, my parents decided it was better to wash their hands of me and ship me off to boarding school. As time ticked away, my envy for friends and their idyllic families turned me into a recluse. I found solace in the small things; I enjoyed listening to the Hammond organ, Morris Dancing, and building up my collection of 20th-century telegraph poles. You could always find me aimlessly wandering around the vast diesel decks at the local spaceport, attempting to rediscover the joy of getting lost. I even took up learning Esperanto in my sleep. But, as I looked up at the stars, where dreams of greatness shimmer like distant galaxies, my story was only just beginning. Arnold Judas Rimmer was destined for glory from the very fabric of stardust. My humble journey commenced not among the celestial bodies but within the labyrinth of obstacles — the very crucible of my stellar aspirations.

It was just another sunny day on Io, spent jesting with my older brothers John, Howard, and Frank. God, we were close — the 'Four Musketeers,' as we used to call ourselves! Well, the three musketeers actually; they always let me be the queen of Spain. What fun we'd have! An occasional practical joke, of course — apple-pie beds, black-eye telescope. They even hid a small landmine in my sandpit! How were they supposed to know it would go off? However, on this particular day, we were all blissfully ignorant of the interstellar smeg about to hit my life!

As my mother casually revealed her plan to send me off to boarding school! My school grades had been gradually slipping, and my parents, having tried absolutely nothing and being fresh out of ideas, thought it would be best to let me be someone else's problem. I, in my infinite pubescent wisdom, hit her with the forceful question, 'Will I still get to see Bruno?' Bruno was the family dog, clearly. You could see where my main priorities lay.

In response, she crouched down, bless her heart—magnificent woman. Very prim, very proper; some say austere. Some people mistook her for being cold and thought she was aloof. Not a bit of it. She crouched down to my eye level, as if we were sharing the secrets of the universe. In a tone that probably sounded more dramatic than she intended, she explained that it was a boarding school on the other side of Io—pretty much as far away from them while still being on the same planet.

Turning to dear old Dad for an explanation or, at the very least, a distraction from the impending familial meltdown, the bearded git was engaged in a staring contest with the sky. It was as if he believed they held the secrets to a lifetime supply of cosmic beer. 'I don't want to go!' I declared, my voice dripping with the gravitas only a nine-year-old prophet could muster.

"Just a couple of years, Arnold, and you can come home for your birthday," she boldly declared, and Dad, ever the spectator in the family circus, continued his stoic gaze into the sky. He never was one for eye contact. Snapping his head, he interjected, "Don't get the weaselly smegger's hopes up." Classic Dad!

Undeterred by the lack of emotional support, she flung a promise of her triumphant return in time for my birthday, as if the universe itself would pause its dance to celebrate my existence. Hugging me, she hoisted me up. 'C'mon, let's get some quiche,' she declared, casting a glance at Dad, who remained emotionally disengaged; he never would give quiche a chance.

The next morning, I was hurled into a transport craft, sharing a seat with Fred 'Thicky' Holden, leaving me to ponder the cosmic absurdity of it all. Suddenly, the predictable rhythms of my boyhood were replaced by the unpredictable chaos of the universe. Leaving behind our modest house on Io—a perfect replica of an Earth house from the 19th and 20th centuries with its hectares of land. There were some parts I wouldn't miss: getting up early in the morning to feed the sheep and cows, and my pet Lemming. Dad's insistence on manual labor became the launching pad for my determination and my brothers to join the Space Corps.

Our house had witnessed the shenanigans of many generations of Rimmers, with stories galore about my great-great-grandfather, Jebediah Rimmer, who legend has it fought off native Ionians to build the house and gardens. Now maintained by my Dad and with help from the local gardener, Dungo. My dad couldn't stand Dungo, and could never understand why. Sure, he was slightly inept at times and egotistical, self-important, lacked confidence, and was socially awkward. But I always liked him; he had a strong moralistic attitude, and my mother always took a shine to him.

My father, a half-crazed military failure, spent his early years amidst the military pioneers. Growing up on Io, his childhood was an exercise in minimalism. Yet, he yearned to be an officer like his father. The dream almost turned into reality when he strutted onto Space Corps Academy grounds, fulfilling an ambition that had marinated in the spartan conditions of an Io upbringing. Grandpa, an eternal optimist, had dreams of his son treading the same starlit path. Destiny pulled a cosmic prank when he was one inch below Corps regulation height.

My mother was born into an austere family that considered space exploration a genetic trait. Her father was part of the Space Corps' third graduating class, and her mother was a part of the cybernautic division—a family with enough star power to make a pulsar blush.

Mum, with dreams of becoming an astrobiologist, found herself on a collision course with Dad in an Introduction to Space Corps History class. Oh, but the Space Corps Directive 2574 about students fraternizing with other students was stricter than a vegan at a butcher shop. They soon found themselves in front of the space corps instructor with a warning.

Fast forward to Dad's posting on the JMC Emerald Nebula. Despite the height restrictions, strings were pulled, and he was made a galley steward. The ship was still three months away from Earth. He'd stayed in touch with my mother throughout, and in a move that combined romantic flair with a dash of desperation, while on leave at Lunar City 7, Dad proposed to my mother. 'Everyone thought we were bloody mad,' Mum once said, 'Maybe it was the wine or the smell of the beef that had seeped into his clothes. But I just couldn't say no to those puppy dog eyes.' Ah, the cosmic irony of hindsight.

My mother was posted on Titan, and my dad was posted on the JMC Emerald Nebula. Over a year passed before she saw Dad again, and almost two more years before she donned the graduation cap and tossed it into the wind. Yet, fate, with its sense of humor, decided that she wouldn't be posted anywhere near my dad.

My mother was freshly stationed on the Axiom II; however, it wasn't long before she found she had a tiny stowaway on board. She was pregnant with my older brother, Frank! 'Your father was in the outer rim at the time; he nearly dropped his spatula,' she said, 'and by the time the message got to him, I was already as big as a cow

So Mum's Space Corps ambitions hit a speed bump; she took a leave of absence and went to shack up on Io with my paternal grandparents. Lacking her parental navigators, who had embarked on the ultimate road trip years earlier, she found herself surrounded by vast farmland of good old terrestrial adventure. Enter Frank, my elder sibling, making his grand entrance. The interstellar escapades of the next generation were officially underway.

With the cosmic clock ticking, Mum had a mere two Earth-bound years before Space Corp's relentless gravitational pull demanded her return. In those terrestrial years, she juggled the titles of astrobiologist and dedicated mum. 'I just felt shagged out all the time,' she reminisced. 'I missed little Frank; this wasn't what I wanted.' Parenthood, it turns out, is the ultimate improvisational act.

With parents who had charted the final frontier of life and having witnessed her mother resigning her commission to raise her and her brother solo during Dad's cosmic escapades as chief slop server, Mum found herself in a parenting predicament. 'I was bored out of my mind, but your dad's career was everything to him,' she admitted. She'd study where she could while my grandparents took care of Frank. 'Your grandparents were like Energizer bunnies,' she shared. Meanwhile, Dad, charting his course through the galactic highways aboard the JMC Emerald Nebula, missed Mum and Frank. As the countdown to Mum's return commenced, Dad, ever the master of cosmic shenanigans, pulled whatever strings he could to get her posted back to Io, where he had assumed the role of Restroom attendant.

Only for calamity to strike again after my Mum's grand return to the Space Corps. Surprise, surprise — John was on the way, stealing the spotlight as the next Rimmer headliner. Dad informing Captain Sulaco was less than thrilled. Shipboard nurseries were not on his playlist. But, that triggered Dad's decision. A message blinked in from the cosmic ether — Dad's old man had punched out his ticket to the great beyond when he was born. His career as a restroom attendant wasn't going anywhere fast. Cue the resignation letter to Space Corps — bye-bye dad's officer career. So from that point on, they began to settle into life on Io together. Mum later shot out my next brother Howard. Then, having a break, they focused on the house and garden, bringing local gardener Dungo to assist. It wasn't long after I arrived on the scene!

In the galactic years since, I've mulled over Dad's plot twist and how it flung my trajectory into the cosmic unknown. The cosmic yarn I spin for the masses: Dad ditching Space Corps lit the afterburners on John, Howard, Frank, and my career quest, filling the void he left.

My brothers, all being older, eventually signed up for the Space Corps, graduating with top marks in their classes. They all got commission postings on the fleet's best ships. John was an astro-navigator on the SSS Augustus, where he shared quarters with a certain Frank Hollister — a captain in the making.

Frank, the rising star in the Space Corps, snagged the first officer position aboard the Nova 4 when the previous first officer, Cheddar Flatheringson, decided he'd rather play captain. Six years of navigating the officer bureaucracy had Frank on a trajectory to break records and become the youngest captain in the Space Corps. But, as I've always said, 'Up, up, up the ziggurat lickety-split.

As for me, at the tender age of nine, my school grades were less than promising, and in a twist of cosmic fate, my parents decided it was better to wash their hands of me and ship me off to boarding school. As time ticked away, my envy for friends and their idyllic families turned me into a recluse. I found solace in the small things; I enjoyed listening to the Hammond organ, Morris Dancing, and building up my collection of 20th-century telegraph poles. You could always find me aimlessly wandering around the vast diesel decks at the local spaceport, attempting to rediscover the joy of getting lost. I even took up learning Esperanto in my sleep. But, as I looked up at the stars, where dreams of greatness shimmer like distant galaxies, my story was only just beginning. Arnold Judas Rimmer was destined for glory from the very fabric of stardust. My humble journey commenced not among the celestial bodies but within the labyrinth of obstacles—the very crucible of my stellar aspirations.

It was just another sunny day on Io, spent jesting with my older brothers John, Howard, and Frank. God, we were close—the 'Four Musketeers,' as we used to call ourselves! Well, the three musketeers actually; they always let me be the queen of Spain. What fun we'd have! An occasional practical joke, of course—apple-pie beds, black-eye telescope. They even hid a small landmine in my sandpit! How were they supposed to know it would go off? However, on this particular day, we were all blissfully ignorant of the interstellar smeg about to hit my life!

As my mother casually revealed her plan to send me off to boarding school! My school grades had been gradually slipping, and my parents, having tried absolutely nothing and being fresh out of ideas, thought it would be best to let me be someone else's problem. I, in my infinite pubescent wisdom, hit her with the forceful question, 'Will I still get to see Bruno?' Bruno was the family dog, clearly. You could see where my main priorities lay.

In response, she crouched down, bless her heart—magnificent woman. Very prim, very proper; some say austere. Some people mistook her for being cold and thought she was aloof. Not a bit of it. She crouched down to my eye level, as if we were sharing the secrets of the universe. In a tone that probably sounded more dramatic than she intended, she explained that it was a boarding school on the other side of Io—pretty much as far away from them while still being on the same planet.

Turning to dear old Dad for an explanation or, at the very least, a distraction from the impending familial meltdown, the bearded git was engaged in a staring contest with the sky. It was as if he believed they held the secrets to a lifetime supply of cosmic beer. 'I don't want to go!' I declared, my voice dripping with the gravitas only a nine-year-old prophet could muster.

"Just a couple of years, Arnold, and you can come home for your birthday," she boldly declared, and Dad, ever the spectator in the family circus, continued his stoic gaze into the sky. He never was one for eye contact. Snapping his head, he interjected, "Don't get the weaselly smegger's hopes up." Classic Dad!

Undeterred by the lack of emotional support, she flung a promise of her triumphant return in time for my birthday, as if the universe itself would pause its dance to celebrate my existence. Hugging me, she hoisted me up. 'C'mon, let's get some quiche,' she declared, casting a glance at Dad, who remained emotionally disengaged; he never would give quiche a chance.

The next morning, I was hurled into a transport craft, sharing a seat with Fred 'Thicky' Holden, leaving me to ponder the cosmic absurdity of it all. Suddenly, the predictable rhythms of my boyhood were replaced by the unpredictable chaos of the universe. Leaving behind our modest house on Io—a perfect replica of an Earth house from the 19th and 20th centuries with its hectares of land. There were some parts I wouldn't miss: getting up early in the morning to feed the sheep and cows, and my pet Lemming. Dad's insistence on manual labor became the launching pad for my determination and my brothers to join the Space Corps.

Our house had witnessed the shenanigans of many generations of Rimmers, with stories galore about my great-great-grandfather, Jebediah Rimmer, who legend has it fought off native Ionians to build the house and gardens. Now maintained by my Dad and with help from the local gardener, Dungo. My dad couldn't stand Dungo, and could never understand why. Sure, he was slightly inept at times and egotistical, self-important, lacked confidence, and was socially awkward. But I always liked him; he had a strong moralistic attitude, and my mother always took a shine to him.

My father, a half-crazed military failure, spent his early years amidst the military pioneers. Growing up on Io, his childhood was an exercise in minimalism. Yet, he yearned to be an officer like his father. The dream almost turned into reality when he strutted onto Space Corps Academy grounds, fulfilling an ambition that had marinated in the spartan conditions of an Io upbringing. Grandpa, an eternal optimist, had dreams of his son treading the same starlit path. Destiny pulled a cosmic prank when he was one inch below Corps regulation height.

My mother was born into an austere family that considered space exploration a genetic trait. Her father was part of the Space Corps' third graduating class, and her mother was a part of the cybernautic division — a family with enough star power to make a pulsar blush.

Mum, with dreams of becoming an astrobiologist, found herself on a collision course with Dad in an Introduction to Space Corps History class. Oh, but the Space Corps Directive 2574 about students fraternizing with other students was stricter than a vegan at a butcher shop. They soon found themselves in front of the space corps instructor with a warning.

Fast forward to Dad's posting on the JMC Emerald Nebula. Despite the height restrictions, strings were pulled, and he was made a galley steward. The ship was still three months away from Earth. He'd stayed in touch with my mother throughout, and in a move that combined romantic flair with a dash of desperation, while on leave at Lunar City 7, Dad proposed to my mother. 'Everyone thought we were bloody mad,' Mum once said, 'Maybe it was the wine or the smell of the beef that had seeped into his clothes. But I just couldn't say no to those puppy dog eyes.' Ah, the cosmic irony of hindsight.

My mother was posted on Titan, and my dad was posted on the JMC Emerald Nebula. Over a year passed before she saw Dad again, and almost two more years before she donned the graduation cap and tossed it into the wind. Yet, fate, with its sense of humor, decided that she wouldn't be posted anywhere near my dad.

My mother was freshly stationed on the Axiom II; however, it wasn't long before she found she had a tiny stowaway on board. She was pregnant with my older brother, Frank! 'Your father was in the outer rim at the time; he nearly dropped his spatula,' she said, 'and by the time the message got to him, I was already as big as a cow

So Mum's Space Corps ambitions hit a speed bump; she took a leave of absence and went to shack up on Io with my paternal grandparents. Lacking her parental navigators, who had embarked on the ultimate road trip years earlier, she found herself surrounded by vast farmland of good old terrestrial adventure. Enter Frank, my elder sibling, making his grand entrance. The interstellar escapades of the next generation were officially underway.

With the cosmic clock ticking, Mum had a mere two Earth-bound years before Space Corp's relentless gravitational pull demanded her return. In those terrestrial years, she juggled the titles of astrobiologist and dedicated mum. 'I just felt shagged out all the time,' she reminisced. 'I missed little Frank; this wasn't what I wanted.' Parenthood, it turns out, is the ultimate improvisational act.

With parents who had charted the final frontier of life and having witnessed her mother resigning her commission to raise her and her brother solo during Dad's cosmic escapades as chief slop server, Mum found herself in a parenting predicament. 'I was bored out of my mind, but your dad's career was everything to him,' she admitted. She'd study where she could while my grandparents took care of Frank. 'Your grandparents were like Energizer bunnies,' she shared. Meanwhile, Dad, charting his course through the galactic highways aboard the JMC Emerald Nebula, missed Mum and Frank. As the countdown to Mum's return commenced, Dad, ever the master of cosmic shenanigans, pulled whatever strings he could to get her posted back to Io, where he had assumed the role of Restroom attendant.

Only for calamity to strike again after my Mum's grand return to the Space Corps. Surprise, surprise—John was on the way, stealing the spotlight as the next Rimmer headliner. Dad informing Captain Sulaco was less than thrilled. Shipboard nurseries were not on his playlist. But, that triggered Dad's decision. A message blinked in from the cosmic ether—Dad's old man had punched out his ticket to the great beyond when he was born. His career as a restroom attendant wasn't going anywhere fast. Cue the resignation letter to Space Corps—bye-bye dad's officer career. So from that point on, they began to settle into life on Io together. Mum later shot out my next brother Howard. Then, having a break, they focused on the house and garden, bringing local gardener Dungo to assist. It wasn't long after I arrived on the scene!

116

In the galactic years since, I've mulled over Dad's plot twist and how it flung my trajectory into the cosmic unknown. The cosmic yarn I spin for the masses: Dad ditching Space Corps lit the afterburners on John, Howard, Frank, and my career quest, filling the void he left.

My brothers, all being older, eventually signed up for the Space Corps, graduating with top marks in their classes. They all got commission postings on the fleet's best ships. John was an astro-navigator on the SSS Augustus, where he shared quarters with a certain Frank Hollister—a captain in the making.

Frank, the rising star in the Space Corps, snagged the first officer position aboard the Nova 4 when the previous first officer, Cheddar Flatheringson, decided he'd rather play captain. Six years of navigating the officer bureaucracy had Frank on a trajectory to break records and become the youngest captain in the Space Corps. But, as I've always said, 'Up, up, up the ziggurat lickety-split.

As for me, at the tender age of nine, my school grades were less than promising, and in a twist of cosmic fate, my parents decided it was better to wash their hands of me and ship me off to boarding school. As time ticked away, my envy for friends and their idyllic families turned me into a recluse. I found solace in the small things; I enjoyed listening to the Hammond organ, Morris Dancing, and building up my collection of 20th-century telegraph poles. You could always find me aimlessly wandering around the vast diesel decks at the local spaceport, attempting to rediscover the joy of getting lost. I even took up learning Esperanto in my sleep. But, as I looked up at the stars, where dreams of greatness shimmer like distant galaxies, my story was only just beginning. Arnold Judas Rimmer was destined for glory from the very fabric of stardust. My humble journey commenced not among the celestial bodies but within the labyrinth of obstacles—the very crucible of my stellar aspirations.

It was just another sunny day on Io, spent jesting with my older brothers John, Howard, and Frank. God, we were close—the 'Four Musketeers,' as we used to call ourselves! Well, the three musketeers actually; they always let me be the queen of Spain. What fun we'd have! An occasional practical joke, of course—apple-pie beds, black-eye telescope. They even hid a small landmine in my sandpit! How were they supposed to know it would go off? However, on this particular day, we were all blissfully ignorant of the interstellar smeg about to hit my life!

As my mother casually revealed her plan to send me off to boarding school! My school grades had been gradually slipping, and my parents, having tried absolutely nothing and being fresh out of ideas, thought it would be best to let me be someone else's problem. I, in my infinite pubescent wisdom, hit her with the forceful question, 'Will I still get to see Bruno?' Bruno was the family dog, clearly. You could see where my main priorities lay.

In response, she crouched down, bless her heart—magnificent woman. Very prim, very proper; some say austere. Some people mistook her for being cold and thought she was aloof. Not a bit of it. She crouched down to my eye level, as if we were sharing the secrets of the universe. In a tone that probably sounded more dramatic than she intended, she explained that it was a boarding school on the other side of Io—pretty much as far away from them while still being on the same planet.

Turning to dear old Dad for an explanation or, at the very least, a distraction from the impending familial meltdown, the bearded git was engaged in a staring contest with the sky. It was as if he believed they held the secrets to a lifetime supply of cosmic beer. 'I don't want to go!' I declared, my voice dripping with the gravitas only a nine-year-old prophet could muster.

"Just a couple of years, Arnold, and you can come home for your birthday," she boldly declared, and Dad, ever the spectator in the family circus, continued his stoic gaze into the sky. He never was one for eye contact. Snapping his head, he interjected, "Don't get the weaselly smegger's hopes up." Classic Dad!

Undeterred by the lack of emotional support, she flung a promise of her triumphant return in time for my birthday, as if the universe itself would pause its dance to celebrate my existence. Hugging me, she hoisted me up. 'C'mon, let's get some quiche,' she declared, casting a glance at Dad, who remained emotionally disengaged; he never would give quiche a chance.

The next morning, I was hurled into a transport craft, sharing a seat with Fred 'Thicky' Holden, leaving me to ponder the cosmic absurdity of it all. Suddenly, the predictable rhythms of my boyhood were replaced by the unpredictable chaos of the universe. Leaving behind our modest house on Io — a perfect replica of an Earth house from the 19th and 20th centuries with its hectares of land. There were some parts I wouldn't miss: getting up early in the morning to feed the sheep and cows, and my pet Lemming. Dad's insistence on manual labor became the launching pad for my determination and my brothers to join the Space Corps.

Our house had witnessed the shenanigans of many generations of Rimmers, with stories galore about my great-great-grandfather, Jebediah Rimmer, who legend has it fought off native Ionians to build the house and gardens. Now maintained by my Dad and with help from the local gardener, Dungo. My dad couldn't stand Dungo, and could never understand why. Sure, he was slightly inept at times and egotistical, self-important, lacked confidence, and was socially awkward. But I always liked him; he had a strong moralistic attitude, and my mother always took a shine to him.

My father, a half-crazed military failure, spent his early years amidst the military pioneers. Growing up on Io, his childhood was an exercise in minimalism. Yet, he yearned to be an officer like his father. The dream almost turned into reality when he strutted onto Space Corps Academy grounds, fulfilling an ambition that had marinated in the spartan conditions of an Io upbringing. Grandpa, an eternal optimist, had dreams of his son treading the same starlit path. Destiny pulled a cosmic prank when he was one inch below Corps regulation height.

My mother was born into an austere family that considered space exploration a genetic trait. Her father was part of the Space Corps' third graduating class, and her mother was a part of the cybernautic division — a family with enough star power to make a pulsar blush.

Mum, with dreams of becoming an astrobiologist, found herself on a collision course with Dad in an Introduction to Space Corps History class. Oh, but the Space Corps Directive 2574 about students fraternizing with other students was stricter than a vegan at a butcher shop. They soon found themselves in front of the space corps instructor with a warning.

Fast forward to Dad's posting on the JMC Emerald Nebula. Despite the height restrictions, strings were pulled, and he was made a galley steward. The ship was still three months away from Earth. He'd stayed in touch with my mother throughout, and in a move that combined romantic flair with a dash of desperation, while on leave at Lunar City 7, Dad proposed to my mother. 'Everyone thought we were bloody mad,' Mum once said, 'Maybe it was the wine or the smell of the beef that had seeped into his clothes. But I just couldn't say no to those puppy dog eyes.' Ah, the cosmic irony of hindsight.

120

My mother was posted on Titan, and my dad was posted on the JMC Emerald Nebula. Over a year passed before she saw Dad again, and almost two more years before she donned the graduation cap and tossed it into the wind. Yet, fate, with its sense of humor, decided that she wouldn't be posted anywhere near my dad.

My mother was freshly stationed on the Axiom II; however, it wasn't long before she found she had a tiny stowaway on board. She was pregnant with my older brother, Frank! 'Your father was in the outer rim at the time; he nearly dropped his spatula,' she said, 'and by the time the message got to him, I was already as big as a cow

So Mum's Space Corps ambitions hit a speed bump; she took a leave of absence and went to shack up on Io with my paternal grandparents. Lacking her parental navigators, who had embarked on the ultimate road trip years earlier, she found herself surrounded by vast farmland of good old terrestrial adventure. Enter Frank, my elder sibling, making his grand entrance. The interstellar escapades of the next generation were officially underway.

With the cosmic clock ticking, Mum had a mere two Earth-bound years before Space Corp's relentless gravitational pull demanded her return. In those terrestrial years, she juggled the titles of astrobiologist and dedicated mum. 'I just felt shagged out all the time,' she reminisced. 'I missed little Frank; this wasn't what I wanted.' Parenthood, it turns out, is the ultimate improvisational act.

With parents who had charted the final frontier of life and having witnessed her mother resigning her commission to raise her and her brother solo during Dad's cosmic escapades as chief slop server, Mum found herself in a parenting predicament. 'I was bored out of my mind, but your dad's career was everything to him,' she admitted. She'd study where she could while my grandparents took care of Frank. 'Your grandparents were like Energizer bunnies,' she shared. Meanwhile, Dad, charting his course through the galactic highways aboard the JMC Emerald Nebula, missed Mum and Frank. As the countdown to Mum's return commenced, Dad, ever the master of cosmic shenanigans, pulled whatever strings he could to get her posted back to Io, where he had assumed the role of Restroom attendant.

Only for calamity to strike again after my Mum's grand return to the Space Corps. Surprise, surprise—John was on the way, stealing the spotlight as the next Rimmer headliner. Dad informing Captain Sulaco was less than thrilled. Shipboard nurseries were not on his playlist. But, that triggered Dad's decision. A message blinked in from the cosmic ether—Dad's old man had punched out his ticket to the great beyond when he was born. His career as a restroom attendant wasn't going anywhere fast. Cue the resignation letter to Space Corps—bye-bye dad's officer career. So from that point on, they began to settle into life on Io together. Mum later shot out my next brother Howard. Then, having a break, they focused on the house and garden, bringing local gardener Dungo to assist. It wasn't long after I arrived on the scene!

In the galactic years since, I've mulled over Dad's plot twist and how it flung my trajectory into the cosmic unknown. The cosmic yarn I spin for the masses: Dad ditching Space Corps lit the afterburners on John, Howard, Frank, and my career quest, filling the void he left.

My brothers, all being older, eventually signed up for the Space Corps, graduating with top marks in their classes. They all got commission postings on the fleet's best ships. John was an astro-navigator on the SSS Augustus, where he shared quarters with a certain Frank Hollister—a captain in the making.

Frank, the rising star in the Space Corps, snagged the first officer position aboard the Nova 4 when the previous first officer, Cheddar Flatheringson, decided he'd rather play captain. Six years of navigating the officer bureaucracy had Frank on a trajectory to break records and become the youngest captain in the Space Corps. But, as I've always said, 'Up, up, up the ziggurat lickety-split.

As for me, at the tender age of nine, my school grades were less than promising, and in a twist of cosmic fate, my parents decided it was better to wash their hands of me and ship me off to boarding school. As time ticked away, my envy for friends and their idyllic families turned me into a recluse. I found solace in the small things; I enjoyed listening to the Hammond organ, Morris Dancing, and building up my collection of 20th-century telegraph poles. You could always find me aimlessly wandering around the vast diesel decks at the local spaceport, attempting to rediscover the joy of getting lost. I even took up learning Esperanto in my sleep. But, as I looked up at the stars, where dreams of greatness shimmer like distant galaxies, my story was only just beginning. Arnold Judas Rimmer was destined for glory from the very fabric of stardust. My humble journey commenced not among the celestial bodies but within the labyrinth of obstacles—the very crucible of my stellar aspirations.

It was just another sunny day on Io, spent jesting with my older brothers John, Howard, and Frank. God, we were close—the 'Four Musketeers,' as we used to call ourselves! Well, the three musketeers actually; they always let me be the queen of Spain. What fun we'd have! An occasional practical joke, of course—apple-pie beds, black-eye telescope. They even hid a small landmine in my sandpit! How were they supposed to know it would go off? However, on this particular day, we were all blissfully ignorant of the interstellar smeg about to hit my life!

As my mother casually revealed her plan to send me off to boarding school! My school grades had been gradually slipping, and my parents, having tried absolutely nothing and being fresh out of ideas, thought it would be best to let me be someone else's problem. I, in my infinite pubescent wisdom, hit her with the forceful question, 'Will I still get to see Bruno?' Bruno was the family dog, clearly. You could see where my main priorities lay.

In response, she crouched down, bless her heart—magnificent woman. Very prim, very proper; some say austere. Some people mistook her for being cold and thought she was aloof. Not a bit of it. She crouched down to my eye level, as if we were sharing the secrets of the universe. In a tone that probably sounded more dramatic than she intended, she explained that it was a boarding school on the other side of Io—pretty much as far away from them while still being on the same planet.

Turning to dear old Dad for an explanation or, at the very least, a distraction from the impending familial meltdown, the bearded git was engaged in a staring contest with the sky. It was as if he believed they held the secrets to a lifetime supply of cosmic beer. 'I don't want to go!' I declared, my voice dripping with the gravitas only a nine-year-old prophet could muster.

"Just a couple of years, Arnold, and you can come home for your birthday," she boldly declared, and Dad, ever the spectator in the family circus, continued his stoic gaze into the sky. He never was one for eye contact. Snapping his head, he interjected, "Don't get the weaselly smegger's hopes up." Classic Dad!

Undeterred by the lack of emotional support, she flung a promise of her triumphant return in time for my birthday, as if the universe itself would pause its dance to celebrate my existence. Hugging me, she hoisted me up. 'C'mon, let's get some quiche,' she declared, casting a glance at Dad, who remained emotionally disengaged; he never would give quiche a chance.

The next morning, I was hurled into a transport craft, sharing a seat with Fred 'Thicky' Holden, leaving me to ponder the cosmic absurdity of it all. Suddenly, the predictable rhythms of my boyhood were replaced by the unpredictable chaos of the universe. Leaving behind our modest house on Io — a perfect replica of an Earth house from the 19th and 20th centuries with its hectares of land. There were some parts I wouldn't miss: getting up early in the morning to feed the sheep and cows, and my pet Lemming. Dad's insistence on manual labor became the launching pad for my determination and my brothers to join the Space Corps.

Our house had witnessed the shenanigans of many generations of Rimmers, with stories galore about my great-great-grandfather, Jebediah Rimmer, who legend has it fought off native Ionians to build the house and gardens. Now maintained by my Dad and with help from the local gardener, Dungo. My dad couldn't stand Dungo, and could never understand why. Sure, he was slightly inept at times and egotistical, self-important, lacked confidence, and was socially awkward. But I always liked him; he had a strong moralistic attitude, and my mother always took a shine to him.

My father, a half-crazed military failure, spent his early years amidst the military pioneers. Growing up on Io, his childhood was an exercise in minimalism. Yet, he yearned to be an officer like his father. The dream almost turned into reality when he strutted onto Space Corps Academy grounds, fulfilling an ambition that had marinated in the spartan

conditions of an Io upbringing. Grandpa, an eternal optimist, had dreams of his son treading the same starlit path. Destiny pulled a cosmic prank when he was one inch below Corps regulation height.

My mother was born into an austere family that considered space exploration a genetic trait. Her father was part of the Space Corps' third graduating class, and her mother was a part of the cybernautic division — a family with enough star power to make a pulsar blush.

Mum, with dreams of becoming an astrobiologist, found herself on a collision course with Dad in an Introduction to Space Corps History class. Oh, but the Space Corps Directive 2574 about students fraternizing with other students was stricter than a vegan at a butcher shop. They soon found themselves in front of the space corps instructor with a warning.

Fast forward to Dad's posting on the JMC Emerald Nebula. Despite the height restrictions, strings were pulled, and he was made a galley steward. The ship was still three months away from Earth. He'd stayed in touch with my mother throughout, and in a move that combined romantic flair with a dash of desperation, while on leave at Lunar City 7, Dad proposed to my mother. 'Everyone thought we were bloody mad,' Mum once said, 'Maybe it was the wine or the smell of the beef that had seeped into his clothes. But I just couldn't say no to those puppy dog eyes.' Ah, the cosmic irony of hindsight.

My mother was posted on Titan, and my dad was posted on the JMC Emerald Nebula. Over a year passed before she saw Dad again, and almost two more years before she donned the graduation cap and tossed it into the wind. Yet, fate, with its sense of humor, decided that she wouldn't be posted anywhere near my dad.

My mother was freshly stationed on the Axiom II; however, it wasn't long before she found she had a tiny stowaway on board. She was pregnant with my older brother, Frank! 'Your father was in the outer rim at the time; he nearly dropped his spatula,' she said, 'and by the time the message got to him, I was already as big as a cow

So Mum's Space Corps ambitions hit a speed bump; she took a leave of absence and went to shack up on Io with my paternal grandparents. Lacking her parental navigators, who had embarked on the ultimate road trip years earlier, she found herself surrounded by vast farmland of good old terrestrial adventure. Enter Frank, my elder sibling, making his grand entrance. The interstellar escapades of the next generation were officially underway.

With the cosmic clock ticking, Mum had a mere two Earth-bound years before Space Corp's relentless gravitational pull demanded her return. In those terrestrial years, she juggled the titles of astrobiologist and dedicated mum. 'I just felt shagged out all the time,' she reminisced. 'I missed little Frank; this wasn't what I wanted.' Parenthood, it turns out, is the ultimate improvisational act.

With parents who had charted the final frontier of life and having witnessed her mother resigning her commission to raise her and her brother solo during Dad's cosmic escapades as chief slop server, Mum found herself in a parenting predicament. 'I was bored out of my mind, but your dad's career was everything to him,' she admitted. She'd study where she could while my grandparents took care of Frank. 'Your grandparents were like Energizer bunnies,' she shared. Meanwhile, Dad, charting his course through the galactic highways aboard the JMC Emerald Nebula, missed Mum and Frank. As the countdown to Mum's return commenced, Dad, ever the master of cosmic shenanigans, pulled whatever strings he could to get her posted back to Io, where he had assumed the role of Restroom attendant.

Only for calamity to strike again after my Mum's grand return to the Space Corps. Surprise, surprise—John was on the way, stealing the spotlight as the next Rimmer headliner. Dad informing Captain Sulaco was less than thrilled. Shipboard nurseries were not on his playlist. But, that triggered Dad's decision. A message blinked in from the cosmic ether—Dad's old man had punched out his ticket to the great beyond when he was born. His career as a restroom attendant wasn't going anywhere fast. Cue the resignation letter to Space Corps—bye-bye dad's officer career. So from that point on, they began to settle into life on Io together. Mum later shot out my next brother Howard. Then, having a break, they focused on the house and garden, bringing local gardener Dungo to assist. It wasn't long after I arrived on the scene!

In the galactic years since, I've mulled over Dad's plot twist and how it flung my trajectory into the cosmic unknown. The cosmic yarn I spin for the masses: Dad ditching Space Corps lit the afterburners on John, Howard, Frank, and my career quest, filling the void he left.

My brothers, all being older, eventually signed up for the Space Corps, graduating with top marks in their classes. They all got commission postings on the fleet's best ships. John was an astro-navigator on the SSS Augustus, where he shared quarters with a certain Frank Hollister—a captain in the making.

Frank, the rising star in the Space Corps, snagged the first officer position aboard the Nova 4 when the previous first officer, Cheddar Flatheringson, decided he'd rather play captain. Six years of navigating the officer bureaucracy had Frank on a trajectory to break records and become the youngest captain in the Space Corps. But, as I've always said, 'Up, up, up the ziggurat lickety-split.

As for me, at the tender age of nine, my school grades were less than promising, and in a twist of cosmic fate, my parents decided it was better to wash their hands of me and ship me off to boarding school. As time ticked away, my envy for friends and their idyllic families turned me into a recluse. I found solace in the small things; I enjoyed listening to the Hammond organ, Morris Dancing, and building up my collection of 20th-century telegraph poles. You could always find me aimlessly wandering around the vast diesel decks at the local spaceport, attempting to rediscover the joy of getting lost. I even took up learning Esperanto in my sleep. But, as I looked up at the stars, where dreams of greatness shimmer like distant galaxies, my story was only just beginning. Arnold Judas Rimmer was destined for glory from the very fabric of stardust. My humble journey commenced not among the celestial bodies but within the labyrinth of obstacles—the very crucible of my stellar aspirations.

# CHAPTER 6
# FIRST ENCOUNTERS AND CELESTIAL CONFLICTS

It was just another sunny day on Io, spent jesting with my older brothers John, Howard, and Frank. God, we were close—the 'Four Musketeers,' as we used to call ourselves! Well, the three musketeers actually; they always let me be the queen of Spain. What fun we'd have! An occasional practical joke, of course—apple-pie beds, black-eye telescope. They even hid a small landmine in my sandpit! How were they supposed to know it would go off? However, on this particular day, we were all blissfully ignorant of the interstellar smeg about to hit my life!

As my mother casually revealed her plan to send me off to boarding school! My school grades had been gradually slipping, and my parents, having tried absolutely nothing and being fresh out of ideas, thought it would be best to let me be someone else's problem. I, in my infinite pubescent wisdom, hit her with the forceful question, 'Will I still get to see Bruno?' Bruno was the family dog, clearly. You could see where my main priorities lay.

In response, she crouched down, bless her heart—magnificent woman. Very prim, very proper; some say austere. Some people mistook her for being cold and thought she was aloof. Not a bit of it. She crouched down to my eye level, as if we were sharing the secrets of the universe. In a tone that probably sounded more dramatic than she intended, she explained that it was a boarding school on the other side of Io—pretty much as far away from them while still being on the same planet.

Turning to dear old Dad for an explanation or, at the very least, a distraction from the impending familial meltdown, the bearded git was engaged in a staring contest with the sky. It was as if he believed they held the secrets to a lifetime supply of cosmic beer. 'I don't want to go!' I declared, my voice dripping with the gravitas only a nine-year-old prophet could muster.

"Just a couple of years, Arnold, and you can come home for your birthday," she boldly declared, and Dad, ever the spectator in the family circus, continued his stoic gaze into the sky. He never was one for eye contact. Snapping his head, he interjected, "Don't get the weaselly smegger's hopes up." Classic Dad!

Undeterred by the lack of emotional support, she flung a promise of her triumphant return in time for my birthday, as if the universe itself would pause its dance to celebrate my existence. Hugging me, she hoisted me up. 'C'mon, let's get some quiche,' she declared, casting a glance at Dad, who remained emotionally disengaged; he never would give quiche a chance.

The next morning, I was hurled into a transport craft, sharing a seat with Fred 'Thicky' Holden, leaving me to ponder the cosmic absurdity of it all. Suddenly, the predictable rhythms of my boyhood were replaced by the unpredictable chaos of the universe. Leaving behind our modest house on Io — a perfect replica of an Earth house from the 19th and 20th centuries with its hectares of land. There were some parts I wouldn't miss: getting up early in the morning to feed the sheep and cows, and my pet Lemming. Dad's insistence on manual labor became the launching pad for my determination and my brothers to join the Space Corps.

Our house had witnessed the shenanigans of many generations of Rimmers, with stories galore about my great-great-grandfather, Jebediah Rimmer, who legend has it fought off native Ionians to build the house and gardens. Now maintained by my Dad and with help from the local gardener, Dungo. My dad couldn't stand Dungo, and could never understand why. Sure, he was slightly inept at times and egotistical, self-important, lacked confidence, and was socially awkward. But I always liked him; he had a strong moralistic attitude, and my mother always took a shine to him.

My father, a half-crazed military failure, spent his early years amidst the military pioneers. Growing up on Io, his childhood was an exercise in minimalism. Yet, he yearned to be an officer like his father. The dream almost turned into reality when he strutted onto Space Corps Academy grounds, fulfilling an ambition that had marinated in the spartan conditions of an Io upbringing. Grandpa, an eternal optimist, had dreams of his son treading the same starlit path. Destiny pulled a cosmic prank when he was one inch below Corps regulation height.

My mother was born into an austere family that considered space exploration a genetic trait. Her father was part of the Space Corps' third graduating class, and her mother was a part of the cybernautic division — a family with enough star power to make a pulsar blush.

Mum, with dreams of becoming an astrobiologist, found herself on a collision course with Dad in an Introduction to Space Corps History class. Oh, but the Space Corps Directive 2574 about students fraternizing with other students was stricter than a vegan at a butcher shop. They soon found themselves in front of the space corps instructor with a warning.

Fast forward to Dad's posting on the JMC Emerald Nebula. Despite the height restrictions, strings were pulled, and he was made a galley steward. The ship was still three months away from Earth. He'd stayed in touch with my mother throughout, and in a move that combined romantic flair with a dash of desperation, while on leave at Lunar City 7, Dad proposed to my mother. 'Everyone thought we were bloody mad,' Mum once said, 'Maybe it was the wine or the smell of the beef that had seeped into his clothes. But I just couldn't say no to those puppy dog eyes.' Ah, the cosmic irony of hindsight.

My mother was posted on Titan, and my dad was posted on the JMC Emerald Nebula. Over a year passed before she saw Dad again, and almost two more years before she donned the graduation cap and tossed it into the wind. Yet, fate, with its sense of humor, decided that she wouldn't be posted anywhere near my dad.

My mother was freshly stationed on the Axiom II; however, it wasn't long before she found she had a tiny stowaway on board. She was pregnant with my older brother, Frank! 'Your father was in the outer rim at the time; he nearly dropped his spatula,' she said, 'and by the time the message got to him, I was already as big as a cow

So Mum's Space Corps ambitions hit a speed bump; she took a leave of absence and went to shack up on Io with my paternal grandparents. Lacking her parental navigators, who had embarked on the ultimate road trip years earlier, she found herself surrounded by vast farmland of good old terrestrial adventure. Enter Frank, my elder sibling, making his grand entrance. The interstellar escapades of the next generation were officially underway.

With the cosmic clock ticking, Mum had a mere two Earth-bound years before Space Corp's relentless gravitational pull demanded her return. In those terrestrial years, she juggled the titles of astrobiologist and dedicated mum. 'I just felt shagged out all the time,' she reminisced. 'I missed little Frank; this wasn't what I wanted.' Parenthood, it turns out, is the ultimate improvisational act.

With parents who had charted the final frontier of life and having witnessed her mother resigning her commission to raise her and her brother solo during Dad's cosmic escapades as chief slop server, Mum found herself in a parenting predicament. 'I was bored out of my mind, but your dad's career was everything to him,' she admitted. She'd study where she could while my grandparents took care of Frank. 'Your grandparents were like Energizer bunnies,' she shared. Meanwhile, Dad, charting his course through the galactic highways aboard the JMC Emerald Nebula, missed Mum and Frank. As the countdown to Mum's return commenced, Dad, ever the master of cosmic shenanigans, pulled whatever strings he could to get her posted back to Io, where he had assumed the role of Restroom attendant.

Only for calamity to strike again after my Mum's grand return to the Space Corps. Surprise, surprise—John was on the way, stealing the spotlight as the next Rimmer headliner. Dad informing Captain Sulaco was less than thrilled. Shipboard nurseries were not on his playlist. But, that triggered Dad's decision. A message blinked in from the cosmic ether—Dad's old man had punched out his ticket to the great beyond when he was born. His career as a restroom attendant wasn't going anywhere fast. Cue the resignation letter to Space Corps—bye-bye dad's officer career. So from that point on, they began to settle into life on Io together. Mum later shot out my next brother Howard. Then, having a break, they focused on the house and garden, bringing local gardener Dungo to assist. It wasn't long after I arrived on the scene!

In the galactic years since, I've mulled over Dad's plot twist and how it flung my trajectory into the cosmic unknown. The cosmic yarn I spin for the masses: Dad ditching Space Corps lit the afterburners on John, Howard, Frank, and my career quest, filling the void he left.

My brothers, all being older, eventually signed up for the Space Corps, graduating with top marks in their classes. They all got commission postings on the fleet's best ships. John was an astro-navigator on the SSS Augustus, where he shared quarters with a certain Frank Hollister—a captain in the making.

Frank, the rising star in the Space Corps, snagged the first officer position aboard the Nova 4 when the previous first officer, Cheddar Flatheringson, decided he'd rather play captain. Six years of navigating the officer bureaucracy had Frank on a trajectory to break records and become the youngest captain in the Space Corps. But, as I've always said, 'Up, up, up the ziggurat lickety-split.

As for me, at the tender age of nine, my school grades were less than promising, and in a twist of cosmic fate, my parents decided it was better to wash their hands of me and ship me off to boarding school. As time ticked away, my envy for friends and their idyllic families turned me into a recluse. I found solace in the small things; I enjoyed listening to the Hammond organ, Morris Dancing, and building up my collection of 20th-century telegraph poles. You could always find me aimlessly wandering around the vast diesel decks at the local spaceport, attempting to rediscover the joy of getting lost. I even took up learning Esperanto in my sleep. But, as I looked up at the stars, where dreams of greatness shimmer like distant galaxies, my story was only just beginning. Arnold Judas Rimmer was destined for glory from the very fabric of stardust. My humble journey commenced not among the celestial bodies but within the labyrinth of obstacles—the very crucible of my stellar aspirations.

It was just another sunny day on Io, spent jesting with my older brothers John, Howard, and Frank. God, we were close — the 'Four Musketeers,' as we used to call ourselves! Well, the three musketeers actually; they always let me be the queen of Spain. What fun we'd have! An occasional practical joke, of course — apple-pie beds, black-eye telescope. They even hid a small landmine in my sandpit! How were they supposed to know it would go off? However, on this particular day, we were all blissfully ignorant of the interstellar smeg about to hit my life!

As my mother casually revealed her plan to send me off to boarding school! My school grades had been gradually slipping, and my parents, having tried absolutely nothing and being fresh out of ideas, thought it would be best to let me be someone else's problem. I, in my infinite pubescent wisdom, hit her with the forceful question, 'Will I still get to see Bruno?' Bruno was the family dog, clearly. You could see where my main priorities lay.

In response, she crouched down, bless her heart — magnificent woman. Very prim, very proper; some say austere. Some people mistook her for being cold and thought she was aloof. Not a bit of it. She crouched down to my eye level, as if we were sharing the secrets of the universe. In a tone that probably sounded more dramatic than she intended, she explained that it was a boarding school on the other side of Io — pretty much as far away from them while still being on the same planet.

Turning to dear old Dad for an explanation or, at the very least, a distraction from the impending familial meltdown, the bearded git was engaged in a staring contest with the sky. It was as if he believed they held the secrets to a lifetime supply of cosmic beer. 'I don't want to go!' I declared, my voice dripping with the gravitas only a nine-year-old prophet could muster.

"Just a couple of years, Arnold, and you can come home for your birthday," she boldly declared, and Dad, ever the spectator in the family circus, continued his stoic gaze into the sky. He never was one for eye contact. Snapping his head, he interjected, "Don't get the weaselly smegger's hopes up." Classic Dad!

Undeterred by the lack of emotional support, she flung a promise of her triumphant return in time for my birthday, as if the universe itself would pause its dance to celebrate my existence. Hugging me, she hoisted me up. 'C'mon, let's get some quiche,' she declared, casting a glance at Dad, who remained emotionally disengaged; he never would give quiche a chance.

The next morning, I was hurled into a transport craft, sharing a seat with Fred 'Thicky' Holden, leaving me to ponder the cosmic absurdity of it all. Suddenly, the predictable rhythms of my boyhood were replaced by the unpredictable chaos of the universe. Leaving behind our modest house on Io — a perfect replica of an Earth house from the 19th and 20th centuries with its hectares of land. There were some parts I wouldn't miss: getting up early in the morning to feed the sheep and cows, and my pet Lemming. Dad's insistence on manual labor became the launching pad for my determination and my brothers to join the Space Corps.

Our house had witnessed the shenanigans of many generations of Rimmers, with stories galore about my great-great-grandfather, Jebediah Rimmer, who legend has it fought off native Ionians to build the house and gardens. Now maintained by my Dad and with help from the local gardener, Dungo. My dad couldn't stand Dungo, and could never understand why. Sure, he was slightly inept at times and egotistical, self-important, lacked confidence, and was socially awkward. But I always liked him; he had a strong moralistic attitude, and my mother always took a shine to him.

My father, a half-crazed military failure, spent his early years amidst the military pioneers. Growing up on Io, his childhood was an exercise in minimalism. Yet, he yearned to be an officer like his father. The dream almost turned into reality when he strutted onto Space Corps Academy grounds, fulfilling an ambition that had marinated in the spartan conditions of an Io upbringing. Grandpa, an eternal optimist, had dreams of his son treading the same starlit path. Destiny pulled a cosmic prank when he was one inch below Corps regulation height.

My mother was born into an austere family that considered space exploration a genetic trait. Her father was part of the Space Corps' third graduating class, and her mother was a part of the cybernautic division — a family with enough star power to make a pulsar blush.

Mum, with dreams of becoming an astrobiologist, found herself on a collision course with Dad in an Introduction to Space Corps History class. Oh, but the Space Corps Directive 2574 about students fraternizing with other students was stricter than a vegan at a butcher shop. They soon found themselves in front of the space corps instructor with a warning.

Fast forward to Dad's posting on the JMC Emerald Nebula. Despite the height restrictions, strings were pulled, and he was made a galley steward. The ship was still three months away from Earth. He'd stayed in touch with my mother throughout, and in a move that combined romantic flair with a dash of desperation, while on leave at Lunar City 7, Dad proposed to my mother. 'Everyone thought we were bloody mad,' Mum once said, 'Maybe it was the wine or the smell of the beef that had seeped into his clothes. But I just couldn't say no to those puppy dog eyes.' Ah, the cosmic irony of hindsight.

My mother was posted on Titan, and my dad was posted on the JMC Emerald Nebula. Over a year passed before she saw Dad again, and almost two more years before she donned the graduation cap and tossed it into the wind. Yet, fate, with its sense of humor, decided that she wouldn't be posted anywhere near my dad.

My mother was freshly stationed on the Axiom II; however, it wasn't long before she found she had a tiny stowaway on board. She was pregnant with my older brother, Frank! 'Your father was in the outer rim at the time; he nearly dropped his spatula,' she said, 'and by the time the message got to him, I was already as big as a cow

So Mum's Space Corps ambitions hit a speed bump; she took a leave of absence and went to shack up on Io with my paternal grandparents. Lacking her parental navigators, who had embarked on the ultimate road trip years earlier, she found herself surrounded by vast farmland of good old terrestrial adventure. Enter Frank, my elder sibling, making his grand entrance. The interstellar escapades of the next generation were officially underway.

With the cosmic clock ticking, Mum had a mere two Earth-bound years before Space Corp's relentless gravitational pull demanded her return. In those terrestrial years, she juggled the titles of astrobiologist and dedicated mum. 'I just felt shagged out all the time,' she reminisced. 'I missed little Frank; this wasn't what I wanted.' Parenthood, it turns out, is the ultimate improvisational act.

With parents who had charted the final frontier of life and having witnessed her mother resigning her commission to raise her and her brother solo during Dad's cosmic escapades as chief slop server, Mum found herself in a parenting predicament. 'I was bored out of my mind, but your dad's career was everything to him,' she admitted. She'd study

139

where she could while my grandparents took care of Frank. 'Your grandparents were like Energizer bunnies,' she shared. Meanwhile, Dad, charting his course through the galactic highways aboard the JMC Emerald Nebula, missed Mum and Frank. As the countdown to Mum's return commenced, Dad, ever the master of cosmic shenanigans, pulled whatever strings he could to get her posted back to Io, where he had assumed the role of Restroom attendant.

Only for calamity to strike again after my Mum's grand return to the Space Corps. Surprise, surprise—John was on the way, stealing the spotlight as the next Rimmer headliner. Dad informing Captain Sulaco was less than thrilled. Shipboard nurseries were not on his playlist. But, that triggered Dad's decision. A message blinked in from the cosmic ether—Dad's old man had punched out his ticket to the great beyond when he was born. His career as a restroom attendant wasn't going anywhere fast. Cue the resignation letter to Space Corps—bye-bye dad's officer career. So from that point on, they began to settle into life on Io together. Mum later shot out my next brother Howard. Then, having a break, they focused on the house and garden, bringing local gardener Dungo to assist. It wasn't long after I arrived on the scene!

In the galactic years since, I've mulled over Dad's plot twist and how it flung my trajectory into the cosmic unknown. The cosmic yarn I spin for the masses: Dad ditching Space Corps lit the afterburners on John, Howard, Frank, and my career quest, filling the void he left.

My brothers, all being older, eventually signed up for the Space Corps, graduating with top marks in their classes. They all got commission postings on the fleet's best ships. John was an astro-navigator on the SSS Augustus, where he shared quarters with a certain Frank Hollister—a captain in the making.

Frank, the rising star in the Space Corps, snagged the first officer position aboard the Nova 4 when the previous first officer, Cheddar Flatheringson, decided he'd rather play captain. Six years of navigating the officer bureaucracy had Frank on a trajectory to break records and become the youngest captain in the Space Corps. But, as I've always said, 'Up, up, up the ziggurat lickety-split.

As for me, at the tender age of nine, my school grades were less than promising, and in a twist of cosmic fate, my parents decided it was better to wash their hands of me and ship me off to boarding school. As time ticked away, my envy for friends and their idyllic families turned me into a recluse. I found solace in the small things; I enjoyed listening to the Hammond organ, Morris Dancing, and building up my collection of 20th-century telegraph poles. You could always find me aimlessly wandering around the vast diesel decks at the local spaceport, attempting to rediscover the joy of getting lost. I even took up learning Esperanto in my sleep. But, as I looked up at the stars, where dreams of greatness shimmer like distant galaxies, my story was only just beginning. Arnold Judas Rimmer was destined for glory from the very fabric of stardust. My humble journey commenced not among the celestial bodies but within the labyrinth of obstacles—the very crucible of my stellar aspirations.

It was just another sunny day on Io, spent jesting with my older brothers John, Howard, and Frank. God, we were close—the 'Four Musketeers,' as we used to call ourselves! Well, the three musketeers actually; they always let me be the queen of Spain. What fun we'd have! An occasional practical joke, of course—apple-pie beds, black-eye telescope. They even hid a small landmine in my sandpit! How were they supposed to know it would go off? However, on this particular day, we were all blissfully ignorant of the interstellar smeg about to hit my life!

As my mother casually revealed her plan to send me off to boarding school! My school grades had been gradually slipping, and my parents, having tried absolutely nothing and being fresh out of ideas, thought it would be best to let me be someone else's problem. I, in my infinite pubescent wisdom, hit her with the forceful question, 'Will I still get to see Bruno?' Bruno was the family dog, clearly. You could see where my main priorities lay.

In response, she crouched down, bless her heart—magnificent woman. Very prim, very proper; some say austere. Some people mistook her for being cold and thought she was aloof. Not a bit of it. She crouched down to my eye level, as if we were sharing the secrets of the universe. In a tone that probably sounded more dramatic than she intended, she explained that it was a boarding school on the other side of Io—pretty much as far away from them while still being on the same planet.

Turning to dear old Dad for an explanation or, at the very least, a distraction from the impending familial meltdown, the bearded git was engaged in a staring contest with the sky. It was as if he believed they held the secrets to a lifetime supply of cosmic beer. 'I don't want to go!' I declared, my voice dripping with the gravitas only a nine-year-old prophet could muster.

"Just a couple of years, Arnold, and you can come home for your birthday," she boldly declared, and Dad, ever the spectator in the family circus, continued his stoic gaze into the sky. He never was one for eye contact. Snapping his head, he interjected, "Don't get the weaselly smegger's hopes up." Classic Dad!

Undeterred by the lack of emotional support, she flung a promise of her triumphant return in time for my birthday, as if the universe itself would pause its dance to celebrate my existence. Hugging me, she hoisted me

up. 'C'mon, let's get some quiche,' she declared, casting a glance at Dad, who remained emotionally disengaged; he never would give quiche a chance.

The next morning, I was hurled into a transport craft, sharing a seat with Fred 'Thicky' Holden, leaving me to ponder the cosmic absurdity of it all. Suddenly, the predictable rhythms of my boyhood were replaced by the unpredictable chaos of the universe. Leaving behind our modest house on Io — a perfect replica of an Earth house from the 19th and 20th centuries with its hectares of land. There were some parts I wouldn't miss: getting up early in the morning to feed the sheep and cows, and my pet Lemming. Dad's insistence on manual labor became the launching pad for my determination and my brothers to join the Space Corps.

Our house had witnessed the shenanigans of many generations of Rimmers, with stories galore about my great-great-grandfather, Jebediah Rimmer, who legend has it fought off native Ionians to build the house and gardens. Now maintained by my Dad and with help from the local gardener, Dungo. My dad couldn't stand Dungo, and could never understand why. Sure, he was slightly inept at times and egotistical, self-important, lacked confidence, and was socially awkward. But I always liked him; he had a strong moralistic attitude, and my mother always took a shine to him.

My father, a half-crazed military failure, spent his early years amidst the military pioneers. Growing up on Io, his childhood was an exercise in minimalism. Yet, he yearned to be an officer like his father. The dream almost turned into reality when he strutted onto Space Corps Academy grounds, fulfilling an ambition that had marinated in the spartan conditions of an Io upbringing. Grandpa, an eternal optimist, had dreams of his son treading the same starlit path. Destiny pulled a cosmic prank when he was one inch below Corps regulation height.

143

My mother was born into an austere family that considered space exploration a genetic trait. Her father was part of the Space Corps' third graduating class, and her mother was a part of the cybernautic division — a family with enough star power to make a pulsar blush.

Mum, with dreams of becoming an astrobiologist, found herself on a collision course with Dad in an Introduction to Space Corps History class. Oh, but the Space Corps Directive 2574 about students fraternizing with other students was stricter than a vegan at a butcher shop. They soon found themselves in front of the space corps instructor with a warning.

Fast forward to Dad's posting on the JMC Emerald Nebula. Despite the height restrictions, strings were pulled, and he was made a galley steward. The ship was still three months away from Earth. He'd stayed in touch with my mother throughout, and in a move that combined romantic flair with a dash of desperation, while on leave at Lunar City 7, Dad proposed to my mother. 'Everyone thought we were bloody mad,' Mum once said, 'Maybe it was the wine or the smell of the beef that had seeped into his clothes. But I just couldn't say no to those puppy dog eyes.' Ah, the cosmic irony of hindsight.

My mother was posted on Titan, and my dad was posted on the JMC Emerald Nebula. Over a year passed before she saw Dad again, and almost two more years before she donned the graduation cap and tossed it into the wind. Yet, fate, with its sense of humor, decided that she wouldn't be posted anywhere near my dad.

My mother was freshly stationed on the Axiom II; however, it wasn't long before she found she had a tiny stowaway on board. She was pregnant with my older brother, Frank! 'Your father was in the outer rim at the time; he nearly dropped his spatula,' she said, 'and by the time the message got to him, I was already as big as a cow

So Mum's Space Corps ambitions hit a speed bump; she took a leave of absence and went to shack up on Io with my paternal grandparents. Lacking her parental navigators, who had embarked on the ultimate road trip years earlier, she found herself surrounded by vast farmland of good old terrestrial adventure. Enter Frank, my elder sibling, making his grand entrance. The interstellar escapades of the next generation were officially underway.

With the cosmic clock ticking, Mum had a mere two Earth-bound years before Space Corp's relentless gravitational pull demanded her return. In those terrestrial years, she juggled the titles of astrobiologist and dedicated mum. 'I just felt shagged out all the time,' she reminisced. 'I missed little Frank; this wasn't what I wanted.' Parenthood, it turns out, is the ultimate improvisational act.

With parents who had charted the final frontier of life and having witnessed her mother resigning her commission to raise her and her brother solo during Dad's cosmic escapades as chief slop server, Mum found herself in a parenting predicament. 'I was bored out of my mind, but your dad's career was everything to him,' she admitted. She'd study where she could while my grandparents took care of Frank. 'Your grandparents were like Energizer bunnies,' she shared. Meanwhile, Dad, charting his course through the galactic highways aboard the JMC Emerald Nebula, missed Mum and Frank. As the countdown to Mum's return commenced, Dad, ever the master of cosmic shenanigans, pulled whatever strings he could to get her posted back to Io, where he had assumed the role of Restroom attendant.

Only for calamity to strike again after my Mum's grand return to the Space Corps. Surprise, surprise—John was on the way, stealing the spotlight as the next Rimmer headliner. Dad informing Captain Sulaco was less than thrilled. Shipboard nurseries were not on his playlist. But, that triggered Dad's decision. A message blinked in from the cosmic ether—Dad's old man had punched out his ticket to the great beyond when he was born. His career as a restroom attendant wasn't going anywhere fast. Cue the resignation letter to Space Corps—bye-bye dad's officer career. So from that point on, they began to settle into life on Io together. Mum later shot out my next brother Howard. Then, having a break, they focused on the house and garden, bringing local gardener Dungo to assist. It wasn't long after I arrived on the scene!

In the galactic years since, I've mulled over Dad's plot twist and how it flung my trajectory into the cosmic unknown. The cosmic yarn I spin for the masses: Dad ditching Space Corps lit the afterburners on John, Howard, Frank, and my career quest, filling the void he left.

My brothers, all being older, eventually signed up for the Space Corps, graduating with top marks in their classes. They all got commission postings on the fleet's best ships. John was an astro-navigator on the SSS Augustus, where he shared quarters with a certain Frank Hollister—a captain in the making.

Frank, the rising star in the Space Corps, snagged the first officer position aboard the Nova 4 when the previous first officer, Cheddar Flatheringson, decided he'd rather play captain. Six years of navigating the officer bureaucracy had Frank on a trajectory to break records and become the youngest captain in the Space Corps. But, as I've always said, 'Up, up, up the ziggurat lickety-split.

As for me, at the tender age of nine, my school grades were less than promising, and in a twist of cosmic fate, my parents decided it was better to wash their hands of me and ship me off to boarding school. As time ticked away, my envy for friends and their idyllic families turned me into a recluse. I found solace in the small things; I enjoyed listening to the Hammond organ, Morris Dancing, and building up my collection of 20th-century telegraph poles. You could always find me aimlessly wandering around the vast diesel decks at the local spaceport, attempting to rediscover the joy of getting lost. I even took up learning Esperanto in my sleep. But, as I looked up at the stars, where dreams of greatness shimmer like distant galaxies, my story was only just beginning. Arnold Judas Rimmer was destined for glory from the very fabric of stardust. My humble journey commenced not among the celestial bodies but within the labyrinth of obstacles—the very crucible of my stellar aspirations.

It was just another sunny day on Io, spent jesting with my older brothers John, Howard, and Frank. God, we were close—the 'Four Musketeers,' as we used to call ourselves! Well, the three musketeers actually; they always let me be the queen of Spain. What fun we'd have! An occasional practical joke, of course—apple-pie beds, black-eye telescope. They even hid a small landmine in my sandpit! How were they supposed to know it would go off? However, on this particular day, we were all blissfully ignorant of the interstellar smeg about to hit my life!

As my mother casually revealed her plan to send me off to boarding school! My school grades had been gradually slipping, and my parents, having tried absolutely nothing and being fresh out of ideas, thought it would be best to let me be someone else's problem. I, in my infinite pubescent wisdom, hit her with the forceful question, 'Will I still get to see Bruno?' Bruno was the family dog, clearly. You could see where my main priorities lay.

In response, she crouched down, bless her heart — magnificent woman. Very prim, very proper; some say austere. Some people mistook her for being cold and thought she was aloof. Not a bit of it. She crouched down to my eye level, as if we were sharing the secrets of the universe. In a tone that probably sounded more dramatic than she intended, she explained that it was a boarding school on the other side of Io — pretty much as far away from them while still being on the same planet.

Turning to dear old Dad for an explanation or, at the very least, a distraction from the impending familial meltdown, the bearded git was engaged in a staring contest with the sky. It was as if he believed they held the secrets to a lifetime supply of cosmic beer. 'I don't want to go!' I declared, my voice dripping with the gravitas only a nine-year-old prophet could muster.

"Just a couple of years, Arnold, and you can come home for your birthday," she boldly declared, and Dad, ever the spectator in the family circus, continued his stoic gaze into the sky. He never was one for eye contact. Snapping his head, he interjected, "Don't get the weaselly smegger's hopes up." Classic Dad!

Undeterred by the lack of emotional support, she flung a promise of her triumphant return in time for my birthday, as if the universe itself would pause its dance to celebrate my existence. Hugging me, she hoisted me up. 'C'mon, let's get some quiche,' she declared, casting a glance at Dad, who remained emotionally disengaged; he never would give quiche a chance.

The next morning, I was hurled into a transport craft, sharing a seat with Fred 'Thicky' Holden, leaving me to ponder the cosmic absurdity of it all. Suddenly, the predictable rhythms of my boyhood were replaced by the unpredictable chaos of the universe. Leaving behind our modest house on Io — a perfect replica of an Earth house from the 19th and 20th centuries with its hectares of land. There were some parts I wouldn't miss: getting up early in the morning to feed the sheep and cows, and my pet Lemming. Dad's insistence on manual labor became the launching pad for my determination and my brothers to join the Space Corps.

Our house had witnessed the shenanigans of many generations of Rimmers, with stories galore about my great-great-grandfather, Jebediah Rimmer, who legend has it fought off native Ionians to build the house and gardens. Now maintained by my Dad and with help from the local gardener, Dungo. My dad couldn't stand Dungo, and could never understand why. Sure, he was slightly inept at times and egotistical, self-important, lacked confidence, and was socially awkward. But I always liked him; he had a strong moralistic attitude, and my mother always took a shine to him.

My father, a half-crazed military failure, spent his early years amidst the military pioneers. Growing up on Io, his childhood was an exercise in minimalism. Yet, he yearned to be an officer like his father. The dream almost turned into reality when he strutted onto Space Corps Academy grounds, fulfilling an ambition that had marinated in the spartan conditions of an Io upbringing. Grandpa, an eternal optimist, had dreams of his son treading the same starlit path. Destiny pulled a cosmic prank when he was one inch below Corps regulation height.

My mother was born into an austere family that considered space exploration a genetic trait. Her father was part of the Space Corps' third graduating class, and her mother was a part of the cybernautic division — a family with enough star power to make a pulsar blush.

Mum, with dreams of becoming an astrobiologist, found herself on a collision course with Dad in an Introduction to Space Corps History class. Oh, but the Space Corps Directive 2574 about students fraternizing with other students was stricter than a vegan at a butcher shop. They soon found themselves in front of the space corps instructor with a warning.

Fast forward to Dad's posting on the JMC Emerald Nebula. Despite the height restrictions, strings were pulled, and he was made a galley steward. The ship was still three months away from Earth. He'd stayed in touch with my mother throughout, and in a move that combined romantic flair with a dash of desperation, while on leave at Lunar City 7, Dad proposed to my mother. 'Everyone thought we were bloody mad,' Mum once said, 'Maybe it was the wine or the smell of the beef that had seeped into his clothes. But I just couldn't say no to those puppy dog eyes.' Ah, the cosmic irony of hindsight.

My mother was posted on Titan, and my dad was posted on the JMC Emerald Nebula. Over a year passed before she saw Dad again, and almost two more years before she donned the graduation cap and tossed it into the wind. Yet, fate, with its sense of humor, decided that she wouldn't be posted anywhere near my dad.

My mother was freshly stationed on the Axiom II; however, it wasn't long before she found she had a tiny stowaway on board. She was pregnant with my older brother, Frank! 'Your father was in the outer rim at the time; he nearly dropped his spatula,' she said, 'and by the time the message got to him, I was already as big as a cow

So Mum's Space Corps ambitions hit a speed bump; she took a leave of absence and went to shack up on Io with my paternal grandparents. Lacking her parental navigators, who had embarked on the ultimate road

150

trip years earlier, she found herself surrounded by vast farmland of good old terrestrial adventure. Enter Frank, my elder sibling, making his grand entrance. The interstellar escapades of the next generation were officially underway.

With the cosmic clock ticking, Mum had a mere two Earth-bound years before Space Corp's relentless gravitational pull demanded her return. In those terrestrial years, she juggled the titles of astrobiologist and dedicated mum. 'I just felt shagged out all the time,' she reminisced. 'I missed little Frank; this wasn't what I wanted.' Parenthood, it turns out, is the ultimate improvisational act.

With parents who had charted the final frontier of life and having witnessed her mother resigning her commission to raise her and her brother solo during Dad's cosmic escapades as chief slop server, Mum found herself in a parenting predicament. 'I was bored out of my mind, but your dad's career was everything to him,' she admitted. She'd study where she could while my grandparents took care of Frank. 'Your grandparents were like Energizer bunnies,' she shared. Meanwhile, Dad, charting his course through the galactic highways aboard the JMC Emerald Nebula, missed Mum and Frank. As the countdown to Mum's return commenced, Dad, ever the master of cosmic shenanigans, pulled whatever strings he could to get her posted back to Io, where he had assumed the role of Restroom attendant.

Only for calamity to strike again after my Mum's grand return to the Space Corps. Surprise, surprise—John was on the way, stealing the spotlight as the next Rimmer headliner. Dad informing Captain Sulaco was less than thrilled. Shipboard nurseries were not on his playlist. But, that triggered Dad's decision. A message blinked in from the cosmic ether—Dad's old man had punched out his ticket to the great beyond when he was born. His career as a restroom attendant wasn't going anywhere fast. Cue the resignation letter to Space Corps — bye-bye dad's officer career. So from that point on, they began to settle into life on Io together. Mum later shot out my next brother Howard. Then, having a break, they focused on the house and garden, bringing local gardener Dungo to assist. It wasn't long after I arrived on the scene!

In the galactic years since, I've mulled over Dad's plot twist and how it flung my trajectory into the cosmic unknown. The cosmic yarn I spin for the masses: Dad ditching Space Corps lit the afterburners on John, Howard, Frank, and my career quest, filling the void he left.

My brothers, all being older, eventually signed up for the Space Corps, graduating with top marks in their classes. They all got commission postings on the fleet's best ships. John was an astro-navigator on the SSS Augustus, where he shared quarters with a certain Frank Hollister — a captain in the making.

Frank, the rising star in the Space Corps, snagged the first officer position aboard the Nova 4 when the previous first officer, Cheddar Flatheringson, decided he'd rather play captain. Six years of navigating the officer bureaucracy had Frank on a trajectory to break records and become the youngest captain in the Space Corps. But, as I've always said, 'Up, up, up the ziggurat lickety-split.

As for me, at the tender age of nine, my school grades were less than promising, and in a twist of cosmic fate, my parents decided it was better to wash their hands of me and ship me off to boarding school. As time ticked away, my envy for friends and their idyllic families turned me into a recluse. I found solace in the small things; I enjoyed listening to the Hammond organ, Morris Dancing, and building up my collection of 20th-century telegraph poles. You could always find me aimlessly wandering around the vast diesel decks at the local spaceport, attempting to rediscover the joy of getting lost. I even took up learning Esperanto in my sleep. But, as I looked up at the stars, where dreams of greatness shimmer like distant galaxies, my story was only just beginning. Arnold Judas Rimmer was destined for glory from the very fabric of stardust. My humble journey commenced not among the celestial bodies but within the labyrinth of obstacles — the very crucible of my stellar aspirations.

# CHAPTER 7
# GALACTIC DIPLOMACY AND THE
# ART OF MICROMANAGEMENT

It was just another sunny day on Io, spent jesting with my older brothers John, Howard, and Frank. God, we were close — the 'Four Musketeers,' as we used to call ourselves! Well, the three musketeers actually; they always let me be the queen of Spain. What fun we'd have! An occasional practical joke, of course — apple-pie beds, black-eye telescope. They even hid a small landmine in my sandpit! How were they supposed to know it would go off? However, on this particular day, we were all blissfully ignorant of the interstellar smeg about to hit my life!

As my mother casually revealed her plan to send me off to boarding school! My school grades had been gradually slipping, and my parents, having tried absolutely nothing and being fresh out of ideas, thought it would be best to let me be someone else's problem. I, in my infinite pubescent wisdom, hit her with the forceful question, 'Will I still get to see Bruno?' Bruno was the family dog, clearly. You could see where my main priorities lay.

In response, she crouched down, bless her heart — magnificent woman. Very prim, very proper; some say austere. Some people mistook her for being cold and thought she was aloof. Not a bit of it. She crouched down to my eye level, as if we were sharing the secrets of the universe. In a tone that probably sounded more dramatic than she intended, she explained that it was a boarding school on the other side of Io — pretty much as far away from them while still being on the same planet.

Turning to dear old Dad for an explanation or, at the very least, a distraction from the impending familial meltdown, the bearded git was engaged in a staring contest with the sky. It was as if he believed they held the secrets to a lifetime supply of cosmic beer. 'I don't want to go!' I declared, my voice dripping with the gravitas only a nine-year-old prophet could muster.

"Just a couple of years, Arnold, and you can come home for your birthday," she boldly declared, and Dad, ever the spectator in the family circus, continued his stoic gaze into the sky. He never was one for eye contact. Snapping his head, he interjected, "Don't get the weaselly smegger's hopes up." Classic Dad!

Undeterred by the lack of emotional support, she flung a promise of her triumphant return in time for my birthday, as if the universe itself would pause its dance to celebrate my existence. Hugging me, she hoisted me up. 'C'mon, let's get some quiche,' she declared, casting a glance at Dad, who remained emotionally disengaged; he never would give quiche a chance.

The next morning, I was hurled into a transport craft, sharing a seat with Fred 'Thicky' Holden, leaving me to ponder the cosmic absurdity of it all. Suddenly, the predictable rhythms of my boyhood were replaced by the unpredictable chaos of the universe. Leaving behind our modest house on Io — a perfect replica of an Earth house from the 19th and 20th centuries with its hectares of land. There were some parts I wouldn't miss: getting up early in the morning to feed the sheep and cows, and my pet Lemming. Dad's insistence on manual labor became the launching pad for my determination and my brothers to join the Space Corps.

Our house had witnessed the shenanigans of many generations of Rimmers, with stories galore about my great-great-grandfather, Jebediah Rimmer, who legend has it fought off native Ionians to build the house and gardens. Now maintained by my Dad and with help from the local gardener, Dungo. My dad couldn't stand Dungo, and could never understand why. Sure, he was slightly inept at times and egotistical, self-important, lacked confidence, and was socially awkward. But I always liked him; he had a strong moralistic attitude, and my mother always took a shine to him.

My father, a half-crazed military failure, spent his early years amidst the military pioneers. Growing up on Io, his childhood was an exercise in minimalism. Yet, he yearned to be an officer like his father. The dream almost turned into reality when he strutted onto Space Corps Academy grounds, fulfilling an ambition that had marinated in the spartan conditions of an Io upbringing. Grandpa, an eternal optimist, had dreams of his son treading the same starlit path. Destiny pulled a cosmic prank when he was one inch below Corps regulation height.

My mother was born into an austere family that considered space exploration a genetic trait. Her father was part of the Space Corps' third graduating class, and her mother was a part of the cybernautic division — a family with enough star power to make a pulsar blush.

Mum, with dreams of becoming an astrobiologist, found herself on a collision course with Dad in an Introduction to Space Corps History class. Oh, but the Space Corps Directive 2574 about students fraternizing with other students was stricter than a vegan at a butcher shop. They soon found themselves in front of the space corps instructor with a warning.

Fast forward to Dad's posting on the JMC Emerald Nebula. Despite the height restrictions, strings were pulled, and he was made a galley steward. The ship was still three months away from Earth. He'd stayed in touch with my mother throughout, and in a move that combined romantic flair with a dash of desperation, while on leave at Lunar City 7, Dad proposed to my mother. 'Everyone thought we were bloody mad,' Mum once said, 'Maybe it was the wine or the smell of the beef that had seeped into his clothes. But I just couldn't say no to those puppy dog eyes.' Ah, the cosmic irony of hindsight.

My mother was posted on Titan, and my dad was posted on the JMC Emerald Nebula. Over a year passed before she saw Dad again, and almost two more years before she donned the graduation cap and tossed it into the wind. Yet, fate, with its sense of humor, decided that she wouldn't be posted anywhere near my dad.

My mother was freshly stationed on the Axiom II; however, it wasn't long before she found she had a tiny stowaway on board. She was pregnant with my older brother, Frank! 'Your father was in the outer rim at the time; he nearly dropped his spatula,' she said, 'and by the time the message got to him, I was already as big as a cow

So Mum's Space Corps ambitions hit a speed bump; she took a leave of absence and went to shack up on Io with my paternal grandparents. Lacking her parental navigators, who had embarked on the ultimate road trip years earlier, she found herself surrounded by vast farmland of good old terrestrial adventure. Enter Frank, my elder sibling, making his grand entrance. The interstellar escapades of the next generation were officially underway.

With the cosmic clock ticking, Mum had a mere two Earth-bound years before Space Corp's relentless gravitational pull demanded her return. In those terrestrial years, she juggled the titles of astrobiologist and dedicated mum. 'I just felt shagged out all the time,' she reminisced. 'I missed little Frank; this wasn't what I wanted.' Parenthood, it turns out, is the ultimate improvisational act.

With parents who had charted the final frontier of life and having witnessed her mother resigning her commission to raise her and her brother solo during Dad's cosmic escapades as chief slop server, Mum found herself in a parenting predicament. 'I was bored out of my mind, but your dad's career was everything to him,' she admitted. She'd study where she could while my grandparents took care of Frank. 'Your grandparents were like Energizer bunnies,' she shared. Meanwhile, Dad, charting his course through the galactic highways aboard the JMC Emerald Nebula, missed Mum and Frank. As the countdown to Mum's return commenced, Dad, ever the master of cosmic shenanigans, pulled whatever strings he could to get her posted back to Io, where he had assumed the role of Restroom attendant.

Only for calamity to strike again after my Mum's grand return to the Space Corps. Surprise, surprise—John was on the way, stealing the spotlight as the next Rimmer headliner. Dad informing Captain Sulaco was less than thrilled. Shipboard nurseries were not on his playlist. But, that triggered Dad's decision. A message blinked in from the cosmic ether—Dad's old man had punched out his ticket to the great beyond when he was born. His career as a restroom attendant wasn't going anywhere fast. Cue the resignation letter to Space Corps—bye-bye dad's officer career. So from that point on, they began to settle into life on Io together. Mum later shot out my next brother Howard. Then, having a break, they focused on the house and garden, bringing local gardener Dungo to assist. It wasn't long after I arrived on the scene!

In the galactic years since, I've mulled over Dad's plot twist and how it flung my trajectory into the cosmic unknown. The cosmic yarn I spin for the masses: Dad ditching Space Corps lit the afterburners on John, Howard, Frank, and my career quest, filling the void he left.

My brothers, all being older, eventually signed up for the Space Corps, graduating with top marks in their classes. They all got commission postings on the fleet's best ships. John was an astro-navigator on the SSS Augustus, where he shared quarters with a certain Frank Hollister—a captain in the making.

Frank, the rising star in the Space Corps, snagged the first officer position aboard the Nova 4 when the previous first officer, Cheddar Flatheringson, decided he'd rather play captain. Six years of navigating the officer bureaucracy had Frank on a trajectory to break records and become the youngest captain in the Space Corps. But, as I've always said, 'Up, up, up the ziggurat lickety-split.

As for me, at the tender age of nine, my school grades were less than promising, and in a twist of cosmic fate, my parents decided it was better to wash their hands of me and ship me off to boarding school. As time ticked away, my envy for friends and their idyllic families turned me into a recluse. I found solace in the small things; I enjoyed listening to the Hammond organ, Morris Dancing, and building up my collection of 20th-century telegraph poles. You could always find me aimlessly wandering around the vast diesel decks at the local spaceport, attempting to rediscover the joy of getting lost. I even took up learning Esperanto in my sleep. But, as I looked up at the stars, where dreams of greatness shimmer like distant galaxies, my story was only just beginning. Arnold Judas Rimmer was destined for glory from the very fabric of stardust. My humble journey commenced not among the celestial bodies but within the labyrinth of obstacles—the very crucible of my stellar aspirations.

It was just another sunny day on Io, spent jesting with my older brothers John, Howard, and Frank. God, we were close — the 'Four Musketeers,' as we used to call ourselves! Well, the three musketeers actually; they always let me be the queen of Spain. What fun we'd have! An occasional practical joke, of course — apple-pie beds, black-eye telescope. They even hid a small landmine in my sandpit! How were they supposed to know it would go off? However, on this particular day, we were all blissfully ignorant of the interstellar smeg about to hit my life!

As my mother casually revealed her plan to send me off to boarding school! My school grades had been gradually slipping, and my parents, having tried absolutely nothing and being fresh out of ideas, thought it would be best to let me be someone else's problem. I, in my infinite pubescent wisdom, hit her with the forceful question, 'Will I still get to see Bruno?' Bruno was the family dog, clearly. You could see where my main priorities lay.

In response, she crouched down, bless her heart — magnificent woman. Very prim, very proper; some say austere. Some people mistook her for being cold and thought she was aloof. Not a bit of it. She crouched down to my eye level, as if we were sharing the secrets of the universe. In a tone that probably sounded more dramatic than she intended, she explained that it was a boarding school on the other side of Io — pretty much as far away from them while still being on the same planet.

Turning to dear old Dad for an explanation or, at the very least, a distraction from the impending familial meltdown, the bearded git was engaged in a staring contest with the sky. It was as if he believed they held the secrets to a lifetime supply of cosmic beer. 'I don't want to go!' I declared, my voice dripping with the gravitas only a nine-year-old prophet could muster.

"Just a couple of years, Arnold, and you can come home for your birthday," she boldly declared, and Dad, ever the spectator in the family circus, continued his stoic gaze into the sky. He never was one for eye contact. Snapping his head, he interjected, "Don't get the weaselly smegger's hopes up." Classic Dad!

Undeterred by the lack of emotional support, she flung a promise of her triumphant return in time for my birthday, as if the universe itself would pause its dance to celebrate my existence. Hugging me, she hoisted me up. 'C'mon, let's get some quiche,' she declared, casting a glance at Dad, who remained emotionally disengaged; he never would give quiche a chance.

The next morning, I was hurled into a transport craft, sharing a seat with Fred 'Thicky' Holden, leaving me to ponder the cosmic absurdity of it all. Suddenly, the predictable rhythms of my boyhood were replaced by the unpredictable chaos of the universe. Leaving behind our modest house on Io — a perfect replica of an Earth house from the 19th and 20th centuries with its hectares of land. There were some parts I wouldn't miss: getting up early in the morning to feed the sheep and cows, and my pet Lemming. Dad's insistence on manual labor became the launching pad for my determination and my brothers to join the Space Corps.

Our house had witnessed the shenanigans of many generations of Rimmers, with stories galore about my great-great-grandfather, Jebediah Rimmer, who legend has it fought off native Ionians to build the house and gardens. Now maintained by my Dad and with help from the local gardener, Dungo. My dad couldn't stand Dungo, and could never understand why. Sure, he was slightly inept at times and egotistical, self-important, lacked confidence, and was socially awkward. But I always liked him; he had a strong moralistic attitude, and my mother always took a shine to him.

My father, a half-crazed military failure, spent his early years amidst the military pioneers. Growing up on Io, his childhood was an exercise in minimalism. Yet, he yearned to be an officer like his father. The dream almost turned into reality when he strutted onto Space Corps Academy grounds, fulfilling an ambition that had marinated in the spartan conditions of an Io upbringing. Grandpa, an eternal optimist, had dreams of his son treading the same starlit path. Destiny pulled a cosmic prank when he was one inch below Corps regulation height.

My mother was born into an austere family that considered space exploration a genetic trait. Her father was part of the Space Corps' third graduating class, and her mother was a part of the cybernautic division — a family with enough star power to make a pulsar blush.

Mum, with dreams of becoming an astrobiologist, found herself on a collision course with Dad in an Introduction to Space Corps History class. Oh, but the Space Corps Directive 2574 about students fraternizing with other students was stricter than a vegan at a butcher shop. They soon found themselves in front of the space corps instructor with a warning.

Fast forward to Dad's posting on the JMC Emerald Nebula. Despite the height restrictions, strings were pulled, and he was made a galley steward. The ship was still three months away from Earth. He'd stayed in touch with my mother throughout, and in a move that combined romantic flair with a dash of desperation, while on leave at Lunar City 7, Dad proposed to my mother. 'Everyone thought we were bloody mad,' Mum once said, 'Maybe it was the wine or the smell of the beef that had seeped into his clothes. But I just couldn't say no to those puppy dog eyes.' Ah, the cosmic irony of hindsight.

My mother was posted on Titan, and my dad was posted on the JMC Emerald Nebula. Over a year passed before she saw Dad again, and almost two more years before she donned the graduation cap and tossed it into the wind. Yet, fate, with its sense of humor, decided that she wouldn't be posted anywhere near my dad.

My mother was freshly stationed on the Axiom II; however, it wasn't long before she found she had a tiny stowaway on board. She was pregnant with my older brother, Frank! 'Your father was in the outer rim at the time; he nearly dropped his spatula,' she said, 'and by the time the message got to him, I was already as big as a cow

So Mum's Space Corps ambitions hit a speed bump; she took a leave of absence and went to shack up on Io with my paternal grandparents. Lacking her parental navigators, who had embarked on the ultimate road trip years earlier, she found herself surrounded by vast farmland of good old terrestrial adventure. Enter Frank, my elder sibling, making his grand entrance. The interstellar escapades of the next generation were officially underway.

With the cosmic clock ticking, Mum had a mere two Earth-bound years before Space Corp's relentless gravitational pull demanded her return. In those terrestrial years, she juggled the titles of astrobiologist and dedicated mum. 'I just felt shagged out all the time,' she reminisced. 'I missed little Frank; this wasn't what I wanted.' Parenthood, it turns out, is the ultimate improvisational act.

With parents who had charted the final frontier of life and having witnessed her mother resigning her commission to raise her and her brother solo during Dad's cosmic escapades as chief slop server, Mum found herself in a parenting predicament. 'I was bored out of my mind, but your dad's career was everything to him,' she admitted. She'd study where she could while my grandparents took care of Frank. 'Your grandparents were like Energizer bunnies,' she shared. Meanwhile, Dad, charting his course through the galactic highways aboard the JMC Emerald Nebula, missed Mum and Frank. As the countdown to Mum's return commenced, Dad, ever the master of cosmic shenanigans, pulled whatever strings he could to get her posted back to Io, where he had assumed the role of Restroom attendant.

Only for calamity to strike again after my Mum's grand return to the Space Corps. Surprise, surprise—John was on the way, stealing the spotlight as the next Rimmer headliner. Dad informing Captain Sulaco was less than thrilled. Shipboard nurseries were not on his playlist. But, that triggered Dad's decision. A message blinked in from the cosmic ether—Dad's old man had punched out his ticket to the great beyond when he was born. His career as a restroom attendant wasn't going anywhere fast. Cue the resignation letter to Space Corps—bye-bye dad's officer career. So from that point on, they began to settle into life on Io together. Mum later shot out my next brother Howard. Then, having a break, they focused on the house and garden, bringing local gardener Dungo to assist. It wasn't long after I arrived on the scene!

In the galactic years since, I've mulled over Dad's plot twist and how it flung my trajectory into the cosmic unknown. The cosmic yarn I spin for the masses: Dad ditching Space Corps lit the afterburners on John, Howard, Frank, and my career quest, filling the void he left.

My brothers, all being older, eventually signed up for the Space Corps, graduating with top marks in their classes. They all got commission postings on the fleet's best ships. John was an astro-navigator on the SSS Augustus, where he shared quarters with a certain Frank Hollister—a captain in the making.

Frank, the rising star in the Space Corps, snagged the first officer position aboard the Nova 4 when the previous first officer, Cheddar Flatheringson, decided he'd rather play captain. Six years of navigating the officer bureaucracy had Frank on a trajectory to break records and become the youngest captain in the Space Corps. But, as I've always said, 'Up, up, up the ziggurat lickety-split.

As for me, at the tender age of nine, my school grades were less than promising, and in a twist of cosmic fate, my parents decided it was better to wash their hands of me and ship me off to boarding school. As time ticked away, my envy for friends and their idyllic families turned me into a recluse. I found solace in the small things; I enjoyed listening to the Hammond organ, Morris Dancing, and building up my collection of 20th-century telegraph poles. You could always find me aimlessly wandering around the vast diesel decks at the local spaceport, attempting to rediscover the joy of getting lost. I even took up learning Esperanto in my sleep. But, as I looked up at the stars, where dreams of greatness shimmer like distant galaxies, my story was only just beginning. Arnold Judas Rimmer was destined for glory from the very fabric of stardust. My humble journey commenced not among the celestial bodies but within the labyrinth of obstacles — the very crucible of my stellar aspirations.

It was just another sunny day on Io, spent jesting with my older brothers John, Howard, and Frank. God, we were close — the 'Four Musketeers,' as we used to call ourselves! Well, the three musketeers actually; they always let me be the queen of Spain. What fun we'd have! An occasional practical joke, of course — apple-pie beds, black-eye telescope. They even hid a small landmine in my sandpit! How were they supposed to know it would go off? However, on this particular day, we were all blissfully ignorant of the interstellar smeg about to hit my life!

As my mother casually revealed her plan to send me off to boarding school! My school grades had been gradually slipping, and my parents, having tried absolutely nothing and being fresh out of ideas, thought it would be best to let me be someone else's problem. I, in my infinite pubescent wisdom, hit her with the forceful question, 'Will I still get to see Bruno?' Bruno was the family dog, clearly. You could see where my main priorities lay.

In response, she crouched down, bless her heart — magnificent woman. Very prim, very proper; some say austere. Some people mistook her for being cold and thought she was aloof. Not a bit of it. She crouched down to my eye level, as if we were sharing the secrets of the universe. In a tone that probably sounded more dramatic than she intended, she explained that it was a boarding school on the other side of Io — pretty much as far away from them while still being on the same planet.

Turning to dear old Dad for an explanation or, at the very least, a distraction from the impending familial meltdown, the bearded git was engaged in a staring contest with the sky. It was as if he believed they held the secrets to a lifetime supply of cosmic beer. 'I don't want to go!' I declared, my voice dripping with the gravitas only a nine-year-old prophet could muster.

"Just a couple of years, Arnold, and you can come home for your birthday," she boldly declared, and Dad, ever the spectator in the family circus, continued his stoic gaze into the sky. He never was one for eye contact. Snapping his head, he interjected, "Don't get the weaselly smegger's hopes up." Classic Dad!

Undeterred by the lack of emotional support, she flung a promise of her triumphant return in time for my birthday, as if the universe itself would pause its dance to celebrate my existence. Hugging me, she hoisted me

up. 'C'mon, let's get some quiche,' she declared, casting a glance at Dad, who remained emotionally disengaged; he never would give quiche a chance.

The next morning, I was hurled into a transport craft, sharing a seat with Fred 'Thicky' Holden, leaving me to ponder the cosmic absurdity of it all. Suddenly, the predictable rhythms of my boyhood were replaced by the unpredictable chaos of the universe. Leaving behind our modest house on Io — a perfect replica of an Earth house from the 19th and 20th centuries with its hectares of land. There were some parts I wouldn't miss: getting up early in the morning to feed the sheep and cows, and my pet Lemming. Dad's insistence on manual labor became the launching pad for my determination and my brothers to join the Space Corps.

Our house had witnessed the shenanigans of many generations of Rimmers, with stories galore about my great-great-grandfather, Jebediah Rimmer, who legend has it fought off native Ionians to build the house and gardens. Now maintained by my Dad and with help from the local gardener, Dungo. My dad couldn't stand Dungo, and could never understand why. Sure, he was slightly inept at times and egotistical, self-important, lacked confidence, and was socially awkward. But I always liked him; he had a strong moralistic attitude, and my mother always took a shine to him.

My father, a half-crazed military failure, spent his early years amidst the military pioneers. Growing up on Io, his childhood was an exercise in minimalism. Yet, he yearned to be an officer like his father. The dream almost turned into reality when he strutted onto Space Corps Academy grounds, fulfilling an ambition that had marinated in the spartan conditions of an Io upbringing. Grandpa, an eternal optimist, had dreams of his son treading the same starlit path. Destiny pulled a cosmic prank when he was one inch below Corps regulation height.

My mother was born into an austere family that considered space exploration a genetic trait. Her father was part of the Space Corps' third graduating class, and her mother was a part of the cybernautic division — a family with enough star power to make a pulsar blush.

Mum, with dreams of becoming an astrobiologist, found herself on a collision course with Dad in an Introduction to Space Corps History class. Oh, but the Space Corps Directive 2574 about students fraternizing with other students was stricter than a vegan at a butcher shop. They soon found themselves in front of the space corps instructor with a warning.

Fast forward to Dad's posting on the JMC Emerald Nebula. Despite the height restrictions, strings were pulled, and he was made a galley steward. The ship was still three months away from Earth. He'd stayed in touch with my mother throughout, and in a move that combined romantic flair with a dash of desperation, while on leave at Lunar City 7, Dad proposed to my mother. 'Everyone thought we were bloody mad,' Mum once said, 'Maybe it was the wine or the smell of the beef that had seeped into his clothes. But I just couldn't say no to those puppy dog eyes.' Ah, the cosmic irony of hindsight.

My mother was posted on Titan, and my dad was posted on the JMC Emerald Nebula. Over a year passed before she saw Dad again, and almost two more years before she donned the graduation cap and tossed it into the wind. Yet, fate, with its sense of humor, decided that she wouldn't be posted anywhere near my dad.

My mother was freshly stationed on the Axiom II; however, it wasn't long before she found she had a tiny stowaway on board. She was pregnant with my older brother, Frank! 'Your father was in the outer rim at the time; he nearly dropped his spatula,' she said, 'and by the time the message got to him, I was already as big as a cow

So Mum's Space Corps ambitions hit a speed bump; she took a leave of absence and went to shack up on Io with my paternal grandparents. Lacking her parental navigators, who had embarked on the ultimate road trip years earlier, she found herself surrounded by vast farmland of good old terrestrial adventure. Enter Frank, my elder sibling, making his grand entrance. The interstellar escapades of the next generation were officially underway.

With the cosmic clock ticking, Mum had a mere two Earth-bound years before Space Corp's relentless gravitational pull demanded her return. In those terrestrial years, she juggled the titles of astrobiologist and dedicated mum. 'I just felt shagged out all the time,' she reminisced. 'I missed little Frank; this wasn't what I wanted.' Parenthood, it turns out, is the ultimate improvisational act.

With parents who had charted the final frontier of life and having witnessed her mother resigning her commission to raise her and her brother solo during Dad's cosmic escapades as chief slop server, Mum found herself in a parenting predicament. 'I was bored out of my mind, but your dad's career was everything to him,' she admitted. She'd study where she could while my grandparents took care of Frank. 'Your grandparents were like Energizer bunnies,' she shared. Meanwhile, Dad, charting his course through the galactic highways aboard the JMC Emerald Nebula, missed Mum and Frank. As the countdown to Mum's return commenced, Dad, ever the master of cosmic shenanigans, pulled whatever strings he could to get her posted back to Io, where he had assumed the role of Restroom attendant.

Only for calamity to strike again after my Mum's grand return to the Space Corps. Surprise, surprise—John was on the way, stealing the spotlight as the next Rimmer headliner. Dad informing Captain Sulaco was less than thrilled. Shipboard nurseries were not on his playlist. But, that triggered Dad's decision. A message blinked in from the cosmic ether — Dad's old man had punched out his ticket to the great beyond when he was born. His career as a restroom attendant wasn't going anywhere fast. Cue the resignation letter to Space Corps — bye-bye dad's officer career. So from that point on, they began to settle into life on Io together. Mum later shot out my next brother Howard. Then, having a break, they focused on the house and garden, bringing local gardener Dungo to assist. It wasn't long after I arrived on the scene!

In the galactic years since, I've mulled over Dad's plot twist and how it flung my trajectory into the cosmic unknown. The cosmic yarn I spin for the masses: Dad ditching Space Corps lit the afterburners on John, Howard, Frank, and my career quest, filling the void he left.

My brothers, all being older, eventually signed up for the Space Corps, graduating with top marks in their classes. They all got commission postings on the fleet's best ships. John was an astro-navigator on the SSS Augustus, where he shared quarters with a certain Frank Hollister — a captain in the making.

Frank, the rising star in the Space Corps, snagged the first officer position aboard the Nova 4 when the previous first officer, Cheddar Flatheringson, decided he'd rather play captain. Six years of navigating the officer bureaucracy had Frank on a trajectory to break records and become the youngest captain in the Space Corps. But, as I've always said, 'Up, up, up the ziggurat lickety-split.

As for me, at the tender age of nine, my school grades were less than promising, and in a twist of cosmic fate, my parents decided it was better to wash their hands of me and ship me off to boarding school. As time ticked away, my envy for friends and their idyllic families turned me into a recluse. I found solace in the small things; I enjoyed listening to the Hammond organ, Morris Dancing, and building up my collection of 20th-century telegraph poles. You could always find me aimlessly wandering around the vast diesel decks at the local spaceport, attempting to rediscover the joy of getting lost. I even took up learning Esperanto in my sleep. But, as I looked up at the stars, where dreams of greatness shimmer like distant galaxies, my story was only just beginning. Arnold Judas Rimmer was destined for glory from the very fabric of stardust. My humble journey commenced not among the celestial bodies but within the labyrinth of obstacles—the very crucible of my stellar aspirations.

It was just another sunny day on Io, spent jesting with my older brothers John, Howard, and Frank. God, we were close—the 'Four Musketeers,' as we used to call ourselves! Well, the three musketeers actually; they always let me be the queen of Spain. What fun we'd have! An occasional practical joke, of course—apple-pie beds, black-eye telescope. They even hid a small landmine in my sandpit! How were they supposed to know it would go off? However, on this particular day, we were all blissfully ignorant of the interstellar smeg about to hit my life!

As my mother casually revealed her plan to send me off to boarding school! My school grades had been gradually slipping, and my parents, having tried absolutely nothing and being fresh out of ideas, thought it would be best to let me be someone else's problem. I, in my infinite pubescent wisdom, hit her with the forceful question, 'Will I still get to see Bruno?' Bruno was the family dog, clearly. You could see where my main priorities lay.

In response, she crouched down, bless her heart—magnificent woman. Very prim, very proper; some say austere. Some people mistook her for being cold and thought she was aloof. Not a bit of it. She crouched down to my eye level, as if we were sharing the secrets of the universe. In a tone that probably sounded more dramatic than she intended, she explained that it was a boarding school on the other side of Io—pretty much as farway from them while still being on the same planet.

171

Turning to dear old Dad for an explanation or, at the very least, a distraction from the impending familial meltdown, the bearded git was engaged in a staring contest with the sky. It was as if he believed they held the secrets to a lifetime supply of cosmic beer. 'I don't want to go!' I declared, my voice dripping with the gravitas only a nine-year-old prophet could muster.

"Just a couple of years, Arnold, and you can come home for your birthday," she boldly declared, and Dad, ever the spectator in the family circus, continued his stoic gaze into the sky. He never was one for eye contact. Snapping his head, he interjected, "Don't get the weaselly smegger's hopes up." Classic Dad!

Undeterred by the lack of emotional support, she flung a promise of her triumphant return in time for my birthday, as if the universe itself would pause its dance to celebrate my existence. Hugging me, she hoisted me up. 'C'mon, let's get some quiche,' she declared, casting a glance at Dad, who remained emotionally disengaged; he never would give quiche a chance.

The next morning, I was hurled into a transport craft, sharing a seat with Fred 'Thicky' Holden, leaving me to ponder the cosmic absurdity of it all. Suddenly, the predictable rhythms of my boyhood were replaced by the unpredictable chaos of the universe. Leaving behind our modest house on Io — a perfect replica of an Earth house from the 19th and 20th centuries with its hectares of land. There were some parts I wouldn't miss: getting up early in the morning to feed the sheep and cows, and my pet Lemming. Dad's insistence on manual labor became the launching pad for my determination and my brothers to join the Space Corps.

Our house had witnessed the shenanigans of many generations of Rimmers, with stories galore about my great-great-grandfather, Jebediah Rimmer, who legend has it fought off native Ionians to build the house and gardens. Now maintained by my Dad and with help from the local gardener, Dungo. My dad couldn't stand Dungo, and could never understand why. Sure, he was slightly inept at times and egotistical, self-important, lacked confidence, and was socially awkward. But I always liked him; he had a strong moralistic attitude, and my mother always took a shine to him.

My father, a half-crazed military failure, spent his early years amidst the military pioneers. Growing up on Io, his childhood was an exercise in minimalism. Yet, he yearned to be an officer like his father. The dream almost turned into reality when he strutted onto Space Corps Academy grounds, fulfilling an ambition that had marinated in the spartan conditions of an Io upbringing. Grandpa, an eternal optimist, had dreams of his son treading the same starlit path. Destiny pulled a cosmic prank when he was one inch below Corps regulation height.

My mother was born into an austere family that considered space exploration a genetic trait. Her father was part of the Space Corps' third graduating class, and her mother was a part of the cybernautic division — a family with enough star power to make a pulsar blush.

Mum, with dreams of becoming an astrobiologist, found herself on a collision course with Dad in an Introduction to Space Corps History class. Oh, but the Space Corps Directive 2574 about students fraternizing with other students was stricter than a vegan at a butcher shop. They soon found themselves in front of the space corps instructor with a warning.

Fast forward to Dad's posting on the JMC Emerald Nebula. Despite the height restrictions, strings were pulled, and he was made a galley steward. The ship was still three months away from Earth. He'd stayed in touch with my mother throughout, and in a move that combined romantic flair with a dash of desperation, while on leave at Lunar City 7, Dad proposed to my mother. 'Everyone thought we were bloody mad,' Mum once said, 'Maybe it was the wine or the smell of the beef that had seeped into his clothes. But I just couldn't say no to those puppy dog eyes.' Ah, the cosmic irony of hindsight.

My mother was posted on Titan, and my dad was posted on the JMC Emerald Nebula. Over a year passed before she saw Dad again, and almost two more years before she donned the graduation cap and tossed it into the wind. Yet, fate, with its sense of humor, decided that she wouldn't be posted anywhere near my dad.

My mother was freshly stationed on the Axiom II; however, it wasn't long before she found she had a tiny stowaway on board. She was pregnant with my older brother, Frank! 'Your father was in the outer rim at the time; he nearly dropped his spatula,' she said, 'and by the time the message got to him, I was already as big as a cow

So Mum's Space Corps ambitions hit a speed bump; she took a leave of absence and went to shack up on Io with my paternal grandparents. Lacking her parental navigators, who had embarked on the ultimate road trip years earlier, she found herself surrounded by vast farmland of good old terrestrial adventure. Enter Frank, my elder sibling, making his grand entrance. The interstellar escapades of the next generation were officially underway.

With the cosmic clock ticking, Mum had a mere two Earth-bound years before Space Corp's relentless gravitational pull demanded her return. In those terrestrial years, she juggled the titles of astrobiologist and dedicated mum. 'I just felt shagged out all the time,' she reminisced. 'I missed little Frank; this wasn't what I wanted.' Parenthood, it turns out, is the ultimate improvisational act.

With parents who had charted the final frontier of life and having witnessed her mother resigning her commission to raise her and her brother solo during Dad's cosmic escapades as chief slop server, Mum found herself in a parenting predicament. 'I was bored out of my mind, but your dad's career was everything to him,' she admitted. She'd study where she could while my grandparents took care of Frank. 'Your grandparents were like Energizer bunnies,' she shared. Meanwhile, Dad, charting his course through the galactic highways aboard the JMC Emerald Nebula, missed Mum and Frank. As the countdown to Mum's return commenced, Dad, ever the master of cosmic shenanigans, pulled whatever strings he could to get her posted back to Io, where he had assumed the role of Restroom attendant.

Only for calamity to strike again after my Mum's grand return to the Space Corps. Surprise, surprise—John was on the way, stealing the spotlight as the next Rimmer headliner. Dad informing Captain Sulaco was less than thrilled. Shipboard nurseries were not on his playlist. But, that triggered Dad's decision. A message blinked in from the cosmic ether—Dad's old man had punched out his ticket to the great beyond when he was born. His career as a restroom attendant wasn't going anywhere fast. Cue the resignation letter to Space Corps—bye-bye dad's officer career. So from that point on, they began to settle into life on Io together. Mum later shot out my next brother Howard. Then, having a break, they focused on the house and garden, bringing local gardener Dungo to assist. It wasn't long after I arrived on the scene!

In the galactic years since, I've mulled over Dad's plot twist and how it flung my trajectory into the cosmic unknown. The cosmic yarn I spin for the masses: Dad ditching Space Corps lit the afterburners on John, Howard, Frank, and my career quest, filling the void he left.

My brothers, all being older, eventually signed up for the Space Corps, graduating with top marks in their classes. They all got commission postings on the fleet's best ships. John was an astro-navigator on the SSS Augustus, where he shared quarters with a certain Frank Hollister — a captain in the making.

Frank, the rising star in the Space Corps, snagged the first officer position aboard the Nova 4 when the previous first officer, Cheddar Flatheringson, decided he'd rather play captain. Six years of navigating the officer bureaucracy had Frank on a trajectory to break records and become the youngest captain in the Space Corps. But, as I've always said, 'Up, up, up the ziggurat lickety-split.

As for me, at the tender age of nine, my school grades were less than promising, and in a twist of cosmic fate, my parents decided it was better to wash their hands of me and ship me off to boarding school. As time ticked away, my envy for friends and their idyllic families turned me into a recluse. I found solace in the small things; I enjoyed listening to the Hammond organ, Morris Dancing, and building up my collection of 20th-century telegraph poles. You could always find me aimlessly wandering around the vast diesel decks at the local spaceport, attempting to rediscover the joy of getting lost. I even took up learning Esperanto in my sleep. But, as I looked up at the stars, where dreams of greatness shimmer like distant galaxies, my story was only just beginning. Arnold Judas Rimmer was destined for glory from the very fabric of stardust. My humble journey commenced not among the celestial bodies but within the labyrinth of obstacles — the very crucible of my stellar aspirations.

# FINAL CHAPTER
# LEGACY AMONG THE STARS

It was just another sunny day on Io, spent jesting with my older brothers John, Howard, and Frank. God, we were close—the 'Four Musketeers,' as we used to call ourselves! Well, the three musketeers actually; they always let me be the queen of Spain. What fun we'd have! An occasional practical joke, of course—apple-pie beds, black-eye telescope. They even hid a small landmine in my sandpit! How were they supposed to know it would go off? However, on this particular day, we were all blissfully ignorant of the interstellar smeg about to hit my life!

As my mother casually revealed her plan to send me off to boarding school! My school grades had been gradually slipping, and my parents, having tried absolutely nothing and being fresh out of ideas, thought it would be best to let me be someone else's problem. I, in my infinite pubescent wisdom, hit her with the forceful question, 'Will I still get to see Bruno?' Bruno was the family dog, clearly. You could see where my main priorities lay.

In response, she crouched down, bless her heart—magnificent woman. Very prim, very proper; some say austere. Some people mistook her for being cold and thought she was aloof. Not a bit of it. She crouched down to my eye level, as if we were sharing the secrets of the universe. In a tone that probably sounded more dramatic than she intended, she explained that it was a boarding school on the other side of Io—pretty much as far away from them while still being on the same planet.

Turning to dear old Dad for an explanation or, at the very least, a distraction from the impending familial meltdown, the bearded git was engaged in a staring contest with the sky. It was as if he believed they held the secrets to a lifetime supply of cosmic beer. 'I don't want to go!' I declared, my voice dripping with the gravitas only a nine-year-old prophet could muster.

"Just a couple of years, Arnold, and you can come home for your birthday," she boldly declared, and Dad, ever the spectator in the family circus, continued his stoic gaze into the sky. He never was one for eye contact. Snapping his head, he interjected, "Don't get the weaselly smegger's hopes up." Classic Dad!

Undeterred by the lack of emotional support, she flung a promise of her triumphant return in time for my birthday, as if the universe itself would pause its dance to celebrate my existence. Hugging me, she hoisted me up. 'C'mon, let's get some quiche,' she declared, casting a glance at Dad, who remained emotionally disengaged; he never would give quiche a chance.

The next morning, I was hurled into a transport craft, sharing a seat with Fred 'Thicky' Holden, leaving me to ponder the cosmic absurdity of it all. Suddenly, the predictable rhythms of my boyhood were replaced by the unpredictable chaos of the universe. Leaving behind our modest house on Io — a perfect replica of an Earth house from the 19th and 20th centuries with its hectares of land. There were some parts I wouldn't miss: getting up early in the morning to feed the sheep and cows, and my pet Lemming. Dad's insistence on manual labor became the launching pad for my determination and my brothers to join the Space Corps.

Our house had witnessed the shenanigans of many generations of Rimmers, with stories galore about my great-great-grandfather, Jebediah Rimmer, who legend has it fought off native Ionians to build the house and gardens. Now maintained by my Dad and with help from the local gardener, Dungo. My dad couldn't stand Dungo, and could never understand why. Sure, he was slightly inept at times and egotistical, self-important, lacked confidence, and was socially awkward. But I always liked him; he had a strong moralistic attitude, and my mother always took a shine to him.

My father, a half-crazed military failure, spent his early years amidst the military pioneers. Growing up on Io, his childhood was an exercise in minimalism. Yet, he yearned to be an officer like his father. The dream almost turned into reality when he strutted onto Space Corps Academy grounds, fulfilling an ambition that had marinated in the spartan conditions of an Io upbringing. Grandpa, an eternal optimist, had dreams of his son treading the same starlit path. Destiny pulled a cosmic prank when he was one inch below Corps regulation height.

My mother was born into an austere family that considered space exploration a genetic trait. Her father was part of the Space Corps' third graduating class, and her mother was a part of the cybernautic division — a family with enough star power to make a pulsar blush.

Mum, with dreams of becoming an astrobiologist, found herself on a collision course with Dad in an Introduction to Space Corps History class. Oh, but the Space Corps Directive 2574 about students fraternizing with other students was stricter than a vegan at a butcher shop. They soon found themselves in front of the space corps instructor with a warning.

Fast forward to Dad's posting on the JMC Emerald Nebula. Despite the height restrictions, strings were pulled, and he was made a galley steward. The ship was still three months away from Earth. He'd stayed in touch with my mother throughout, and in a move that combined romantic flair with a dash of desperation, while on leave at Lunar City 7, Dad proposed to my mother. 'Everyone thought we were bloody mad,' Mum once said, 'Maybe it was the wine or the smell of the beef that had seeped into his clothes. But I just couldn't say no to those puppy dog eyes.' Ah, the cosmic irony of hindsight.

My mother was posted on Titan, and my dad was posted on the JMC Emerald Nebula. Over a year passed before she saw Dad again, and almost two more years before she donned the graduation cap and tossed it into the wind. Yet, fate, with its sense of humor, decided that she wouldn't be posted anywhere near my dad.

My mother was freshly stationed on the Axiom II; however, it wasn't long before she found she had a tiny stowaway on board. She was pregnant with my older brother, Frank! 'Your father was in the outer rim at the time; he nearly dropped his spatula,' she said, 'and by the time the message got to him, I was already as big as a cow

So Mum's Space Corps ambitions hit a speed bump; she took a leave of absence and went to shack up on Io with my paternal grandparents. Lacking her parental navigators, who had embarked on the ultimate road trip years earlier, she found herself surrounded by vast farmland of good old terrestrial adventure. Enter Frank, my elder sibling, making his grand entrance. The interstellar escapades of the next generation were officially underway.

With the cosmic clock ticking, Mum had a mere two Earth-bound years before Space Corp's relentless gravitational pull demanded her return. In those terrestrial years, she juggled the titles of astrobiologist and dedicated mum. 'I just felt shagged out all the time,' she reminisced. 'I missed little Frank; this wasn't what I wanted.' Parenthood, it turns out, is the ultimate improvisational act.

With parents who had charted the final frontier of life and having witnessed her mother resigning her commission to raise her and her brother solo during Dad's cosmic escapades as chief slop server, Mum found herself in a parenting predicament. 'I was bored out of my mind, but your dad's career was everything to him,' she admitted. She'd study where she could while my grandparents took care of Frank. 'Your grandparents were like Energizer bunnies,' she shared. Meanwhile, Dad, charting his course through the galactic highways aboard the JMC Emerald Nebula, missed Mum and Frank. As the countdown to Mum's return commenced, Dad, ever the master of cosmic shenanigans, pulled whatever strings he could to get her posted back to Io, where he had assumed the role of Restroom attendant.

Only for calamity to strike again after my Mum's grand return to the Space Corps. Surprise, surprise—John was on the way, stealing the spotlight as the next Rimmer headliner. Dad informing Captain Sulaco was less than thrilled. Shipboard nurseries were not on his playlist. But, that triggered Dad's decision. A message blinked in from the cosmic ether—Dad's old man had punched out his ticket to the great beyond when he was born. His career as a restroom attendant wasn't going anywhere fast. Cue the resignation letter to Space Corps—bye-bye dad's officer career. So from that point on, they began to settle into life on Io together. Mum later shot out my next brother Howard. Then, having a break, they focused on the house and garden, bringing local gardener Dungo to assist. It wasn't long after I arrived on the scene!

In the galactic years since, I've mulled over Dad's plot twist and how it flung my trajectory into the cosmic unknown. The cosmic yarn I spin for the masses: Dad ditching Space Corps lit the afterburners on John, Howard, Frank, and my career quest, filling the void he left.

My brothers, all being older, eventually signed up for the Space Corps, graduating with top marks in their classes. They all got commission postings on the fleet's best ships. John was an astro-navigator on the SSS Augustus, where he shared quarters with a certain Frank Hollister — a captain in the making.

Frank, the rising star in the Space Corps, snagged the first officer position aboard the Nova 4 when the previous first officer, Cheddar Flatheringson, decided he'd rather play captain. Six years of navigating the officer bureaucracy had Frank on a trajectory to break records and become the youngest captain in the Space Corps. But, as I've always said, 'Up, up, up the ziggurat lickety-split.

As for me, at the tender age of nine, my school grades were less than promising, and in a twist of cosmic fate, my parents decided it was better to wash their hands of me and ship me off to boarding school. As time ticked away, my envy for friends and their idyllic families turned me into a recluse. I found solace in the small things; I enjoyed listening to the Hammond organ, Morris Dancing, and building up my collection of 20th-century telegraph poles. You could always find me aimlessly wandering around the vast diesel decks at the local spaceport, attempting to rediscover the joy of getting lost. I even took up learning Esperanto in my sleep. But, as I looked up at the stars, where dreams of greatness shimmer like distant galaxies, my story was only just beginning. Arnold Judas Rimmer was destined for glory from the very fabric of stardust. My humble journey commenced not among the celestial bodies but within the labyrinth of obstacles — the very crucible of my stellar aspirations.

It was just another sunny day on Io, spent jesting with my older brothers John, Howard, and Frank. God, we were close — the 'Four Musketeers,' as we used to call ourselves! Well, the three musketeers actually; they always let me be the queen of Spain. What fun we'd have! An occasional practical joke, of course — apple-pie beds, black-eye telescope. They even hid a small landmine in my sandpit! How were they supposed to know it would go off? However, on this particular day, we were all blissfully ignorant of the interstellar smeg about to hit my life!

As my mother casually revealed her plan to send me off to boarding school! My school grades had been gradually slipping, and my parents, having tried absolutely nothing and being fresh out of ideas, thought it would be best to let me be someone else's problem. I, in my infinite pubescent wisdom, hit her with the forceful question, 'Will I still get to see Bruno?' Bruno was the family dog, clearly. You could see where my main priorities lay.

In response, she crouched down, bless her heart — magnificent woman. Very prim, very proper; some say austere. Some people mistook her for being cold and thought she was aloof. Not a bit of it. She crouched down to my eye level, as if we were sharing the secrets of the universe. In a tone that probably sounded more dramatic than she intended, she explained that it was a boarding school on the other side of Io — pretty much as far away from them while still being on the same planet.

Turning to dear old Dad for an explanation or, at the very least, a distraction from the impending familial meltdown, the bearded git was engaged in a staring contest with the sky. It was as if he believed they held the secrets to a lifetime supply of cosmic beer. 'I don't want to go!' I declared, my voice dripping with the gravitas only a nine-year-old prophet could muster.

"Just a couple of years, Arnold, and you can come home for your birthday," she boldly declared, and Dad, ever the spectator in the family circus, continued his stoic gaze into the sky. He never was one for eye contact. Snapping his head, he interjected, "Don't get the weaselly smegger's hopes up." Classic Dad!

Undeterred by the lack of emotional support, she flung a promise of her triumphant return in time for my birthday, as if the universe itself would pause its dance to celebrate my existence. Hugging me, she hoisted me up. 'C'mon, let's get some quiche,' she declared, casting a glance at Dad, who remained emotionally disengaged; he never would give quiche a chance.

The next morning, I was hurled into a transport craft, sharing a seat with Fred 'Thicky' Holden, leaving me to ponder the cosmic absurdity of it all. Suddenly, the predictable rhythms of my boyhood were replaced by the unpredictable chaos of the universe. Leaving behind our modest house on Io — a perfect replica of an Earth house from the 19th and 20th centuries with its hectares of land. There were some parts I wouldn't miss: getting up early in the morning to feed the sheep and cows, and my pet Lemming. Dad's insistence on manual labor became the launching pad for my determination and my brothers to join the Space Corps.

Our house had witnessed the shenanigans of many generations of Rimmers, with stories galore about my great-great-grandfather, Jebediah Rimmer, who legend has it fought off native Ionians to build the house and gardens. Now maintained by my Dad and with help from the local gardener, Dungo. My dad couldn't stand Dungo, and could never understand why. Sure, he was slightly inept at times and egotistical, self-important, lacked confidence, and was socially awkward. But I always liked him; he had a strong moralistic attitude, and my mother always took a shine to him.

My father, a half-crazed military failure, spent his early years amidst the military pioneers. Growing up on Io, his childhood was an exercise in minimalism. Yet, he yearned to be an officer like his father. The dream almost turned into reality when he strutted onto Space Corps Academy grounds, fulfilling an ambition that had marinated in the spartan conditions of an Io upbringing. Grandpa, an eternal optimist, had dreams of his son treading the same starlit path. Destiny pulled a cosmic prank when he was one inch below Corps regulation height.

My mother was born into an austere family that considered space exploration a genetic trait. Her father was part of the Space Corps' third graduating class, and her mother was a part of the cybernautic division — a family with enough star power to make a pulsar blush.

Mum, with dreams of becoming an astrobiologist, found herself on a collision course with Dad in an Introduction to Space Corps History class. Oh, but the Space Corps Directive 2574 about students fraternizing with other students was stricter than a vegan at a butcher shop. They soon found themselves in front of the space corps instructor with a warning.

Fast forward to Dad's posting on the JMC Emerald Nebula. Despite the height restrictions, strings were pulled, and he was made a galley steward. The ship was still three months away from Earth. He'd stayed in touch with my mother throughout, and in a move that combined romantic flair with a dash of desperation, while on leave at Lunar City 7, Dad proposed to my mother. 'Everyone thought we were bloody mad,' Mum once said, 'Maybe it was the wine or the smell of the beef that had seeped into his clothes. But I just couldn't say no to those puppy dog eyes.' Ah, the cosmic irony of hindsight.

My mother was posted on Titan, and my dad was posted on the JMC Emerald Nebula. Over a year passed before she saw Dad again, and almost two more years before she donned the graduation cap and tossed it into the wind. Yet, fate, with its sense of humor, decided that she wouldn't be posted anywhere near my dad.

My mother was freshly stationed on the Axiom II; however, it wasn't long before she found she had a tiny stowaway on board. She was pregnant with my older brother, Frank! 'Your father was in the outer rim at the time; he nearly dropped his spatula,' she said, 'and by the time the message got to him, I was already as big as a cow

So Mum's Space Corps ambitions hit a speed bump; she took a leave of absence and went to shack up on Io with my paternal grandparents. Lacking her parental navigators, who had embarked on the ultimate road trip years earlier, she found herself surrounded by vast farmland of good old terrestrial adventure. Enter Frank, my elder sibling, making his grand entrance. The interstellar escapades of the next generation were officially underway.

With the cosmic clock ticking, Mum had a mere two Earth-bound years before Space Corp's relentless gravitational pull demanded her return. In those terrestrial years, she juggled the titles of astrobiologist and dedicated mum. 'I just felt shagged out all the time,' she reminisced. 'I missed little Frank; this wasn't what I wanted.' Parenthood, it turns out, is the ultimate improvisational act.

With parents who had charted the final frontier of life and having witnessed her mother resigning her commission to raise her and her brother solo during Dad's cosmic escapades as chief slop server, Mum found herself in a parenting predicament. 'I was bored out of my mind, but your dad's career was everything to him,' she admitted. She'd study where she could while my grandparents took care of Frank. 'Your grandparents were like Energizer bunnies,' she shared. Meanwhile, Dad, charting his course through the galactic highways aboard the JMC Emerald Nebula, missed Mum and Frank. As the countdown to Mum's return commenced, Dad, ever the master of cosmic shenanigans, pulled whatever strings he could to get her posted back to Io, where he had assumed the role of Restroom attendant.

Only for calamity to strike again after my Mum's grand return to the Space Corps. Surprise, surprise—John was on the way, stealing the spotlight as the next Rimmer headliner. Dad informing Captain Sulaco was less than thrilled. Shipboard nurseries were not on his playlist. But, that triggered Dad's decision. A message blinked in from the cosmic ether—Dad's old man had punched out his ticket to the great beyond when he was born. His career as a restroom attendant wasn't going anywhere fast. Cue the resignation letter to Space Corps—bye-bye dad's officer career. So from that point on, they began to settle into life on Io together. Mum later shot out my next brother Howard. Then, having a break, they focused on the house and garden, bringing local gardener Dungo to assist. It wasn't long after I arrived on the scene!

In the galactic years since, I've mulled over Dad's plot twist and how it flung my trajectory into the cosmic unknown. The cosmic yarn I spin for the masses: Dad ditching Space Corps lit the afterburners on John, Howard, Frank, and my career quest, filling the void he left.

My brothers, all being older, eventually signed up for the Space Corps, graduating with top marks in their classes. They all got commission postings on the fleet's best ships. John was an astro-navigator on the SSS Augustus, where he shared quarters with a certain Frank Hollister—a captain in the making.

Frank, the rising star in the Space Corps, snagged the first officer position aboard the Nova 4 when the previous first officer, Cheddar Flatheringson, decided he'd rather play captain. Six years of navigating the officer bureaucracy had Frank on a trajectory to break records and become the youngest captain in the Space Corps. But, as I've always said, 'Up, up, up the ziggurat lickety-split.

As for me, at the tender age of nine, my school grades were less than promising, and in a twist of cosmic fate, my parents decided it was better to wash their hands of me and ship me off to boarding school. As time ticked away, my envy for friends and their idyllic families turned me into a recluse. I found solace in the small things; I enjoyed listening to the Hammond organ, Morris Dancing, and building up my collection of 20th-century telegraph poles. You could always find me aimlessly wandering around the vast diesel decks at the local spaceport, attempting to rediscover the joy of getting lost. I even took up learning Esperanto in my sleep. But, as I looked up at the stars, where dreams of greatness shimmer like distant galaxies, my story was only just beginning. Arnold Judas Rimmer was destined for glory from the very fabric of stardust. My humble journey commenced not among the celestial bodies but within the labyrinth of obstacles — the very crucible of my stellar aspirations.

It was just another sunny day on Io, spent jesting with my older brothers John, Howard, and Frank. God, we were close — the 'Four Musketeers,' as we used to call ourselves! Well, the three musketeers actually; they always let me be the queen of Spain. What fun we'd have! An occasional practical joke, of course — apple-pie beds, black-eye telescope. They even hid a small landmine in my sandpit! How were they supposed to know it would go off? However, on this particular day, we were all blissfully ignorant of the interstellar smeg about to hit my life!

As my mother casually revealed her plan to send me off to boarding school! My school grades had been gradually slipping, and my parents, having tried absolutely nothing and being fresh out of ideas, thought it would be best to let me be someone else's problem. I, in my infinite pubescent wisdom, hit her with the forceful question, 'Will I still get to see Bruno?' Bruno was the family dog, clearly. You could see where my main priorities lay.

In response, she crouched down, bless her heart — magnificent woman. Very prim, very proper; some say austere. Some people mistook her for being cold and thought she was aloof. Not a bit of it. She crouched down to my eye level, as if we were sharing the secrets of the universe. In a tone that probably sounded more dramatic than she intended, she explained that it was a boarding school on the other side of Io — pretty much as far away from them while still being on the same planet.

Turning to dear old Dad for an explanation or, at the very least, a distraction from the impending familial meltdown, the bearded git was engaged in a staring contest with the sky. It was as if he believed they held the secrets to a lifetime supply of cosmic beer. 'I don't want to go!' I declared, my voice dripping with the gravitas only a nine-year-old prophet could muster.

"Just a couple of years, Arnold, and you can come home for your birthday," she boldly declared, and Dad, ever the spectator in the family circus, continued his stoic gaze into the sky. He never was one for eye contact. Snapping his head, he interjected, "Don't get the weaselly smegger's hopes up." Classic Dad!

Undeterred by the lack of emotional support, she flung a promise of her triumphant return in time for my birthday, as if the universe itself would pause its dance to celebrate my existence. Hugging me, she hoisted me up. 'C'mon, let's get some quiche,' she declared, casting a glance at Dad, who remained emotionally disengaged; he never would give quiche a chance.

The next morning, I was hurled into a transport craft, sharing a seat with Fred 'Thicky' Holden, leaving me to ponder the cosmic absurdity of it all. Suddenly, the predictable rhythms of my boyhood were replaced by the unpredictable chaos of the universe. Leaving behind our modest house on Io — a perfect replica of an Earth house from the 19th and 20th centuries with its hectares of land. There were some parts I wouldn't miss: getting up early in the morning to feed the sheep and cows, and my pet Lemming. Dad's insistence on manual labor became the launching pad for my determination and my brothers to join the Space Corps.

Our house had witnessed the shenanigans of many generations of Rimmers, with stories galore about my great-great-grandfather, Jebediah Rimmer, who legend has it fought off native Ionians to build the house and gardens. Now maintained by my Dad and with help from the local gardener, Dungo. My dad couldn't stand Dungo, and could never understand why. Sure, he was slightly inept at times and egotistical, self-important, lacked confidence, and was socially awkward. But I always liked him; he had a strong moralistic attitude, and my mother always took a shine to him.

My father, a half-crazed military failure, spent his early years amidst the military pioneers. Growing up on Io, his childhood was an exercise in minimalism. Yet, he yearned to be an officer like his father. The dream almost turned into reality when he strutted onto Space Corps Academy grounds, fulfilling an ambition that had marinated in the spartan conditions of an Io upbringing. Grandpa, an eternal optimist, had dreams of his son treading the same starlit path. Destiny pulled a cosmic prank when he was one inch below Corps regulation height.

My mother was born into an austere family that considered space exploration a genetic trait. Her father was part of the Space Corps' third graduating class, and her mother was a part of the cybernautic division — a family with enough star power to make a pulsar blush.

Mum, with dreams of becoming an astrobiologist, found herself on a collision course with Dad in an Introduction to Space Corps History class. Oh, but the Space Corps Directive 2574 about students fraternizing with other students was stricter than a vegan at a butcher shop. They soon found themselves in front of the space corps instructor with a warning.

Fast forward to Dad's posting on the JMC Emerald Nebula. Despite the height restrictions, strings were pulled, and he was made a galley steward. The ship was still three months away from Earth. He'd stayed in touch with my mother throughout, and in a move that combined romantic flair with a dash of desperation, while on leave at Lunar City 7, Dad proposed to my mother. 'Everyone thought we were bloody mad,' Mum once said, 'Maybe it was the wine or the smell of the beef that had seeped into his clothes. But I just couldn't say no to those puppy dog eyes.' Ah, the cosmic irony of hindsight.

My mother was posted on Titan, and my dad was posted on the JMC Emerald Nebula. Over a year passed before she saw Dad again, and almost two more years before she donned the graduation cap and tossed it into the wind. Yet, fate, with its sense of humor, decided that she wouldn't be posted anywhere near my dad.

My mother was freshly stationed on the Axiom II; however, it wasn't long before she found she had a tiny stowaway on board. She was pregnant with my older brother, Frank! 'Your father was in the outer rim at the time; he nearly dropped his spatula,' she said, 'and by the time the message got to him, I was already as big as a cow

So Mum's Space Corps ambitions hit a speed bump; she took a leave of absence and went to shack up on Io with my paternal grandparents. Lacking her parental navigators, who had embarked on the ultimate road

trip years earlier, she found herself surrounded by vast farmland of good old terrestrial adventure. Enter Frank, my elder sibling, making his grand entrance. The interstellar escapades of the next generation were officially underway.

With the cosmic clock ticking, Mum had a mere two Earth-bound years before Space Corp's relentless gravitational pull demanded her return. In those terrestrial years, she juggled the titles of astrobiologist and dedicated mum. 'I just felt shagged out all the time,' she reminisced. 'I missed little Frank; this wasn't what I wanted.' Parenthood, it turns out, is the ultimate improvisational act.

With parents who had charted the final frontier of life and having witnessed her mother resigning her commission to raise her and her brother solo during Dad's cosmic escapades as chief slop server, Mum found herself in a parenting predicament. 'I was bored out of my mind, but your dad's career was everything to him,' she admitted. She'd study where she could while my grandparents took care of Frank. 'Your grandparents were like Energizer bunnies,' she shared. Meanwhile, Dad, charting his course through the galactic highways aboard the JMC Emerald Nebula, missed Mum and Frank. As the countdown to Mum's return commenced, Dad, ever the master of cosmic shenanigans, pulled whatever strings he could to get her posted back to Io, where he had assumed the role of Restroom attendant.

Only for calamity to strike again after my Mum's grand return to the Space Corps. Surprise, surprise—John was on the way, stealing the spotlight as the next Rimmer headliner. Dad informing Captain Sulaco was less than thrilled. Shipboard nurseries were not on his playlist. But, that triggered Dad's decision. A message blinked in from the cosmic ether—Dad's old man had punched out his ticket to the great beyond when he was born. His career as a restroom attendant wasn't going anywhere fast. Cue the resignation letter to Space Corps—bye-bye dad's

officer career. So from that point on, they began to settle into life on Io together. Mum later shot out my next brother Howard. Then, having a break, they focused on the house and garden, bringing local gardener Dungo to assist. It wasn't long after I arrived on the scene!

In the galactic years since, I've mulled over Dad's plot twist and how it flung my trajectory into the cosmic unknown. The cosmic yarn I spin for the masses: Dad ditching Space Corps lit the afterburners on John, Howard, Frank, and my career quest, filling the void he left.

My brothers, all being older, eventually signed up for the Space Corps, graduating with top marks in their classes. They all got commission postings on the fleet's best ships. John was an astro-navigator on the SSS Augustus, where he shared quarters with a certain Frank Hollister—a captain in the making.

Frank, the rising star in the Space Corps, snagged the first officer position aboard the Nova 4 when the previous first officer, Cheddar Flatheringson, decided he'd rather play captain. Six years of navigating the officer bureaucracy had Frank on a trajectory to break records and become the youngest captain in the Space Corps. But, as I've always said, 'Up, up, up the ziggurat lickety-split.

As for me, at the tender age of nine, my school grades were less than promising, and in a twist of cosmic fate, my parents decided it was better to wash their hands of me and ship me off to boarding school. As time ticked away, my envy for friends and their idyllic families turned me into a recluse. I found solace in the small things; I enjoyed listening to the Hammond organ, Morris Dancing, and building up my collection of 20th-century telegraph poles. You could always find me aimlessly wandering around the vast diesel decks at the local spaceport, attempting to rediscover the joy of getting lost. I even took up learning Esperanto in my

sleep. But, as I looked up at the stars, where dreams of greatness shimmer like distant galaxies, my story was only just beginning. Arnold Judas Rimmer was destined for glory from the very fabric of stardust. My humble journey commenced not among the celestial bodies but within the labyrinth of obstacles — the very crucible of my stellar aspirations.

It was just another sunny day on Io, spent jesting with my older brothers John, Howard, and Frank. God, we were close — the 'Four Musketeers,' as we used to call ourselves! Well, the three musketeers actually; they always let me be the queen of Spain. What fun we'd have! An occasional practical joke, of course — apple-pie beds, black-eye telescope. They even hid a small landmine in my sandpit! How were they supposed to know it would go off? However, on this particular day, we were all blissfully ignorant of the interstellar smeg about to hit my life!

As my mother casually revealed her plan to send me off to boarding school! My school grades had been gradually slipping, and my parents, having tried absolutely nothing and being fresh out of ideas, thought it would be best to let me be someone else's problem. I, in my infinite pubescent wisdom, hit her with the forceful question, 'Will I still get to see Bruno?' Bruno was the family dog, clearly. You could see where my main priorities lay.

In response, she crouched down, bless her heart — magnificent woman. Very prim, very proper; some say austere. Some people mistook her for being cold and thought she was aloof. Not a bit of it. She crouched down to my eye level, as if we were sharing the secrets of the universe. In a tone that probably sounded more dramatic than she intended, she explained that it was a boarding school on the other side of Io — pretty much as far away from them while still being on the same planet.

Turning to dear old Dad for an explanation or, at the very least, a distraction from the impending familial meltdown, the bearded git was engaged in a staring contest with the sky. It was as if he believed they held the secrets to a lifetime supply of cosmic beer. 'I don't want to go!' I declared, my voice dripping with the gravitas only a nine-year-old prophet could muster.

"Just a couple of years, Arnold, and you can come home for your birthday," she boldly declared, and Dad, ever the spectator in the family circus, continued his stoic gaze into the sky. He never was one for eye contact. Snapping his head, he interjected, "Don't get the weaselly smegger's hopes up." Classic Dad!

Undeterred by the lack of emotional support, she flung a promise of her triumphant return in time for my birthday, as if the universe itself would pause its dance to celebrate my existence. Hugging me, she hoisted me up. 'C'mon, let's get some quiche,' she declared, casting a glance at Dad, who remained emotionally disengaged; he never would give quiche a chance.

The next morning, I was hurled into a transport craft, sharing a seat with Fred 'Thicky' Holden, leaving me to ponder the cosmic absurdity of it all. Suddenly, the predictable rhythms of my boyhood were replaced by the unpredictable chaos of the universe. Leaving behind our modest house on Io — a perfect replica of an Earth house from the 19th and 20th centuries with its hectares of land. There were some parts I wouldn't miss: getting up early in the morning to feed the sheep and cows, and my pet Lemming. Dad's insistence on manual labor became the launching pad for my determination and my brothers to join the Space Corps.

Our house had witnessed the shenanigans of many generations of Rimmers, with stories galore about my great-great-grandfather, Jebediah Rimmer, who legend has it fought off native Ionians to build the house and gardens. Now maintained by my Dad and with help from the local gardener, Dungo. My dad couldn't stand Dungo, and could never understand why. Sure, he was slightly inept at times and egotistical, self-important, lacked confidence, and was socially awkward. But I always liked him; he had a strong moralistic attitude, and my mother always took a shine to him.

My father, a half-crazed military failure, spent his early years amidst the military pioneers. Growing up on Io, his childhood was an exercise in minimalism. Yet, he yearned to be an officer like his father. The dream almost turned into reality when he strutted onto Space Corps Academy grounds, fulfilling an ambition that had marinated in the spartan conditions of an Io upbringing. Grandpa, an eternal optimist, had dreams of his son treading the same starlit path. Destiny pulled a cosmic prank when he was one inch below Corps regulation height.

My mother was born into an austere family that considered space exploration a genetic trait. Her father was part of the Space Corps' third graduating class, and her mother was a part of the cybernautic division — a family with enough star power to make a pulsar blush.

Mum, with dreams of becoming an astrobiologist, found herself on a collision course with Dad in an Introduction to Space Corps History class. Oh, but the Space Corps Directive 2574 about students fraternizing with other students was stricter than a vegan at a butcher shop. They soon found themselves in front of the space corps instructor with a warning.

Fast forward to Dad's posting on the JMC Emerald Nebula. Despite the height restrictions, strings were pulled, and he was made a galley steward. The ship was still three months away from Earth. He'd stayed in touch with my mother throughout, and in a move that combined romantic flair with a dash of desperation, while on leave at Lunar City 7, Dad proposed to my mother. 'Everyone thought we were bloody mad,' Mum once said, 'Maybe it was the wine or the smell of the beef that had seeped into his clothes. But I just couldn't say no to those puppy dog eyes.' Ah, the cosmic irony of hindsight.

My mother was posted on Titan, and my dad was posted on the JMC Emerald Nebula. Over a year passed before she saw Dad again, and almost two more years before she donned the graduation cap and tossed it into the wind. Yet, fate, with its sense of humor, decided that she wouldn't be posted anywhere near my dad.

My mother was freshly stationed on the Axiom II; however, it wasn't long before she found she had a tiny stowaway on board. She was pregnant with my older brother, Frank! 'Your father was in the outer rim at the time; he nearly dropped his spatula,' she said, 'and by the time the message got to him, I was already as big as a cow

So Mum's Space Corps ambitions hit a speed bump; she took a leave of absence and went to shack up on Io with my paternal grandparents. Lacking her parental navigators, who had embarked on the ultimate road trip years earlier, she found herself surrounded by vast farmland of good old terrestrial adventure. Enter Frank, my elder sibling, making his grand entrance. The interstellar escapades of the next generation were officially underway.

With the cosmic clock ticking, Mum had a mere two Earth-bound years before Space Corp's relentless gravitational pull demanded her return. In those terrestrial years, she juggled the titles of astrobiologist and dedicated mum. 'I just felt shagged out all the time,' she reminisced. 'I missed little Frank; this wasn't what I wanted.' Parenthood, it turns out, is the ultimate improvisational act.

With parents who had charted the final frontier of life and having witnessed her mother resigning her commission to raise her and her brother solo during Dad's cosmic escapades as chief slop server, Mum found herself in a parenting predicament. 'I was bored out of my mind, but your dad's career was everything to him,' she admitted. She'd study where she could while my grandparents took care of Frank. 'Your grandparents were like Energizer bunnies,' she shared. Meanwhile, Dad, charting his course through the galactic highways aboard the JMC Emerald Nebula, missed Mum and Frank. As the countdown to Mum's return commenced, Dad, ever the master of cosmic shenanigans, pulled whatever strings he could to get her posted back to Io, where he had assumed the role of Restroom attendant.

Only for calamity to strike again after my Mum's grand return to the Space Corps. Surprise, surprise—John was on the way, stealing the spotlight as the next Rimmer headliner. Dad informing Captain Sulaco was less than thrilled. Shipboard nurseries were not on his playlist. But, that triggered Dad's decision. A message blinked in from the cosmic ether—Dad's old man had punched out his ticket to the great beyond when he was born. His career as a restroom attendant wasn't going anywhere fast. Cue the resignation letter to Space Corps—bye-bye dad's officer career. So from that point on, they began to settle into life on Io together. Mum later shot out my next brother Howard. Then, having a break, they focused on the house and garden, bringing local gardener Dungo to assist. It wasn't long after I arrived on the scene!

In the galactic years since, I've mulled over Dad's plot twist and how it flung my trajectory into the cosmic unknown. The cosmic yarn I spin for the masses: Dad ditching Space Corps lit the afterburners on John, Howard, Frank, and my career quest, filling the void he left.

My brothers, all being older, eventually signed up for the Space Corps, graduating with top marks in their classes. They all got commission postings on the fleet's best ships. John was an astro-navigator on the SSS Augustus, where he shared quarters with a certain Frank Hollister — a captain in the making.

Frank, the rising star in the Space Corps, snagged the first officer position aboard the Nova 4 when the previous first officer, Cheddar Flatheringson, decided he'd rather play captain. Six years of navigating the officer bureaucracy had Frank on a trajectory to break records and become the youngest captain in the Space Corps. But, as I've always said, 'Up, up, up the ziggurat lickety-split.

As for me, at the tender age of nine, my school grades were less than promising, and in a twist of cosmic fate, my parents decided it was better to wash their hands of me and ship me off to boarding school. As time ticked away, my envy for friends and their idyllic families turned me into a recluse. I found solace in the small things; I enjoyed listening to the Hammond organ, Morris Dancing, and building up my collection of 20th-century telegraph poles. You could always find me aimlessly wandering around the vast diesel decks at the local spaceport, attempting to rediscover the joy of getting lost. I even took up learning Esperanto in my sleep. But, as I looked up at the stars, where dreams of greatness shimmer like distant galaxies, my story was only just beginning. Arnold Judas Rimmer was destined for glory from the very fabric of stardust. My humble journey commenced not among the celestial bodies but within the labyrinth of obstacles — the very crucible of my stellar aspirations.

It was just another sunny day on Io, spent jesting with my older brothers John, Howard, and Frank. God, we were close — the 'Four Musketeers,' as we used to call ourselves! Well, the three musketeers actually; they always let me be the queen of Spain. What fun we'd have! An occasional practical joke, of course — apple-pie beds, black-eye telescope. They even hid a small landmine in my sandpit! How were they supposed to know it would go off? However, on this particular day, we were all blissfully ignorant of the interstellar smeg about to hit my life!

As my mother casually revealed her plan to send me off to boarding school! My school grades had been gradually slipping, and my parents, having tried absolutely nothing and being fresh out of ideas, thought it would be best to let me be someone else's problem. I, in my infinite pubescent wisdom, hit her with the forceful question, 'Will I still get to see Bruno?' Bruno was the family dog, clearly. You could see where my main priorities lay.

In response, she crouched down, bless her heart — magnificent woman. Very prim, very proper; some say austere. Some people mistook her for being cold and thought she was aloof. Not a bit of it. She crouched down to my eye level, as if we were sharing the secrets of the universe. In a tone that probably sounded more dramatic than she intended, she explained that it was a boarding school on the other side of Io — pretty much as far away from them while still being on the same planet.

Turning to dear old Dad for an explanation or, at the very least, a distraction from the impending familial meltdown, the bearded git was engaged in a staring contest with the sky. It was as if he believed they held the secrets to a lifetime supply of cosmic beer. 'I don't want to go!' I declared, my voice dripping with the gravitas only a nine-year-old prophet could muster.

"Just a couple of years, Arnold, and you can come home for your birthday," she boldly declared, and Dad, ever the spectator in the family circus, continued his stoic gaze into the sky. He never was one for eye contact. Snapping his head, he interjected, "Don't get the weaselly smegger's hopes up." Classic Dad!

Undeterred by the lack of emotional support, she flung a promise of her triumphant return in time for my birthday, as if the universe itself would pause its dance to celebrate my existence. Hugging me, she hoisted me up. 'C'mon, let's get some quiche,' she declared, casting a glance at Dad, who remained emotionally disengaged; he never would give quiche a chance.

The next morning, I was hurled into a transport craft, sharing a seat with Fred 'Thicky' Holden, leaving me to ponder the cosmic absurdity of it all. Suddenly, the predictable rhythms of my boyhood were replaced by the unpredictable chaos of the universe. Leaving behind our modest house on Io — a perfect replica of an Earth house from the 19th and 20th centuries with its hectares of land. There were some parts I wouldn't miss: getting up early in the morning to feed the sheep and cows, and my pet Lemming. Dad's insistence on manual labor became the launching pad for my determination and my brothers to join the Space Corps.

Our house had witnessed the shenanigans of many generations of Rimmers, with stories galore about my great-great-grandfather, Jebediah Rimmer, who legend has it fought off native Ionians to build the house and gardens. Now maintained by my Dad and with help from the local gardener, Dungo. My dad couldn't stand Dungo, and could never understand why. Sure, he was slightly inept at times and egotistical, self-important, lacked confidence, and was socially awkward. But I always liked him; he had a strong moralistic attitude, and my mother always took a shine to him.

My father, a half-crazed military failure, spent his early years amidst the military pioneers. Growing up on Io, his childhood was an exercise in minimalism. Yet, he yearned to be an officer like his father. The dream almost turned into reality when he strutted onto Space Corps Academy grounds, fulfilling an ambition that had marinated in the spartan conditions of an Io upbringing. Grandpa, an eternal optimist, had dreams of his son treading the same starlit path. Destiny pulled a cosmic prank when he was one inch below Corps regulation height.

My mother was born into an austere family that considered space exploration a genetic trait. Her father was part of the Space Corps' third graduating class, and her mother was a part of the cybernautic division — a family with enough star power to make a pulsar blush.

Mum, with dreams of becoming an astrobiologist, found herself on a collision course with Dad in an Introduction to Space Corps History class. Oh, but the Space Corps Directive 2574 about students fraternizing with other students was stricter than a vegan at a butcher shop. They soon found themselves in front of the space corps instructor with a warning.

Fast forward to Dad's posting on the JMC Emerald Nebula. Despite the height restrictions, strings were pulled, and he was made a galley steward. The ship was still three months away from Earth. He'd stayed in touch with my mother throughout, and in a move that combined romantic flair with a dash of desperation, while on leave at Lunar City 7, Dad proposed to my mother. 'Everyone thought we were bloody mad,' Mum once said, 'Maybe it was the wine or the smell of the beef that had seeped into his clothes. But I just couldn't say no to those puppy dog eyes.' Ah, the cosmic irony of hindsight.

My mother was posted on Titan, and my dad was posted on the JMC Emerald Nebula. Over a year passed before she saw Dad again, and almost two more years before she donned the graduation cap and tossed it into the wind. Yet, fate, with its sense of humor, decided that she wouldn't be posted anywhere near my dad.

My mother was freshly stationed on the Axiom II; however, it wasn't long before she found she had a tiny stowaway on board. She was pregnant with my older brother, Frank! 'Your father was in the outer rim at the time; he nearly dropped his spatula,' she said, 'and by the time the message got to him, I was already as big as a cow

So Mum's Space Corps ambitions hit a speed bump; she took a leave of absence and went to shack up on Io with my paternal grandparents. Lacking her parental navigators, who had embarked on the ultimate road trip years earlier, she found herself surrounded by vast farmland of good old terrestrial adventure. Enter Frank, my elder sibling, making his grand entrance. The interstellar escapades of the next generation were officially underway.

With the cosmic clock ticking, Mum had a mere two Earth-bound years before Space Corp's relentless gravitational pull demanded her return. In those terrestrial years, she juggled the titles of astrobiologist and dedicated mum. 'I just felt shagged out all the time,' she reminisced. 'I missed little Frank; this wasn't what I wanted.' Parenthood, it turns out, is the ultimate improvisational act.

With parents who had charted the final frontier of life and having witnessed her mother resigning her commission to raise her and her brother solo during Dad's cosmic escapades as chief slop server, Mum found herself in a parenting predicament. 'I was bored out of my mind,

but your dad's career was everything to him,' she admitted. She'd study where she could while my grandparents took care of Frank. 'Your grandparents were like Energizer bunnies,' she shared. Meanwhile, Dad, charting his course through the galactic highways aboard the JMC Emerald Nebula, missed Mum and Frank. As the countdown to Mum's return commenced, Dad, ever the master of cosmic shenanigans, pulled whatever strings he could to get her posted back to Io, where he had assumed the role of Restroom attendant.

Only for calamity to strike again after my Mum's grand return to the Space Corps. Surprise, surprise—John was on the way, stealing the spotlight as the next Rimmer headliner. Dad informing Captain Sulaco was less than thrilled. Shipboard nurseries were not on his playlist. But, that triggered Dad's decision. A message blinked in from the cosmic ether—Dad's old man had punched out his ticket to the great beyond when he was born. His career as a restroom attendant wasn't going anywhere fast. Cue the resignation letter to Space Corps—bye-bye dad's officer career. So from that point on, they began to settle into life on Io together. Mum later shot out my next brother Howard. Then, having a break, they focused on the house and garden, bringing local gardener Dungo to assist. It wasn't long after I arrived on the scene!

In the galactic years since, I've mulled over Dad's plot twist and how it flung my trajectory into the cosmic unknown. The cosmic yarn I spin for the masses: Dad ditching Space Corps lit the afterburners on John, Howard, Frank, and my career quest, filling the void he left.

My brothers, all being older, eventually signed up for the Space Corps, graduating with top marks in their classes. They all got commission postings on the fleet's best ships. John was an astro-navigator on the SSS Augustus, where he shared quarters with a certain Frank Hollister—a captain in the making.

Frank, the rising star in the Space Corps, snagged the first officer position aboard the Nova 4 when the previous first officer, Cheddar Flatheringson, decided he'd rather play captain. Six years of navigating the officer bureaucracy had Frank on a trajectory to break records and become the youngest captain in the Space Corps. But, as I've always said, 'Up, up, up the ziggurat lickety-split.

As for me, at the tender age of nine, my school grades were less than promising, and in a twist of cosmic fate, my parents decided it was better to wash their hands of me and ship me off to boarding school. As time ticked away, my envy for friends and their idyllic families turned me into a recluse. I found solace in the small things; I enjoyed listening to the Hammond organ, Morris Dancing, and building up my collection of 20th-century telegraph poles. You could always find me aimlessly wandering around the vast diesel decks at the local spaceport, attempting to rediscover the joy of getting lost. I even took up learning Esperanto in my sleep. But, as I looked up at the stars, where dreams of greatness shimmer like distant galaxies, my story was only just beginning. Arnold Judas Rimmer was destined for glory from the very fabric of stardust. My humble journey commenced not among the celestial bodies but within the labyrinth of obstacles — the very crucible of my stellar aspirations.

It was just another sunny day on Io, spent jesting with my older brothers John, Howard, and Frank. God, we were close — the 'Four Musketeers,' as we used to call ourselves! Well, the three musketeers actually; they always let me be the queen of Spain. What fun we'd have! An occasional practical joke, of course — apple-pie beds, black-eye telescope. They even hid a small landmine in my sandpit! How were they supposed to know it would go off? However, on this particular day, we were all blissfully ignorant of the interstellar smeg about to hit my life!

As my mother casually revealed her plan to send me off to boarding school! My school grades had been gradually slipping, and my parents, having tried absolutely nothing and being fresh out of ideas, thought it would be best to let me be someone else's problem. I, in my infinite pubescent wisdom, hit her with the forceful question, 'Will I still get to see Bruno?' Bruno was the family dog, clearly. You could see where my main priorities lay.

In response, she crouched down, bless her heart—magnificent woman. Very prim, very proper; some say austere. Some people mistook her for being cold and thought she was aloof. Not a bit of it. She crouched down to my eye level, as if we were sharing the secrets of the universe. In a tone that probably sounded more dramatic than she intended, she explained that it was a boarding school on the other side of Io—pretty much as far away from them while still being on the same planet.

Turning to dear old Dad for an explanation or, at the very least, a distraction from the impending familial meltdown, the bearded git was engaged in a staring contest with the sky. It was as if he believed they held the secrets to a lifetime supply of cosmic beer. 'I don't want to go!' I declared, my voice dripping with the gravitas only a nine-year-old prophet could muster.

"Just a couple of years, Arnold, and you can come home for your birthday," she boldly declared, and Dad, ever the spectator in the family circus, continued his stoic gaze into the sky. He never was one for eye contact. Snapping his head, he interjected, "Don't get the weaselly smegger's hopes up." Classic Dad!

Undeterred by the lack of emotional support, she flung a promise of her triumphant return in time for my birthday, as if the universe itself would pause its dance to celebrate my existence. Hugging me, she hoisted me

up. 'C'mon, let's get some quiche,' she declared, casting a glance at Dad, who remained emotionally disengaged; he never would give quiche a chance.

The next morning, I was hurled into a transport craft, sharing a seat with Fred 'Thicky' Holden, leaving me to ponder the cosmic absurdity of it all. Suddenly, the predictable rhythms of my boyhood were replaced by the unpredictable chaos of the universe. Leaving behind our modest house on Io — a perfect replica of an Earth house from the 19th and 20th centuries with its hectares of land. There were some parts I wouldn't miss: getting up early in the morning to feed the sheep and cows, and my pet Lemming. Dad's insistence on manual labor became the launching pad for my determination and my brothers to join the Space Corps.

Our house had witnessed the shenanigans of many generations of Rimmers, with stories galore about my great-great-grandfather, Jebediah Rimmer, who legend has it fought off native Ionians to build the house and gardens. Now maintained by my Dad and with help from the local gardener, Dungo. My dad couldn't stand Dungo, and could never understand why. Sure, he was slightly inept at times and egotistical, self-important, lacked confidence, and was socially awkward. But I always liked him; he had a strong moralistic attitude, and my mother always took a shine to him.

My father, a half-crazed military failure, spent his early years amidst the military pioneers. Growing up on Io, his childhood was an exercise in minimalism. Yet, he yearned to be an officer like his father. The dream almost turned into reality when he strutted onto Space Corps Academy grounds, fulfilling an ambition that had marinated in the spartan conditions of an Io upbringing. Grandpa, an eternal optimist, had dreams of his son treading the same starlit path. Destiny pulled a cosmic prank when he was one inch below Corps regulation height.

My mother was born into an austere family that considered space exploration a genetic trait. Her father was part of the Space Corps' third graduating class, and her mother was a part of the cybernautic division — a family with enough star power to make a pulsar blush.

Mum, with dreams of becoming an astrobiologist, found herself on a collision course with Dad in an Introduction to Space Corps History class. Oh, but the Space Corps Directive 2574 about students fraternizing with other students was stricter than a vegan at a butcher shop. They soon found themselves in front of the space corps instructor with a warning.

Fast forward to Dad's posting on the JMC Emerald Nebula. Despite the height restrictions, strings were pulled, and he was made a galley steward. The ship was still three months away from Earth. He'd stayed in touch with my mother throughout, and in a move that combined romantic flair with a dash of desperation, while on leave at Lunar City 7, Dad proposed to my mother. 'Everyone thought we were bloody mad,' Mum once said, 'Maybe it was the wine or the smell of the beef that had seeped into his clothes. But I just couldn't say no to those puppy dog eyes.' Ah, the cosmic irony of hindsight.

My mother was posted on Titan, and my dad was posted on the JMC Emerald Nebula. Over a year passed before she saw Dad again, and almost two more years before she donned the graduation cap and tossed it into the wind. Yet, fate, with its sense of humor, decided that she wouldn't be posted anywhere near my dad.

My mother was freshly stationed on the Axiom II; however, it wasn't long before she found she had a tiny stowaway on board. She was pregnant with my older brother, Frank! 'Your father was in the outer rim at the time; he nearly dropped his spatula,' she said, 'and by the time the message got to him, I was already as big as a cow

So Mum's Space Corps ambitions hit a speed bump; she took a leave of absence and went to shack up on Io with my paternal grandparents. Lacking her parental navigators, who had embarked on the ultimate road trip years earlier, she found herself surrounded by vast farmland of good old terrestrial adventure. Enter Frank, my elder sibling, making his grand entrance. The interstellar escapades of the next generation were officially underway.

With the cosmic clock ticking, Mum had a mere two Earth-bound years before Space Corp's relentless gravitational pull demanded her return. In those terrestrial years, she juggled the titles of astrobiologist and dedicated mum. 'I just felt shagged out all the time,' she reminisced. 'I missed little Frank; this wasn't what I wanted.' Parenthood, it turns out, is the ultimate improvisational act.

With parents who had charted the final frontier of life and having witnessed her mother resigning her commission to raise her and her brother solo during Dad's cosmic escapades as chief slop server, Mum found herself in a parenting predicament. 'I was bored out of my mind, but your dad's career was everything to him,' she admitted. She'd study where she could while my grandparents took care of Frank. 'Your grandparents were like Energizer bunnies,' she shared. Meanwhile, Dad, charting his course through the galactic highways aboard the JMC Emerald Nebula, missed Mum and Frank. As the countdown to Mum's return commenced, Dad, ever the master of cosmic shenanigans, pulled whatever strings he could to get her posted back to Io, where he had assumed the role of Restroom attendant.

Only for calamity to strike again after my Mum's grand return to the Space Corps. Surprise, surprise—John was on the way, stealing the spotlight as the next Rimmer headliner. Dad informing Captain Sulaco was less than thrilled. Shipboard nurseries were not on his playlist. But, that triggered Dad's decision. A message blinked in from the cosmic ether—Dad's old man had punched out his ticket to the great beyond when he was born. His career as a restroom attendant wasn't going anywhere fast. Cue the resignation letter to Space Corps—bye-bye dad's officer career. So from that point on, they began to settle into life on Io together. Mum later shot out my next brother Howard. Then, having a break, they focused on the house and garden, bringing local gardener Dungo to assist. It wasn't long after I arrived on the scene!

In the galactic years since, I've mulled over Dad's plot twist and how it flung my trajectory into the cosmic unknown. The cosmic yarn I spin for the masses: Dad ditching Space Corps lit the afterburners on John, Howard, Frank, and my career quest, filling the void he left.

My brothers, all being older, eventually signed up for the Space Corps, graduating with top marks in their classes. They all got commission postings on the fleet's best ships. John was an astro-navigator on the SSS Augustus, where he shared quarters with a certain Frank Hollister—a captain in the making.

Frank, the rising star in the Space Corps, snagged the first officer position aboard the Nova 4 when the previous first officer, Cheddar Flatheringson, decided he'd rather play captain. Six years of navigating the officer bureaucracy had Frank on a trajectory to break records and become the youngest captain in the Space Corps. But, as I've always said, 'Up, up, up the ziggurat lickety-split.

As for me, at the tender age of nine, my school grades were less than promising, and in a twist of cosmic fate, my parents decided it was better to wash their hands of me and ship me off to boarding school. As time ticked away, my envy for friends and their idyllic families turned me into a recluse. I found solace in the small things; I enjoyed listening to the Hammond organ, Morris Dancing, and building up my collection of 20th-century telegraph poles. You could always find me aimlessly wandering around the vast diesel decks at the local spaceport, attempting to rediscover the joy of getting lost. I even took up learning Esperanto in my sleep. But, as I looked up at the stars, where dreams of greatness shimmer like distant galaxies, my story was only just beginning. Arnold Judas Rimmer was destined for glory from the very fabric of stardust. My humble journey commenced not among the celestial bodies but within the labyrinth of obstacles — the very crucible of my stellar aspirations.

It was just another sunny day on Io, spent jesting with my older brothers John, Howard, and Frank. God, we were close — the 'Four Musketeers,' as we used to call ourselves! Well, the three musketeers actually; they always let me be the queen of Spain. What fun we'd have! An occasional practical joke, of course — apple-pie beds, black-eye telescope. They even hid a small landmine in my sandpit! How were they supposed to know it would go off? However, on this particular day, we were all blissfully ignorant of the interstellar smeg about to hit my life!

As my mother casually revealed her plan to send me off to boarding school! My school grades had been gradually slipping, and my parents, having tried absolutely nothing and being fresh out of ideas, thought it would be best to let me be someone else's problem. I, in my infinite pubescent wisdom, hit her with the forceful question, 'Will I still get to see Bruno?' Bruno was the family dog, clearly. You could see where my main priorities lay.

In response, she crouched down, bless her heart — magnificent woman. Very prim, very proper; some say austere. Some people mistook her for being cold and thought she was aloof. Not a bit of it. She crouched down to my eye level, as if we were sharing the secrets of the universe. In a tone that probably sounded more dramatic than she intended, she explained that it was a boarding school on the other side of Io — pretty much as far away from them while still being on the same planet.

211

Turning to dear old Dad for an explanation or, at the very least, a distraction from the impending familial meltdown, the bearded git was engaged in a staring contest with the sky. It was as if he believed they held the secrets to a lifetime supply of cosmic beer. 'I don't want to go!' I declared, my voice dripping with the gravitas only a nine-year-old prophet could muster.

"Just a couple of years, Arnold, and you can come home for your birthday," she boldly declared, and Dad, ever the spectator in the family circus, continued his stoic gaze into the sky. He never was one for eye contact. Snapping his head, he interjected, "Don't get the weaselly smegger's hopes up." Classic Dad!

Undeterred by the lack of emotional support, she flung a promise of her triumphant return in time for my birthday, as if the universe itself would pause its dance to celebrate my existence. Hugging me, she hoisted me up. 'C'mon, let's get some quiche,' she declared, casting a glance at Dad, who remained emotionally disengaged; he never would give quiche a chance.

The next morning, I was hurled into a transport craft, sharing a seat with Fred 'Thicky' Holden, leaving me to ponder the cosmic absurdity of it all. Suddenly, the predictable rhythms of my boyhood were replaced by the unpredictable chaos of the universe. Leaving behind our modest house on Io—a perfect replica of an Earth house from the 19th and 20th centuries with its hectares of land. There were some parts I wouldn't miss: getting up early in the morning to feed the sheep and cows, and my pet Lemming. Dad's insistence on manual labor became the launching pad for my determination and my brothers to join the Space Corps.

Our house had witnessed the shenanigans of many generations of Rimmers, with stories galore about my great-great-grandfather, Jebediah Rimmer, who legend has it fought off native Ionians to build the house and gardens. Now maintained by my Dad and with help from the local gardener, Dungo. My dad couldn't stand Dungo, and could never understand why. Sure, he was slightly inept at times and egotistical, self-important, lacked confidence, and was socially awkward. But I always liked him; he had a strong moralistic attitude, and my mother always took a shine to him.

My father, a half-crazed military failure, spent his early years amidst the military pioneers. Growing up on Io, his childhood was an exercise in minimalism. Yet, he yearned to be an officer like his father. The dream almost turned into reality when he strutted onto Space Corps Academy grounds, fulfilling an ambition that had marinated in the spartan conditions of an Io upbringing. Grandpa, an eternal optimist, had dreams of his son treading the same starlit path. Destiny pulled a cosmic prank when he was one inch below Corps regulation height.

My mother was born into an austere family that considered space exploration a genetic trait. Her father was part of the Space Corps' third graduating class, and her mother was a part of the cybernautic division — a family with enough star power to make a pulsar blush.

Mum, with dreams of becoming an astrobiologist, found herself on a collision course with Dad in an Introduction to Space Corps History class. Oh, but the Space Corps Directive 2574 about students fraternizing with other students was stricter than a vegan at a butcher shop. They soon found themselves in front of the space corps instructor with a warning.

Fast forward to Dad's posting on the JMC Emerald Nebula. Despite the height restrictions, strings were pulled, and he was made a galley steward. The ship was still three months away from Earth. He'd stayed in touch with my mother throughout, and in a move that combined romantic flair with a dash of desperation, while on leave at Lunar City 7, Dad proposed to my mother. 'Everyone thought we were bloody mad,' Mum once said, 'Maybe it was the wine or the smell of the beef that had seeped into his clothes. But I just couldn't say no to those puppy dog eyes.' Ah, the cosmic irony of hindsight.

My mother was posted on Titan, and my dad was posted on the JMC Emerald Nebula. Over a year passed before she saw Dad again, and almost two more years before she donned the graduation cap and tossed it into the wind. Yet, fate, with its sense of humor, decided that she wouldn't be posted anywhere near my dad.

My mother was freshly stationed on the Axiom II; however, it wasn't long before she found she had a tiny stowaway on board. She was pregnant with my older brother, Frank! 'Your father was in the outer rim at the time; he nearly dropped his spatula,' she said, 'and by the time the message got to him, I was already as big as a cow

So Mum's Space Corps ambitions hit a speed bump; she took a leave of absence and went to shack up on Io with my paternal grandparents. Lacking her parental navigators, who had embarked on the ultimate road trip years earlier, she found herself surrounded by vast farmland of good old terrestrial adventure. Enter Frank, my elder sibling, making his grand entrance. The interstellar escapades of the next generation were officially underway.

With the cosmic clock ticking, Mum had a mere two Earth-bound years before Space Corp's relentless gravitational pull demanded her return. In those terrestrial years, she juggled the titles of astrobiologist and dedicated mum. 'I just felt shagged out all the time,' she reminisced. 'I missed little Frank; this wasn't what I wanted.' Parenthood, it turns out, is the ultimate improvisational act.

With parents who had charted the final frontier of life and having witnessed her mother resigning her commission to raise her and her brother solo during Dad's cosmic escapades as chief slop server, Mum found herself in a parenting predicament. 'I was bored out of my mind, but your dad's career was everything to him,' she admitted. She'd study where she could while my grandparents took care of Frank. 'Your grandparents were like Energizer bunnies,' she shared. Meanwhile, Dad, charting his course through the galactic highways aboard the JMC Emerald Nebula, missed Mum and Frank. As the countdown to Mum's return commenced, Dad, ever the master of cosmic shenanigans, pulled whatever strings he could to get her posted back to Io, where he had assumed the role of Restroom attendant.

Only for calamity to strike again after my Mum's grand return to the Space Corps. Surprise, surprise — John was on the way, stealing the spotlight as the next Rimmer headliner. Dad informing Captain Sulaco was less than thrilled. Shipboard nurseries were not on his playlist. But, that triggered Dad's decision. A message blinked in from the cosmic ether — Dad's old man had punched out his ticket to the great beyond when he was born. His career as a restroom attendant wasn't going anywhere fast. Cue the resignation letter to Space Corps — bye-bye dad's officer career. So from that point on, they began to settle into life on Io together. Mum later shot out my next brother Howard. Then, having a break, they focused on the house and garden, bringing local gardener Dungo to assist. It wasn't long after I arrived on the scene!

215

In the galactic years since, I've mulled over Dad's plot twist and how it flung my trajectory into the cosmic unknown. The cosmic yarn I spin for the masses: Dad ditching Space Corps lit the afterburners on John, Howard, Frank, and my career quest, filling the void he left.

My brothers, all being older, eventually signed up for the Space Corps, graduating with top marks in their classes. They all got commission postings on the fleet's best ships. John was an astro-navigator on the SSS Augustus, where he shared quarters with a certain Frank Hollister—a captain in the making.

Frank, the rising star in the Space Corps, snagged the first officer position aboard the Nova 4 when the previous first officer, Cheddar Flatheringson, decided he'd rather play captain. Six years of navigating the officer bureaucracy had Frank on a trajectory to break records and become the youngest captain in the Space Corps. But, as I've always said, 'Up, up, up the ziggurat lickety-split.

As for me, at the tender age of nine, my school grades were less than promising, and in a twist of cosmic fate, my parents decided it was better to wash their hands of me and ship me off to boarding school. As time ticked away, my envy for friends and their idyllic families turned me into a recluse. I found solace in the small things; I enjoyed listening to the Hammond organ, Morris Dancing, and building up my collection of 20th-century telegraph poles. You could always find me aimlessly wandering around the vast diesel decks at the local spaceport, attempting to rediscover the joy of getting lost. I even took up learning Esperanto in my sleep. But, as I looked up at the stars, where dreams of greatness shimmer like distant galaxies, my story was only just beginning. Arnold Judas Rimmer was destined for glory from the very fabric of stardust. My humble journey commenced not among the celestial bodies but within the labyrinth of obstacles—the very crucible of my stellar aspirations.

It was just another sunny day on Io, spent jesting with my older brothers John, Howard, and Frank. God, we were close — the 'Four Musketeers,' as we used to call ourselves! Well, the three musketeers actually; they always let me be the queen of Spain. What fun we'd have! An occasional practical joke, of course — apple-pie beds, black-eye telescope. They even hid a small landmine in my sandpit! How were they supposed to know it would go off? However, on this particular day, we were all blissfully ignorant of the interstellar smeg about to hit my life!

As my mother casually revealed her plan to send me off to boarding school! My school grades had been gradually slipping, and my parents, having tried absolutely nothing and being fresh out of ideas, thought it would be best to let me be someone else's problem. I, in my infinite pubescent wisdom, hit her with the forceful question, 'Will I still get to see Bruno?' Bruno was the family dog, clearly. You could see where my main priorities lay.

In response, she crouched down, bless her heart — magnificent woman. Very prim, very proper; some say austere. Some people mistook her for being cold and thought she was aloof. Not a bit of it. She crouched down to my eye level, as if we were sharing the secrets of the universe. In a tone that probably sounded more dramatic than she intended, she explained that it was a boarding school on the other side of Io — pretty much as far away from them while still being on the same planet.

Turning to dear old Dad for an explanation or, at the very least, a distraction from the impending familial meltdown, the bearded git was engaged in a staring contest with the sky. It was as if he believed they held the secrets to a lifetime supply of cosmic beer. 'I don't want to go!' I declared, my voice dripping with the gravitas only a nine-year-old prophet could muster.

"Just a couple of years, Arnold, and you can come home for your birthday," she boldly declared, and Dad, ever the spectator in the family circus, continued his stoic gaze into the sky. He never was one for eye contact. Snapping his head, he interjected, "Don't get the weaselly smegger's hopes up." Classic Dad!

Undeterred by the lack of emotional support, she flung a promise of her triumphant return in time for my birthday, as if the universe itself would pause its dance to celebrate my existence. Hugging me, she hoisted me up. 'C'mon, let's get some quiche,' she declared, casting a glance at Dad, who remained emotionally disengaged; he never would give quiche a chance.

The next morning, I was hurled into a transport craft, sharing a seat with Fred 'Thicky' Holden, leaving me to ponder the cosmic absurdity of it all. Suddenly, the predictable rhythms of my boyhood were replaced by the unpredictable chaos of the universe. Leaving behind our modest house on Io—a perfect replica of an Earth house from the 19th and 20th centuries with its hectares of land. There were some parts I wouldn't miss: getting up early in the morning to feed the sheep and cows, and my pet Lemming. Dad's insistence on manual labor became the launching pad for my determination and my brothers to join the Space Corps.

Our house had witnessed the shenanigans of many generations of Rimmers, with stories galore about my great-great-grandfather, Jebediah Rimmer, who legend has it fought off native Ionians to build the house and gardens. Now maintained by my Dad and with help from the local gardener, Dungo. My dad couldn't stand Dungo, and could never understand why. Sure, he was slightly inept at times and egotistical, self-important, lacked confidence, and was socially awkward. But I always liked him; he had a strong moralistic attitude, and my mother always took a shine to him.

My father, a half-crazed military failure, spent his early years amidst the military pioneers. Growing up on Io, his childhood was an exercise in minimalism. Yet, he yearned to be an officer like his father. The dream almost turned into reality when he strutted onto Space Corps Academy grounds, fulfilling an ambition that had marinated in the spartan conditions of an Io upbringing. Grandpa, an eternal optimist, had dreams of his son treading the same starlit path. Destiny pulled a cosmic prank when he was one inch below Corps regulation height.

My mother was born into an austere family that considered space exploration a genetic trait. Her father was part of the Space Corps' third graduating class, and her mother was a part of the cybernautic division — a family with enough star power to make a pulsar blush.

Mum, with dreams of becoming an astrobiologist, found herself on a collision course with Dad in an Introduction to Space Corps History class. Oh, but the Space Corps Directive 2574 about students fraternizing with other students was stricter than a vegan at a butcher shop. They soon found themselves in front of the space corps instructor with a warning.

Fast forward to Dad's posting on the JMC Emerald Nebula. Despite the height restrictions, strings were pulled, and he was made a galley steward. The ship was still three months away from Earth. He'd stayed in touch with my mother throughout, and in a move that combined romantic flair with a dash of desperation, while on leave at Lunar City 7, Dad proposed to my mother. 'Everyone thought we were bloody mad,' Mum once said, 'Maybe it was the wine or the smell of the beef that had seeped into his clothes. But I just couldn't say no to those puppy dog eyes.' Ah, the cosmic irony of hindsight.

My mother was posted on Titan, and my dad was posted on the JMC Emerald Nebula. Over a year passed before she saw Dad again, and almost two more years before she donned the graduation cap and tossed it into the wind. Yet, fate, with its sense of humor, decided that she wouldn't be posted anywhere near my dad.

My mother was freshly stationed on the Axiom II; however, it wasn't long before she found she had a tiny stowaway on board. She was pregnant with my older brother, Frank! 'Your father was in the outer rim at the time; he nearly dropped his spatula,' she said, 'and by the time the message got to him, I was already as big as a cow

So Mum's Space Corps ambitions hit a speed bump; she took a leave of absence and went to shack up on Io with my paternal grandparents. Lacking her parental navigators, who had embarked on the ultimate road trip years earlier, she found herself surrounded by vast farmland of good old terrestrial adventure. Enter Frank, my elder sibling, making his grand entrance. The interstellar escapades of the next generation were officially underway.

With the cosmic clock ticking, Mum had a mere two Earth-bound years before Space Corp's relentless gravitational pull demanded her return. In those terrestrial years, she juggled the titles of astrobiologist and dedicated mum. 'I just felt shagged out all the time,' she reminisced. 'I missed little Frank; this wasn't what I wanted.' Parenthood, it turns out, is the ultimate improvisational act.

With parents who had charted the final frontier of life and having witnessed her mother resigning her commission to raise her and her brother solo during Dad's cosmic escapades as chief slop server, Mum found herself in a parenting predicament. 'I was bored out of my mind,

220

but your dad's career was everything to him,' she admitted. She'd study where she could while my grandparents took care of Frank. 'Your grandparents were like Energizer bunnies,' she shared. Meanwhile, Dad, charting his course through the galactic highways aboard the JMC Emerald Nebula, missed Mum and Frank. As the countdown to Mum's return commenced, Dad, ever the master of cosmic shenanigans, pulled whatever strings he could to get her posted back to Io, where he had assumed the role of Restroom attendant.

Only for calamity to strike again after my Mum's grand return to the Space Corps. Surprise, surprise—John was on the way, stealing the spotlight as the next Rimmer headliner. Dad informing Captain Sulaco was less than thrilled. Shipboard nurseries were not on his playlist. But, that triggered Dad's decision. A message blinked in from the cosmic ether—Dad's old man had punched out his ticket to the great beyond when he was born. His career as a restroom attendant wasn't going anywhere fast. Cue the resignation letter to Space Corps—bye-bye dad's officer career. So from that point on, they began to settle into life on Io together. Mum later shot out my next brother Howard. Then, having a break, they focused on the house and garden, bringing local gardener Dungo to assist. It wasn't long after I arrived on the scene!

In the galactic years since, I've mulled over Dad's plot twist and how it flung my trajectory into the cosmic unknown. The cosmic yarn I spin for the masses: Dad ditching Space Corps lit the afterburners on John, Howard, Frank, and my career quest, filling the void he left.

My brothers, all being older, eventually signed up for the Space Corps, graduating with top marks in their classes. They all got commission postings on the fleet's best ships. John was an astro-navigator on the SSS Augustus, where he shared quarters with a certain Frank Hollister—a captain in the making.

Frank, the rising star in the Space Corps, snagged the first officer position aboard the Nova 4 when the previous first officer, Cheddar Flatheringson, decided he'd rather play captain. Six years of navigating the officer bureaucracy had Frank on a trajectory to break records and become the youngest captain in the Space Corps. But, as I've always said, 'Up, up, up the ziggurat lickety-split.

As for me, at the tender age of nine, my school grades were less than promising, and in a twist of cosmic fate, my parents decided it was better to wash their hands of me and ship me off to boarding school. As time ticked away, my envy for friends and their idyllic families turned me into a recluse. I found solace in the small things; I enjoyed listening to the Hammond organ, Morris Dancing, and building up my collection of 20th-century telegraph poles. You could always find me aimlessly wandering around the vast diesel decks at the local spaceport, attempting to rediscover the joy of getting lost. I even took up learning Esperanto in my sleep. But, as I looked up at the stars, where dreams of greatness shimmer like distant galaxies, my story was only just beginning. Arnold Judas Rimmer was destined for glory from the very fabric of stardust. My humble journey commenced not among the celestial bodies but within the labyrinth of obstacles — the very crucible of my stellar aspirations.